THE
LAST
DAYS OF
WILLIAM
SHAKESPEARE

Also by Vlady Kociancich

Novels
La Octava Maravilla
Abisinia

Short Stories
Coraje

Vlady Kociancich

THE
LAST
DAYS OF
WILLIAM
SHAKESPEARE

A NOVEL

Translated from the Spanish by
Margaret Jull Costa

William Morrow and Company, Inc.
New York

The translator would like to thank the author, Nadia Lawrence at William Heinemann, Annella McDermott, and Faye Carney for all their help and advice.

First published in English in Great Britain by William Heinemann Limited, 1990

Recognizing the importance of preserving what has been written, it is the policy of William Morrow and Company, Inc., and its imprints and affiliates to have the books it publishes printed on acid-free paper, and we exert our best efforts to that end.

Library of Congress Cataloging-in-Publication Data

Kociancich, Vlady.
[Ultimos días de William Shakespeare, English]
The last days of William Shakespeare : a novel / Vlady Kociancich; translated from the Spanish by Margaret Jull Costa.
p. cm.
Translation of: Ultimos días de William Shakespeare.
ISBN 0-688-10432-0
I. Title.
PQ7798.21.03U413   1991
863—dc20   90-20520
                                                                  CIP

Printed in the United States of America

First Edition

1 2 3 4 5 6 7 8 9 10

BOOK DESIGN BY MARSHA COHEN

To the victims of stupidity in power

o 1 o

NERVOUSLY SHREDDING his invitation to the first night of *Hamlet,* which he'd failed to hand in at the door because of the overwhelming press of people greeting him, shaking him by the hand, even, to his great embarrassment, embracing him, Emilio Rauch sits slumped in his seat, looking in vain for some trace of past events.

But he can detect nothing. Only the smell of fresh paint in the auditorium of the National Theater; the slight dip in the center of the stage that causes an inept Hamlet to stumble; and the white full-dress uniforms packing the front row and the boxes.

And yet he'd been away such a short time. In the foyer, before the usher announced the start of this wretched performance, Rauch had energetically resisted the warm welcome. No, he hadn't been in exile. It had been a working holiday. He'd visited some friends in Varennes and had spent the rest of his time in Paris, checking the translation of his second novel. Yes, he'd seen some pretty unbelievable stories in the European press, but all mixed up with reports of floods in Brazil, a wheat war in Uruguay, some Ecuadorian beauty winning the Miss World contest. He hadn't realized, he'd been in France alone, working. Why this special performance of Shakespeare's play? To celebrate the liberation, they answered, looking at him in amazement.

This is only his second night in the city. The first night he didn't sleep. His body was crying out for rest after the long journey, but he wouldn't give in to it, holding on stubbornly to wakefulness, afraid of falling asleep and dreaming. He stayed up waiting for morning to come, for the first light of another day, which he again spent constantly on the move, trying to get information out of people who should have been able to help him but didn't want to. Until sunset, that is, until the Catholic priest came to the hotel and brought him Renata's letters and diary.

Thunderous applause jolts him out of his torpor. The lights haven't gone up yet, but Rauch rises from his seat. He pushes his way with difficulty through the enraptured audience; the applause and the cries of "Bravo!" follow him out into the foyer. Stunned and exhausted, he stares at himself in an enormous mirror tarnished with age and mounted in a gold baroque frame. How can he find the red office with no one to guide him? The National Theater is a labyrinth of corridors, rooms, steep staircases, and perilous drops. Rauch has never been beyond the foyer.

"My dear Rauch, this *is* a pleasure."

Another writer appears in the mirror. With dismay Rauch recognizes the tall, elegant figure, the attentive gray eyes, the pipe held in his hand like a small intellectual torch: the prizewinning writer Santiago Bonday, or "the Master," as he is known. Bonday has also returned from Europe in the last few days, and he basks in the moral aura of exile.

"I knew our young writers wouldn't desert us on a night of such deep historic significance."

Like every other member of his country's cultured class, Rauch has a past history of dialogues with Bonday; he knows that no one gets away from the Master without a struggle.

"I'm going to have a look around the theater. Why don't you come with me?"

"Now?" Bonday arches his eyebrows. "They're giving a cocktail party for us. . . ."

Rauch insists. They'll be back in no time. Just a quick look. He resorts to flattery, congratulating the Master on his recent, richly deserved prize and applauding his brave statement to the newspapers, until, reluctant but visibly pleased by this praise from a younger writer, Bonday accepts. Rauch wonders then if he's really capable of hating this poor fool, of dragging him along to the red office.

They walk through the empty theater. A few minutes later, despite Bonday's initial confidence—"I know this place like the back of my hand"—they're lost in a maze of corridors. Now it's Rauch who leads, with Bonday behind him looking anxiously at his watch. The red office is somewhere here, on one of these floors, and Rauch, driven against his better judgment to search for it, won't give up until he's found it.

"We'd better go back," says Bonday.

"You go back if you like," replies Rauch, brusquely now, because they've gone beyond the bounds of courtesy and because Bonday would never have the nerve to undertake the difficult return journey on his own.

They go down another dark corridor and take the third turning on the right. Bonday is pale with the effort of having run upstairs so as not to lose sight of Rauch. "The cocktail party . . ." he pants. But Rauch pushes open the door and turns on the light.

The room is bare of furniture. The walls are painted

a bright red—so like the color of fresh blood that involuntarily Rauch shuts his eyes.

The only sound in the long silence that follows is Bonday's labored breathing.

"How is it possible," Rauch murmurs at last, "how is it possible that in such a short time . . . ?"

Bonday takes up the question. "How could a madness like that be conceived, grow, and die? There's no doubt about it, Rauch, it all happened very fast. And to you, leaving as you did some time before, it must seem incomprehensible. Let's say it's as if you were starting the novel on the last page, with the happy ending."

Rauch goes over to the window. It's open. The night is very clear. He can see the glinting tips of the weeds growing along the shore, the calm surface of the river, the unfinished wall.

"Some critics," says Bonday, puffing on his pipe, "despise happy endings, they say they smack of crass sentimentality. I, on the other hand, join the common man in welcoming the liberation. Do you know, when I heard that immortal soliloquy again, when I realized we had recovered the genius of Shakespeare, my eyes filled with tears."

Rauch tells himself, There's no point in getting angry, he's not worth it. But nevertheless he turns his head and asks hoarsely, "So nothing really happened, then? Everything is just as it was when I left?"

Bonday looks away. "Well, perhaps not *everything*. But it's taught us a lesson," and he adds hurriedly, "The spirit, my young friend, is tempered by pain."

"But whose pain?" cries Rauch.

Startled, Bonday takes a step back. "Please, calm down."

He's right, thinks Rauch, turning back to the window. The fool's right to tell me to calm down.

"The new director of the theater wants to meet you, Rauch. I've told him a lot about you, how talented you are. Shall we go? I'll introduce you. Captain Beh is an admirable man, and he too has suffered." Bonday lowers his voice. "Believe me, Emilio, we've all suffered in one way or another."

Leaning out the window, Rauch remains still and silent.

"I don't know what you're looking for out there," sighs Bonday. "I don't understand."

"You will," says Rauch, calm now. "I'm sorry, Master."

"Sorry?" There's a look of confusion in Bonday's gray eyes and a hesitant smile hovers on his lips. Rauch doesn't reply. The silence grows longer, awkward. Then, in a bitter, weary voice, Santiago Bonday says to the young writer looking out at the river, "We'll be late for the cocktail party, Rauch."

∘ 2 ∘

Dear Emilio,

Since you left for France, I've done nothing but feel how much I miss our conversations. Now that we're separated by an ocean, I realize how little in fact we saw of each other. That's why, when you come back, I won't let work, love affairs, or idleness get in the way of meetings that are so necessary to me. Since I've no interesting news to pass on, I'm writing to you now out of pure nostalgia.

However, I will take this opportunity to point out, conceited as ever, that if it weren't for us writers of fiction, nothing would happen in this flat, gray, tedious city with its river. Even the most unexpected event is just another step down the slippery slope to the murky depths of apathy.

Now I have the courage to tell you that I can't write the diary you told me I should keep. But thank you for that final act of considerateness (so like you). You knew I was having difficulties with my first novel and wanted to take my mind off an enterprise still in its painful throes. But, dear Emilio, my observations on life, people,

books, or my own humble self were always addressed to you; they were to be spoken, not
written down. So in your absence I'll carry on
with the novel, and you'll be spared having to
read the diary that you so generously, if impru-
dently, suggested when we said good-bye.

Love,
Renata

Emilio has the advantage of being eight years and two
books older than me, and, I should add, has an enormous amount of talent. I'm all beginnings. Here I am,
docile and lazy, into the first lines of a blank notebook,
the diary he suggested, and without Emilio here, I've
nothing to say. No one could accuse me of not taking
myself seriously enough, but even I find my life boring.
How can I write down these dull facts without yawning:
the job in a farm-machinery office, the shared room in
the Pension Stella Maris, the sweat and tears expended
over the first chapters of a first novel against a background of Gertrudis's chatter, the radio blaring on the
other side of the paper-thin walls, and the voices of
the other women squabbling over whose turn it is for
the bathroom.

What was it that wrenched me away from my village
in the provinces, from a secure future as a teacher in
the local school, as an ordinary wife and mother? *Literature*, I told my tearful aunt, who never missed a
chance to reproach me with all the worry I'd given her,
and the years she'd spent standing in for my dead parents, they would have been horrified, they would never
have allowed me to go to the city, that monstrous de-
vourer of young girls. *Literature*, I cried. And all I found
were musty examination subjects and stale lessons in

how to dissect books—until, that is, I met Emilio Rauch, who really was a writer and who taught me, at the very least, to read widely and with pleasure. Thanks to Emilio, I've survived these four years of poverty, of chaotic boardinghouse life, of my own lack of talent and my inability to make friends. Because of him I've written a few mediocre stories, made a vague stab at starting to write a novel, and I'm attempting (though I'm ashamed to tell him so) the diary that he asked me to write.

Emilio Rauch believes that my destiny is to be a writer. I just move blindly forward as best I can. Perhaps he's lying to me and I'm lying to myself. Perhaps there's no such thing as a writer's destiny and it's all just a pathetic exploration of loneliness, a search for an escape route out of all the confusion and silence. And what if it is? Emilio would ask. You have to start somewhere: with a story, a novel, jottings in a notebook. I take his advice. If, in order to achieve this destiny, he told me to run barefoot to the river or light candles to the Virgin of Casamanta, I'd do it. I put so much effort into this stupid, fruitless venture that sometimes I wonder if I only do it because Emilio tells me to.

Good grief, I've actually started the diary. But nothing I do comes out right. This doesn't read like a page in a diary. Oh, well, another beginning.

· 3 ·

BONDAY SLOWLY FOLDED the newspaper, put it down next to his empty cup, and stretched lazily.

"I'm going to do some work."

On the other side of the breakfast table his wife continued plucking her eyebrows. She nodded, absorbed in the task, her elbows on the tablecloth, her wan, puffy face turned to the busy tweezers pecking away above a slack eyelid, furrowed with wrinkles. Bonday looked away in disgust. After almost a quarter of a century of marriage to this person who had once been young and possibly even beautiful, he demanded little, only, perhaps, complicity in his slothfulness.

"I don't suppose there's anything to stop me from getting down to work on my novel, is there? That boy, the poet, who was so keen to see me . . ."

His wife shook her head almost imperceptibly, keeping one eye closed, the other open to the mirror and the tweezers.

"Isn't it today I'm supposed to be signing some books?"

"That's next week, Tacho."

Tacho! And to think there was a time when I found the nickname touching. ". . . All right, then, a whole day to spend on my work." At the door he turned around. "Won't the lawyer who's dealing with the plagiarism case need to see me today?"

9

"No, dear."

Drained of energy, irritated and yawning, Bonday slouched toward the library.

As happened for a few minutes every day, the contents of his workroom injected Bonday with a dose of literary adrenaline. The armchairs upholstered in soft, fragrant leather, the exquisitely bound books that lined the walls; the table piled with the Greek and Latin classics for easy, though always postponed, reference. In his office there was his electric typewriter, half a ream of A4 paper, notebooks full of jottings, loose leaves of paper with whole paragraphs crossed out, and a bottle of aspirin: the everyday tools of creativity.

To prolong the sweet joys of idleness, Bonday sat down in an armchair, picked up his pipe, crossed his legs, and looked at himself in the mirror. He liked this large, colonial-style mirror, heavy and majestic in its gilded baroque frame, taking up almost the whole of one wall. He enjoyed seeing his present image, that of the prizewinning author, reflected in the antique glass of a priceless work of art. He tried to look at himself with a stranger's eye, and was pleasantly, mildly surprised to recognize himself in the man whom his own fame reflected back from among the garlands of gold; the flowers and fruits of his celebrity as a writer.

Although he was over fifty, Santiago Bonday retained a youthful slenderness. In his clear gray eyes shone the curiosity of a boy, the attentive gleam that people mistake for intelligence. The graying mustache, abundant but neatly trimmed, sat with measured grace above his melancholy smile. He didn't really smoke (he had a delicate throat and the lungs of a newborn babe), but he couldn't deny himself the pleasure of underlining his words with puffs on a pipeful of the Dutch tobacco he smoked without inhaling, confining himself to savoring its smell and taste.

All that's missing is a dog, he thought, contemplating himself in the mirror. The dog interposed itself between Bonday and his novel. He tried to imagine a Platonic dog, one that would not chew the leather armchairs or ruin the carpet or require tedious walks in the park. He spent half an hour trying to choose the right dog, all to no avail. Inside every ideal dog, perfectly suited to the image of the writer with his pipe and his melancholy smile, lurked a hellhound trying to get out.

At last, conscious of and weighed down by the literary destiny that awaited him in the form of the blank sheets of paper on his desk, he dragged himself from the armchair, put on his glasses, and began to read the draft of his second chapter.

> *Dark and stormy night white cross of lightning the half-wit was moaning Laura in the park and the rain the half-wit my sister the smell of the trees my sister . . .*

Half-wit. Bonday yawned. *Half-wit.* The word was like the longed-for but impossible dog. It howled at him from the page and grated on his ears. How could he improve on it? *Mental defective? Cretin?* Exhausted by the effort, the uphill struggle, his sense of duty in hand-to-hand combat with his sloth, his lack of inspiration, his lack of some friendly muse, he fell asleep.

The doorbell pitched him violently awake. "I'll get it," he shouted to the maid, and shot out toward the temporary freedom that the mail afforded him each morning.

But there was little to keep him from Laura and the half-wit. Some junk mail, the telephone bill, a letter from his brother-in-law asking him for money, a large missive from some government department, and a small

pink envelope. Bonday didn't hesitate: He opened the
small pink envelope first.

It was signed by María Inés, who wrote in the unmis-
takable style, the laborious handwriting, of his adoles-
cent admirers. She'd have bitten nails and faulty
grammar and would be easy enough to carry off to a
hotel but so dreary in bed, talking all the time, and then
there would be the handwritten pages that one would
have to read and, even worse, praise. How come I get
landed with the intellectuals while someone else gets the
pretty ones ׃. . . ? On the point of tearing up the letter, he recalled sad times when love had been in short
supply, blank afternoons inadequately filled by women
friends faithful to a past in which Bonday might very
well have boasted of his conquests (but he was a gentleman and never did), women friends loyal to other
afternoons less languid, less evocative than those of the
present. Just in case, he stowed the pink note, in all its
syntactical innocence, in a drawer in his desk.

Before opening the large envelope, he looked at the
sender's address. Whom did Bonday know in the Ministry of Agriculture and Tourism? No one. But someone there knew him, because they'd spelled his surname
correctly. He reflected a moment. "Not another special
tax." For the first time he felt like sitting down to work
on his novel. "I'll just say I never got the notification."
And he threw the letter unopened into the wastepaper
basket. But then he felt curious, and his curiosity got
the better of him. He picked up the envelope and
smoothed it out.

He had to read the letter twice before grasping that
no one was demanding payment for anything.

Dear Sir,
    With reference to events which are now com-
mon knowledge and which affect one of the most

important of our institutions in the international arena, the President Herrero National Theater, the authorities concerned wish to inform you of your appointment as a member of the Special Investigative Commission.

The said Commission will seek to clarify the causes which have led to the collapse of our prestige in that sector of the South American continent which falls within our domain.

Please contact:

José Castro Miranda
Foreign Affairs Department
Avenida Roma Antica 3, Office 158B

Yours faithfully,
Hugh Pantaenius

Bonday knew nothing about these events that were apparently common knowledge. He hurried off to find the newspaper.

• 4 •

Dear Emilio,

I must just write you a few lines to tell you that I got a telephone call from your friend, the director of Abé Publishers.

Ah, faithful Emilio! I used to like to think that I never complained too much about my eight hours a day of invoices and filing. But if you took the trouble to recommend me secretly to these publishers, I obviously didn't keep *that* quiet about my sorrows.

Last night I couldn't sleep for thinking about the interview. Gertrudis heard me tossing and turning in bed and switched on the light. "You're dreaming again," she complained. My nightmares are the most exciting thing in her life. I could see it coming: the sermon, the interrogation, and the cup of lime-flower tea. It was a good dream, I said. And nothing more. (On the principle that to avert failure, one never talks about success.)

At last, a world of books. A paradise. If I get the job, I can escape from this sordid pension and Gertrudis and go somewhere else to start a totally new existence.

I'm not building up any false hopes. They just rise to the surface on their own, of their own accord.

Love,
Renata

Life always makes my decisions for me. It's like a novel without a plot, a short story without a story. In the end, after making full use of rhetorical devices past and present—reversing chronology, sprinkling the page with quotes, multiple viewpoints, stream of consciousness, collage, etc.—one looks at the last sad dot dot dot, the final miserable square bracket that marks the frontier of one's desperation, and discovers that in fact one has nothing to say, and then one declares, with suicidal arrogance, that the value of this work lies in its experimental nature and its use of language. That's why life and I have come to an agreement; my creative freedom consists merely in providing explanations for what has happened.

Dear Emilio,
    I didn't get the job. But your friend was very kind. I was shaking with nerves, so to calm me down, he began by talking to me about your books, about how intelligent you are, how sensitive, about your way with people. Then he asked me straight out, "Any previous experience?" (I exhausted my curriculum vitae in two stuttered seconds.) "University degree?" (I've no

evidence of my brief attendance at classes in the Arts Faculty.) "Typing?" (Only with two fingers.) "Bookkeeping?"

He looked at me long and hard. I know that look. When I was a little girl, they took me to a local healer to cure a stomach upset. They tried the treatment twice, magic passes, invocations. It was on the third visit and the third failure that I got that look, the same look your friend the director gave me.

And I admit it: I'm your classic loser. Some people say I show promise. But the owner of the pension, the shopkeeper on the corner, the director of the publishing house, they all want results *now*. I could see him looking (the poor man, he so wanted to do you a favor) for some indication of ability in my slight frame, my old-fashioned dress, and my face stiff with shyness. With a terribly sad smile he held out his hand. "Fine. You'll be hearing from me soon. And if you write to Emilio, give him my regards. He's got real talent, genius even."

The ghost of failure is very real. I went out into the street. I could hardly believe it was the same summer morning I'd set out on, heading toward a better future.

It was drizzling. You'd call it some kind of sentimental pathetic fallacy, but the rain joined forces with my misfortune and almost made me cry, standing there with no umbrella. Blindly I stopped a bus. I got off at the block the agricultural machinery office is on, and only then did I realize that there is some value in routine. And who should be in my office but Lucy. A first-class shorthand-typist, speed-reader, and expert administrator of excellent appearance. *She* doesn't just show promise. "Mr. Smithford would like to see you," she said, adding with a charming smile, "you're late."

Again I let myself be looked over by a pair of friendly eyes that reconnoitered with pained embarrassment the brief terrain of my ineptitude. Then I was told that the firm no longer required my services. They weren't giving me the sack, they just no longer required me. After only three months in a job you don't get any compensation.

I went back to the Pension Stella Maris and, like a beaten dog retreating to its kennel, threw myself on the bed. A minute later came a howl from Gertrudis, who yanked the bedspread out from under me to save it from my muddy shoes. Poor Gertrudis. Reasonably enough, she was furious. I'm the bane of her life. She's the one who cleans, polishes, tidies, pins up little posters that say "Home Sweet Home" and "Haste Ye Back." I refuse to wear the felt slippers she gives me, I leave my books all over the floor, and I take up our one small table with my typewriter. Oh yes, and I get depressed and have nightmares.

If you could see her (with her bathrobe only just covering her flashy underwear), and hear her (she'd be late reporting to the police station and the boys would make a terrible fuss), you couldn't help admiring her. Gertrudis has such faith in life! She puts so much energy into her loves and hates! Obediently I removed my shoes, obediently I drank the cup of lime-flower tea.

I let myself imagine you in France. It's eve-

ning, it's not raining, and you're reading or
writing by the light of a lamp. Now you see your
friend Renata as you did so many times at that
café on the south side. With a book between us,
an ocean between us, we begin to talk. I tell you
(you're far away, and distance cures the sin of
pride) that I'm afraid I won't find a job. And
then suddenly I'm joking with you, laughing.

You were right. Even in my sadness I'm not
constant.

> Love,
> Renata

• 5 •

THERE WAS NOTHING about it in the editorial, nothing in the financial section, nothing in the society pages. There were only the sports and the children's section left when Bonday spotted the prominently displayed article:

WHAT A NERVE!
The magazine *Trap*, of Belville West, Ohio, USA, has published an outrageous lie about our country. Once again foreign ignorance gives birth to a calumny. *We will not stand idly by.* We give below, without comment, the offending article.

"Honestly, the lengths the foreign press will go to," Bonday said to his wife as he settled down in an armchair in the living room.

Fact or fiction? This capital city, often referred to as the Paris of South America, *denies* the existence of its own National Theater. And yet your correspondent has visited and admired its imposing Spanish baroque-style architecture. The President Herrero National Theater occupies a

19

block circumscribed by the following streets: Main Street, Boulevard des Lilas, Calle San Felipe Mago, and Calle Los Gracos. But it isn't its position in the center of this charming city that's odd. A series of interviews with top-ranking officials and with notable figures in the artistic and intellectual worlds confirms that they do not even know of its existence.

Bonday stopped reading. "Unbelievable," he said.

"What theater do they mean, Tacho?" his wife asked, raising her eyes from her embroidery.

"Don't be so impatient, Elsa. Let us first drain this bitter cup to the last drop. 'Not without some difficulty I managed to take one of my interviewees with me to the palace . . .' "

"There isn't a palace in the city," said his wife.

"Don't interrupt, Elsa. 'Not without some difficulty I managed to take one of my interviewees with me to the palace, and there was no way he could deny the solid reality of the building: its wrought-iron balconies, its friezes with garlands and cupids, and its imposing bronze doors.' The nerve of the man." Bonday rustled the paper furiously. "And what about this? 'I will not weary my readers with a full description of my investigation. Here are the surprising facts I gleaned . . .' "

As he paused to light his pipe, Bonday's hand was trembling. Then, slowly, angrily enunciating each word, he read out loud:

(a) The President Herrero National Theater not only exists but is subsidized by the Ministry of Education, the Municipal Council, and the Association of Libraries and Affiliated Institutions.

(b) It employs 435 people including 8 permanent actors and 10 understudies.

(c) Since 1920 they have staged only one play: *Hamlet* by William Shakespeare.

"Unbelievable!" Bonday exclaimed, rolling up the newspaper and thumping the table with it. "Not only do they invent this idea that we don't know about our own National Theater, they go on to say that in a list of this country's presidents there isn't a single Herrero."

"Herrero? Which Herrero?"

Bonday stroked his mustache thoughtfully. "Have you noticed how fast news travels these days? The letter arrived the same day the newspaper article appeared. And still people complain about how slow the government is to act!" Santiago Bonday stood up and, firmly and with dignity, announced to his wife, "I won't be working on my novel today. I'm going to sit down this instant and write a reply to that letter."

Instead of summer we're having a premature autumn. It's rainy, cold, and windy. I felt as if I was suffocating in the pension, so I went out for a walk. Out of sheer habit I ended up in the center. I strolled round the square, looked in some shop windows, and stopped at a café. I wanted to talk to someone, preferably a stranger, because I was ashamed of the sadness that I knew would be impossible to conceal from a friend.

It was after lunch when I reached the port with its huge ships that I would have gladly sailed away in just to escape this prison. There were trapped-looking people leaning on the wall along the coast road, gazing sadly out toward the gray horizon, imagining the ocean beyond those turbid, grubby waters. I shivered in the wind, my stomach aching with hunger. But if you're cold and hungry, it's best to walk. So I left the wall and set off. With my eyes glued to the pavement and the asphalt, I walked first in a straight line, then in circles, until I was exhausted. I looked for a café; there wasn't one. There wasn't even a square. It was siesta time, and in the deserted streets there didn't even seem to be a bus. My feet were really sore. I couldn't bring myself to sit down on the pavement. The city, despite its proliferation of huge buildings, is like a tightly closed door unless you happen to know the right password. Then I saw the church, and I intend no sarcasm when I say, Give thanks, weary traveler, for religion and the temples it builds, where you can at least sit down for a while.

The church was shut. I rapped on the door several times. I could hear the noise echo round the empty nave. I resisted the temptation to leave. I beat on the door with my fists. "If the priest is hiding in there somewhere, I'll flush him out." No one answered, despite the fact that I was talking out loud now. The church was set in a garden. I went across the grass in the wind and the rain and found a door at the back. By the door there was a bell. I pressed it.

"Yes?"

A very thin, slight old man appeared, with bright blue eyes and a small head crowned by a mop of snow-white hair.

"I want to talk to the priest."

The old man put a pair of round glasses on his tiny nose and looked at me distrustfully.

"What for?"

"Can I come in?"

"The church is closed. We open at five."

I got angry. If hunger trains you in anything, it's aggression. "So the priest is having his siesta, is he?"

The little blue eyes flashed. "And why shouldn't he?"

"Tell him to get up. There's a . . ." I floundered around for a good lie ". . . there's a lost soul here, that's it, a lost soul."

Above the glasses, the white eyebrows arched. "You're from the film club."

"No, I'm not."

"The laundry then."

"Listen, I want to talk to the priest. Or is the church just here for decoration?"

I heard a little laugh.

"That's what a lot of people think. Come in," he said, putting a hand on my shoulder. The hand, small as a child's, appeared from a long gray sleeve, part of a vast, ill-knitted cardigan. "Sit down and wait a moment. The priest has to get dressed."

Ah, the rock on which the church is built: a spacious carpeted room with bookshelves, comfortable arm-chairs, and a fire in the grate.

"Look," I said, "don't wake him up just yet. The truth is, I'm not in that much of a hurry. Let the poor man sleep."

The old man took off his glasses and rubbed his eyes. Shrugging his shoulders, he said, "Actually, I am the poor man."

"Father, I didn't . . ." I leaped up, but he'd already left the room.

When he returned in his cassock and white dog-collar, I tried to apologize. "Really, there was no need . . ."

But he was already sitting down in the armchair op-posite me, folding his hands and saying calmly, "Come on then, I'm listening."

His kind face, the honest blue eyes, made me dumb with shame.

"You wanted to talk to the priest, the priest was asleep, and that annoyed you, right?"

"Father . . ."

"Father Collins. Don't apologize for interrupting my siesta. At my age one sleeps all the time. Except at night. If you like, I'll forgive you. That will save time. Sooner or later I'd have to forgive you anyway. Let's see. How long is it since you visited the Lord's house?"

I rapidly juggled with dates. But there was some-thing so clear and honest about the old man I couldn't deceive him. I confessed that I wasn't a Catholic. Then that I wasn't a Christian, or a Jew for that matter. Or a Protestant. At last, with an unintentional hauteur born of shyness and a fear of offending him, I said rather incoherently, "I know I've no right to waste your time. It's just that I'm, how can I put it, an agnostic."

He laughed. He had a very young laugh.

"Ah, agnostics are our best customers! If you knew the number of agnostics I've married on Saturday night, baptized on Sunday morning, and consoled on their deathbeds when their time comes. On the other hand we have our faithful Catholic flock. Either they don't come at all or they come to ask us to put on all kinds of activities that have nothing to do with our mission in the world. They're either absentees or fanatics, I never know what the devil they're up to, so to speak. Still, we all have our cross to bear." He looked at me over the top of his glasses, still smiling. "But agnostics, my child, are always prepared to accept the will of God. And do you know why? Because their politeness gets the better of their skepticism."

He turned his head toward the door and shouted at the top of his voice. "Filomena! Filomena!"

A small gray-haired woman appeared, gaunt and fearful.

"Tea, Father?"

Father Collins pointed to me, laughing.

"Yes please, tea for a lost soul. And a big plate of cakes."

Dear Emilio,

I can't find a job, autumn is already upon us, and all this worry is making a different person of me. And if I'm a different person, why shouldn't Emilio be a different person over there in France, a person who doesn't write to me?

You can judge how worried I am by the fact that today I had a long talk with an old Irish priest. But we didn't talk about religion. Odd though it may seem, we talked about Gilgamesh. Some remark about the rain got us talking about the Great Flood; from the flood we got on to Noah and from Noah to the poor Sumerian hero seeking immortality. And how I talked. When he said good-bye to me at the door, the priest gave me a sly smile. "You didn't interrupt my siesta just to talk about an epic Sumerian poem." I think I blushed, but I didn't say anything. Nor would you if you'd been fixed with that same clear gaze. "Trust in God, my child. He always provides. If He didn't provide, why would we bother to conceive the idea of His charity?"

I'm so stupid. I came back to the boarding-house, dead tired, my stomach full, glad to have talked about a poem, a poet, rather than my ridiculous fears, the awfulness of these last few days. And then I realized that I hadn't noted down the name of the street, that I don't know where the church is, that I'll never again see the remarkable Father Collins who befriended me on this foul autumn day.

I look forward to hearing your news.

Love,
Renata

∘ 7 ∘

"I'M SANTIAGO BONDAY."

Across a table overflowing with papers, Castro Miranda held out his hand. Bonday shook it.

"I got your letter yesterday."

The other man smiled, but his face remained a blank. He was short, heavily built, with thick gray hair plastered down with brilliantine and the rosy cheeks of a prosperous peasant. The smile he gave Bonday was as broad as it was perplexed. "Ah, yes, the letter," he said, nodding vigorously.

"I sat down to answer it at once," said Bonday, "then I remembered how bad the mail is, and decided to bring it myself. So here I am."

Castro Miranda blinked.

"You were quite right, quite right," he said, adding, with a sweeping gesture, "Do sit down, please, make yourself comfortable."

"I'm fine as I am," said Bonday, after a quick glance about him.

Apart from the table at which the official sat, and a ladder, there wasn't a stick of furniture in the room. Folders and rolls of paper fastened with rubber bands were scattered over the recently sanded wooden floor, which was still waiting to be varnished. The office was tiny and smelled of fresh paint. There was one picture on the wall. It showed a pair of golden scales against a starry sky. Surrealism, thought Bonday. No doubt about it, surrealism will always be a strong influence. And then he spoke because he couldn't bear the silence, especially when he was forced to stand up with nothing to lean on but his pipe. He had lit it partly to hide his embarrassment and partly to avoid succumbing to a desire to sit down on the ladder.

"Your decision to appeal to members of the Establishment has my wholehearted support. Never let it be said that Santiago Bonday is one of those ivory-tower writers. The pains and joys of the people are my pains and joys, and I . . . ."

He couldn't go on. To his astonishment, the man's lips trembled, and he took out his handkerchief to cover his face. Bonday thought he heard a sob. He instinctively stepped back.

"No, please, don't go." Castro Miranda mopped up invisible tears and took a deep breath. "You must understand, sir. It's the pressure of the job. Stress. And one isn't made of stone. Whenever anyone talks about the pain of the people, I always think something bad is going to happen." Castro Miranda shook himself like a wet dog. "Something bad! In fact, nothing ever happens here. But I get upset. Like a babe-in-arms. You'd never think I'd passed with honors in Don Patricio Montes's futurology course. Do you know Don Patricio?"

Someone knocked at the door.

"You see, not a moment's peace. Come in!" The door opened a crack and no more. "Come in! Come in!"

In came an old man with long white hair, a vast, veiny nose, and a body so thin it looked as if it might break in two. He went straight up to Bonday, holding out a small packet, his smile revealing two solitary teeth in a cavernous mouth.

"No, dear lady," sighed Castro Miranda. "Don't give it to the gentleman, give it to me."

Only then, horrified, did Bonday notice the dress and the handbag swinging from a bony shoulder. He promised himself he would die before he got that old.

"Just look at this lady," said Castro Miranda, with a tenderness that disgusted Bonday, who could more readily imagine the horrors of old age. "Young people these days lack her vigor. Just look at her, the little flirt, look at the high heels she's put on. Tomorrow she'll be back in her wheelchair. But what an example for the depressed youth of today. Thank you, dear. No, no time to talk, go straight back home now, this gentleman and I are very busy. That's it, mind the ladder."

With a combination of affectionate taps and shoves, Castro Miranda showed her to the door. Then he held out the package to Bonday.

"I can assure you, Señor . . . Señor . . ."

"Bonday."

"That's it, Señor Bonday. I can assure you that I haven't the slightest interest in opening it. You know what it is, don't you?"

"Perhaps we could return to the matter that brought me here?"

"Just a second. If you'll allow me, I'd like you to read an important document." He opened the packet and took out a yellowing piece of paper. "Read it, please."

It was a theater program. Beneath a blurred emblem that had once been a woman's head, Bonday read:

THE PRESIDENT HERRERO THEATER
HAMLET, PRINCE OF DENMARK
Last few days

"Ah, the source of all the scandal!" Bonday explained.

Castro Miranda let out a laugh. "So you knew. Of

course, the Herrero Affair. Now I understand, you're the writer. Of course. I knew the name rang a bell. Believe me, Master"—solemnly he opened his arms wide—"my admiration for your work knows no bounds. I'm proud of names such as yours, reputations that project a positive image of our country abroad."

"It's a disgraceful affair," said Bonday, flattered and embarrassed.

The other man shook his head and smiled sadly. "You're right there. Since the news got out, we haven't had a moment's peace. People are up in arms about it."

He dived into the sea of papers that flooded the desk, took out a newspaper, and showed Bonday the headlines.

COUNTRY A LAUGHINGSTOCK
WHO SAYS THE NATIONAL THEATER DOESN'T EXIST?

"It may not exist, but it costs us a lot of money," said the official with an abrupt laugh. "The budget allowance for that wretched theater costs us a fortune. And with the economic crisis the country's in . . ."

"It'll be a question then of proving them wrong."

Castro Miranda sighed. "There is a crisis, Master, there is a crisis. But let's not talk about that now."

"I was referring to the theater."

"Oh, the National Theater!" Castro Miranda nodded in the direction of the door. "You've seen the proof yourself. You saw the lady who brought the package? An *ingenue* in the company in 1932. Hundreds of people like her have turned up. Several generations of actors carrying photos, programs, documents. And if anyone imagines the theater doesn't exist, just let them go along to the corner of Main Street and Calle Los Gracos."

He brought out another cutting from a drawer in his desk.

"Look at this moving letter written to the Sunday supplement of *La Presse*. Really, Master, I think the letters column in newspapers deserves more attention from the critics. That's where you find our really committed literature. Just listen to what a lady from the best society has to say:

"How unjust to forget the great leaders of our country when in their place come only hordes of *parvenus*, intent on destroying our traditions. As if it weren't enough to have the municipal gardeners lopping off the branches of those trees which the poet, in words of untranslatable beauty, called *arbres magnifiques; ces arbres* that line our boulevards and are the wonder of foreign visitors. Few people today remember President Celmiro G. Herrero, who, brief flower, ruled over the fate of this country for one unforgettable week in March. Having had the honor to receive His Excellency *chez moi* on the last Sunday of his term in office, I find myself forced to say publicly: We are not amused."

Castro Miranda looked at the cutting glumly. "If you leave out the words you can't understand, you have to admit that the lady's hit the nail on the head. We do have short memories."

So it was *that* Herrero, thought Bonday. "We certainly do," he agreed.

For a moment they felt happy, united in their condemnation of this great national defect.

"And that's where you come in, Bonday."

"The Investigative Commission."

"Right. I must warn you, it's going to be a tough job. Your efforts won't be rewarded by any . . . Well, apart from the recognition of your country and a medal from the government . . ."

"I see. . . ."

"Thank you, Master. I knew you wouldn't withhold your support. Ah no, you intellectuals aren't like us, you don't sell yourselves for thirty pieces of silver!"

"No, but I . . ."

"No, don't say another word. I used to be a bit of a poet myself. I've probably got some verses around here somewhere."

"Perhaps this isn't the best time."

"I was fifteen with a rather lyrical bent. . . ."

"What's the first step for the Investigative Commission?" asked Bonday desperately.

"Ah, a man of action!" Castro Miranda smiled, taking up a piece of paper and writing a few lines on it. "Go to this address and ask for Captain Beh."

"Captain?"

"Captain of cavalry—retired—Saturnino Beh. Say Don Castro sent you, and he'll see you at once."

Bonday hurriedly shook the other's hand. He feared further disconcerting instructions.

"It's been a pleasure, Don Castro."

The other burst out laughing.

"You intellectuals! You're all the same. Living in a world of your own, distracted, blinded by the effort of creation. I'm not Castro Miranda."

"What?"

"Castro Miranda has gone to Las Vegas as our country's distinguished representative at an international conference on the impact of inflation on developing countries. I merely have the honor of being your humble servant." He bowed ceremoniously and with a honey-eyed smile said, "My name is Hugo Pantaenius."

· 8 ·

Dear Emilio,

Why do people insist that poverty is such a virtuous state? I've had firsthand experience of it lately, and I'm hard put to find any good effects on my character. All that seems to have happened is that I've split into several people: the resigned drinker of white coffees at the bar on the corner; the person who gets offended when Gertrudis advises her to offer herself up to the boys at the police station; the brilliant orator who just about manages to placate her main creditor, the Catalan landlord of my shared room; the woman who reads nothing but the newspaper (and then only the classified ads); another who watches horrified as the soles wear thin on her one pair of shoes. No, there's no virtue in these brand-new Renatas born of the daily exercise of abstinence. But life is endlessly rich in ironies. Do you remember Marga Arregui? How could you forget Marga (you'll say), that face, that hair, those eyes, that creature of the night, who recited Lorca, all orange blossom and lemon-lime, all *verde que te quiero verde*, tall, pale, intense Marga, all passion and honey, the ruin of young men's hearts and of mature minds, whom you used to call (mockingly but no less in love with her than all the others) the Passionflower.

Well, I met her a few days ago, after not having seen her for ages. I didn't recognize her. She stopped me in the street, screeching out my name and swamping me in French perfume. She's cut off that mane of hair you liked so much and married a German engineer. She has a house in a very classy area, a son, a lover (sorry, she was the one who included him in her list of recent acquisitions), and an art gallery where, she confessed, she escapes from the travails of domestic life. She made me promise to visit her. "There'll be just a few close friends," she said, "because I loathe parties."

The house of Señora Hedelstoff, as she is now (or is it Hesseldof? Her husband whistles through his false teeth when he says the name) is large, luxurious, and packed with close friends. Her close friends are all well-fed, well-dressed, and well-read people. They talk—how they talk!—but always rather querulously. They talk about books, paintings, music, etc., but always with that querulous note in their voices. They talk about life here, so mediocre, they say, so provincial. What about me? Do I listen to their profound dialogues and gloomily shake my head? No. The first and only thing I'm aware of at these gatherings of Marga's is a marvelous, fascinating creation, the exquisite work of some anonymous artist: The Buffet. Yes, the buffet with its delicious-smelling platters of meat, fine sauces, delicate fruits. My body trembles with emotion. The blood runs wild in my veins. Ah, but I've forgotten the other Renata, Renata the Proud. Confronted by that table, I know that I am hungry, know it more painfully than when I am seated before coffee and a bun or the plate of pasta I allow myself every other day. I know why. Quite honestly, the answer lacks poetry. It's just hunger. And my humiliation at being hungry because I'm out of work sticks in my throat. The one mouthful I dare to try tastes hard, insipid, gritty.

My present thinness, the result of this period of privation, lends interest to my appearance. As I don't say a word (to save breath, because I tire easily), people think I'm intelligent and (something that would have been unthinkable when I used to eat regularly) wise. I've no shortage of suitors. One gentleman *chez* Marga said to me, "Your eyes reflect all the world's sorrows, and in them lies an eternity of time." Idiot. The only things lying in my eyes are the classified ads, the Catalan's threats to put me out on the street, and Gertrudis and her propositions.

But when Marga asks me about my job, when she asks if I really am well, I reply languidly that I dedicate my life to literature! What demon of pride possesses me? Why don't I humbly ask for help? A teaching post, secretary to the engineer, a salesgirl, something, dear God, to haul me out of this quagmire. But no, not me. No, I have to make my way alone. Me and my soul, independent and free. And dying of hunger.

Last night I fled the house of your Passionflower without even saying good-bye. I wasn't fleeing from her, from her friends, or her world. I was fleeing from my conscience. Last night I had the horrific realization that I accepted her hospitality in the sordid expectation that I would find protection, a roof over my head, food.

You see what a poor foundation poverty provides for building a system of ethics.

Renata

Last night the girl in room 4, Alba, turned up with a pile of photographs her boyfriend had taken of her. He's a cab driver, married with four children. Alba was happy. While she showed us the photos in the kitchenette in the boardinghouse, she laughed a lot, her broad, dark face shining. The girls from room 7 passed me the photos, laughing along with Alba.

Alba sitting on the edge of the bed, naked, lax, smiling a foolish, grateful smile. Alba posing in front of the mirror. Alba stretched out, facedown. Alba holding up a breast to the camera. Her lover took the photos of her because he loves her; you're so pretty, sweetheart, he'd said. I congratulated her. "You look lovely, Alba." "I look really pretty in that one, don't I?" I got up and, without bothering to put on a coat, went out into the street, along the square where I sat down on a bench. Luckily no one else was there.

It was my twenty-third birthday today. I didn't celebrate.

· 9 ·

The Special Investigative Commission, comprising Captain of Cavalry (retd.) Saturnino Beh and the writer Santiago Bonday, now confronted the first obstacle in their investigation. Twice Bonday had been up and down the street where, according to the journalist from Belville West, Ohio, the baroque palace of the National Theater was to be found. It was raining in torrents. Barely protected by an umbrella that the wind threatened to snatch from him, Bonday read the address he had written down in his notebook.

"The street names are right—Main Street, Boulevard des Lilas, Calle San Felipe Mago, Calle Los Gracos."

But no sign of a theater. There was much that was familiar to him about that particular block of streets: the corner where, what seemed a century ago, he used to rendezvous with Marga Hedelstoff (when she was still Arregui); the gloomy barred windows of the tax office; the line of pensioners that, despite the rain, already reached around the block; the Friends of the Arts Exhibition Hall; the goods-vehicle entrance to the Central Market. . . . Water began to seep through the soles of his shoes. With a sudden decisiveness born of ill-humor, Bonday stuffed his notebook into his pocket, crossed the road, and went into a café. He sat down at a table by the window and ordered a coffee. It tasted of nothing. He gulped down some of the insipid brew and looked out of the window, hoping the rain might have eased. It had. He was thinking of calling the waiter when the moment of enlightenment occurred. He almost dropped the cup he was raising to his lips.

The National Theater was right there, before his eyes. The baroque palace with its garlands, wrought-iron balconies, and imposing bronze doors. Hidden among the litter of advertisements for cigarettes and mineral water, edged by the line of pensioners numb with cold, concealed behind the comings and goings of the trucks loaded with fruit and vegetables, encumbered with signs with arrows indicating the window for payments, deposits, and various debts.

Bonday threw some money on the table and ran over to the bronze doors. They were closed. Impatience and the rain that now came down in buckets overwhelmed him. He looked for an entrance. Apart from the one for trucks there didn't appear to be any. Exhausted, soaked to the skin, frozen, he said to himself, "I'll go back to the café and see if I can spot it from there. At least the palace exists."

It was then that he saw the arrow. It was to the left of the bronze doors and pointed to a small, padlocked side door with no handle. Bonday succumbed to his curiosity and peered through the keyhole. He saw a lighted corridor at the end of which was a whitewashed wall. On the wall, painted in green in a childish script, was this announcement:

WILLIAM SHAKESPEARE'S
HAMLET
LAST FEW DAYS

∘ 10 ∘

Dear Emilio,

Yesterday, instead of dropping my letter into the mailbox on the corner, I went to the Main Post Office. There's a postal strike. For several weeks now no letters have entered or left the country. A clerk gave me back my letters. "Don't put them in the mailbox, *señorita*, there's no point." What can I do? Go on writing, of course. I'll send you my monologues when the "dialogue between management and the postal workers" has reached a successful conclusion. By parcel post, probably.

*   *   *

The gods be praised! It's happened, Emilio. I've just been handed this letter. Happiness comes in the form of a most enigmatic message, but at least it's here. This is what it says:

> We are pleased to inform you that, at the suggestion of Don Carlos Bagliatti, director of the Abé Publishing Company and consultant *ad honorem* to the Manufacturing Section, you have been appointed to post Z-k at the President

Herrero National Theater, as provided for in Decree No. 34528.

Report to the Personnel Office of the said theater, Main Street and Calle San Felipe Mago, between 9 and 5.

I remain your humble servant,

Hugo Pantaenius

Imagine that! A theater! What do you think Z-k means? Who cares? Will they pay me? Who cares? I can say good-bye to invoices for agricultural machinery, to shop counters, to Gertrudis's police station. A theater! It doesn't just bring me closer to the possibility of eating, it brings me closer to what's dearest to me, to my destiny.

Now I remember what my Irish priest said. Whether it's down to fortune, chance, the guilty conscience of your friend the director, you, my loyal friend in France, or Father Collins's Provider, I don't much care.

Ashamed of my skepticism, free from all sorrows,

Love,
Renata

P.S. The letter of redemption was delivered by hand. The postal strike continues.

The typewriter is on the table, which is also our chest of drawers. Everything, Gertrudis's jars of face cream and powder, little folders, vases, our Lady of Casamanta, it all gets piled on the bed while I write. Except for the mirror. I look at myself and I see that I'm quite

right: I'm worthless. Why am I sad, today of all days? I
see a face with prominent cheekbones, dark, cowlike
eyes, long, uneven blond bangs. A timid mouth, a
crooked smile, and a long neck appearing out of the
ridiculous lace edging of this nightdress, which I'm
wearing as I write and which I brought with me four
years ago and never got round to exchanging for something less childish. A chin held exaggeratedly high, a
fictitious obstinacy, false courage, the chin of someone
drowning in the sea, lifted toward the air and the sky.
I'm sad. Freedom arrives and I'm sad. I should cut these
bangs, it's no advantage for a woman of twenty-three
to look younger than she is. If I were a man, I'd grow
a mustache. But I'm a woman, and I like long hair.
Anyway, at least it's a good color, a nice texture. It's
pretty. I'm not, though. Emilio liked my eyes and he
was a severe judge, not given to compliments. I have
more faith in the praises of an impartial friend than in
all the sweet talk of a lover. He's very impartial. Too
impartial. So I won't cut my hair. It would only mean
going to the hairdresser's. And as Marga Hedelstoff says,
"The hairdresser's, my dear, is a whole different world."
A woman is sad, for no reason, against all reason, and
she looks at herself in the mirror. No, it isn't me, it's
this room, it's Gertrudis's. I have to get another room,
just for me. I have to believe in a new beginning. The
theater, that job, is a new beginning. I'm going to leave
here as soon as I can.

   I got a letter from my aunt today, sprinkled with tears.
She asks me to go back because now my cousin has come
to the city too. Another exile, another dreamer. The
headmistress of the school has promised my aunt that
she'll give me a teaching post. She sends me a few pesos, the poor thing. How can I explain to her that I've
just found a wonderful job? That I'm moving toward

what I want to do with my life? That I'm waiting for Emilio, to show him the chapters I've written, to receive the books he'll bring me from France, to tell him stories? For the first time in ages everything's going smoothly, and I'm sad. It's just a momentary tremor. But why? Look in the mirror, *señorita*. There's the truth of the matter: I feel horribly alone. Because I *am* alone.

∘ 11 ∘

THE CLUMSY green letters painted on a whitewashed wall, the cellar (suitable accommodation for a mouse, not the monumental work of William Shakespeare), the sheer poverty of that final bunker where the National Theater had found refuge: It all wounded Bonday's sensibilities so profoundly that he had to retreat to his house in Arroyo Manso in the tranquillity of the suburbs. Some weeks later he was heard to say, "It was an instructive experience. My vision of the culture of this country reached a turning point." And then, emphasizing the words by tapping his pipe on the arm of the chair, "We've had enough of literature. The time has come for writers to show a real commitment to the here and now."

Already celebrated as a writer of letters, Bonday once again demonstrated his mastery of the art. Long, passionate, eloquent letters rained on newspapers and magazines in a bitter denunciation of the financial straits and the neglect into which the National Theater had fallen. A group of disciples found him, lost among gardens and quiet paths, dedicating himself solely to writing in protest against that scandal, exhausted after a hard day at his typewriter. To the young admirers getting off the train there was something touching about the figure of Bonday, sitting on a bench at the railway station at Arroyo Manso, a wan smile on his lips. He epitomized the artist whose commitment to reality has torn him away from the pleasures of fiction and the linguistic dreams of literature. They admired the integrity of the man who stood up now to greet them, surprised to see them there, as if one of the trains that he had watched pass by from the solitary refuge of his bench had brought him an unexpected gift of the friendship and human company that his courage had rejected and that his sociable nature gratefully accepted. Just occasionally during those gatherings, organized secretly to distract him, he would break off in midsentence, rest his head on the back of his armchair, and close his eyes. His wife would explain softly to their friends.

"He's been very depressed."

In the small room where the Special Investigative Commission awaited the arrival of the minister of culture in order to deliver their report, the only furniture was a round table and a few stiff colonial-style chairs. On one of the chairs, in tense silence, sat the erect figure of Captain of Cavalry (retd.) Saturnino Beh. On another, the languid figure of Bonday.

They had shaken hands after a chilly introduction.

"I can't tell you how sorry I am that we've only managed to meet for the first time now, Captain. I told your secretary how keen I was to exchange views before this definitive meeting. . . ."

"There was no need," grunted the other. He took off his three-cornered hat with the red plume, sat down on the chair, crossed his arms, and said not a word more.

Bonday had spent the morning in front of the mirror in his library rehearsing unforgettable phrases, and for a good quarter of an hour now had watched them drop into the void. He played nervously with the gold top of his Parker pen. *Should I quote Shakespeare? Talk to him about the theater? Shall I ask after his family?* He looked furtively at the three-cornered hat on the empty seat. *A three-cornered hat. Pretty ridiculous in this day and age. They're so reluctant to give up their uniforms, get rid of the swords, the feathers, and the hats.*

Another ten minutes went by. Bonday was drowning in the silence.

"Well, the cold weather will soon be on us, Captain."

There was no reply. Bonday was astonished by the severe expression on the inscrutable face, which merely twitched (agreeing? ordering him to be silent?), then turned toward the door. *No room for frivolity in the military world.* His body was starting to ache. The seat was very hard and his spine, since the captain appeared to be comfortable enough, feebly civilian. Bonday crossed and uncrossed his legs, brought his heels together then apart, swung his right foot, leaned forward, and then sat upright. There was nothing to be done; any position, aggravated by the silence, was agony. He said to himself, "I'll use the discomfort of the chair, like Demosthenes' pebbles, to help me to go over my speech again."

Conscious of the importance of being a celebrated writer in that gray world of government officials, and knowing that the media would be there to report on the scene to the public at large, Bonday had carefully memorized the text that would introduce his report. With secret delight, anticipating the applause, mentally smiling to the cameras, he went over the beginning of his address:

I have walked the streets of this city like any other man. It doesn't matter if at the end of my days they put up a stone with no name on it, for time erodes

*even marble. But should the National Theater suffer
this appalling South American fate, this death by barbarism?*

"Lack of punctuality is unforgivable."

Startled, Bonday turned toward Captain Beh.

"It shows a complete lack of respect," repeated the
captain with a grunt and a glance at the door. "A complete lack of respect for morality and order."

"Well, yes," stuttered Bonday, intimidated but thank-
ful for even this rather abrupt opening for a dialogue,
"it's true we're not a very punctual race. It's the climate,
the heat—"

"We're not in the tropics, so they'll have to find some
other excuse. People just aren't capable of getting
up early."

Bonday tried to smile. "The early bird catches the
worm," he murmured uncertainly.

Another silence.

"Tell me, Captain," he said hurriedly, to combat the
silence, "did your secretary give you a copy of my
report?"

"She does what she's told, so she must have."

"I would so much have liked to know what you
thought of it. Especially the speech—"

"Don't ask my opinion on such things."

Bonday fell silent. In what part of the anatomy of
this vast man did the force of his undeniable authority
lie? He had a small head, but the luxuriant black mustache with long, downturned ends made up for his small
face and the cranium with its bristle of reddish hair.
His chubby, freckled hands, held clasped against his
uniform jacket, were covered with a coppery down. They
didn't match the mustache and the dark, narrow eyes
at all, as if they belonged to someone else. *It's the erect*

way he carries himself. And the uniform, of course. The uniform. *Do retired officers usually wear uniform?* He was just about to ask the captain when he remembered the brusque, surly replies he had received earlier.

I have walked the streets of this city . . . He knew he had a beautiful voice, firm, elegant, clear. The acoustics in the room were excellent (the creaking of a chair was deafening, as was Bonday's nervous cough). He began to feel better. "We are such stuff as dreams are made on," he would write in his diary that night. Because it was all so like a dream.

The minister of culture and other officials came in. The captain and Bonday stood up. After the formal greetings a secretary read out the text. The minister of culture signed the decree declaring the building situated on the block delimited by Main Street, Boulevard des Lilas, Calle San Felipe Mago, and Calle Los Gracos to be part of the national heritage. Journalists and photographers burst into the room. They all posed for photographs, smiling affably. Bonday put away his pipe and cleared his throat.

"I have walked the streets of this city . . ."

Word for word his speech was set down in notebooks and captured by tape recorders. The ordinary man walking the streets of the city. The headstone with no name. Time eroding marble. The South American fate. But it wasn't Bonday's voice echoing round the room. It was the hard, solemn voice of Captain Beh. Open-mouthed, Bonday watched the plump, freckled hands following the sentences of his text, soft, damp hands that a few minutes later, in a state of some anguish, he would have to clasp, stuttering out his congratulations.

· 12 ·

For the last few days I just haven't felt like
writing to you. Is it the continuing postal strike
denying me a reader? A week isn't a long time,
and yet a lot has happened.

I should begin with an explanation: I'm happy.
And to say that my happiness is born of relief
is by no means to diminish it. To each his own.
From this safe harbor—the President Herrero
National Theater—I look back on my sordid
voyage through unemployment and I know that
now I'm safe. I've gone back to writing my novel,
and I'm reading again. I enjoy the luxury of
being able to forget about myself.

You should see the palace that houses the
theater! It's a world of empty salons with high
walls adorned by friezes of garlands and cupids,
a marble staircase that ascends from the hall to
a circular gallery, stairs that creak among the
silence and shadows, rooms shut up behind
permanently closed doors, and endless corridors, all placed within another, gray world of
offices and enquiry windows and employees in
white overalls. At the heart of this fabulous,

bruised fruit is a stage where *Hamlet* is eternally
played out. Don't ask me why. I don't think
anyone knows. It's just like the ritual repetition
of the same mistake again and again. I doubt
anyone even cares. It just started one day, and
since then this drama, like the kernel of the fruit,
hard, dry, and sterile, has remained, turned in
on itself, a stone placed against the wheel of a
cart that should be moving on, to other plays,
other scenes and characters.

I never tire of wandering round the theater.
There's so much mystery in its empty rooms, in
the spaces opening onto nothing. I admit it: I
love these long random walks, these inexplicable voids. To understand this shameful passion
for great architectural ruins, you'd have to have
been brought up like me among the four solid
walls of my village, or to have lived in the same
room with Gertrudis. The desire to raise it up
in my imagination, to make it beautiful, to con-
vert it into something habitable and useful, goes
hand in hand with a simple instinct to grow, to
make myself tall and strong within it.

I know, you're laughing. You see, on occasion
I can be lyrical as well as scathing.

Love,
Renata

My first day at the theater. It's odd, but it felt hostile.
I'm glad that I didn't let it frighten me, though. With
my letter of appointment in my hand, I went through
the main door of the building on Main Street and Calle
Los Gracos. From behind a desk and a notice that said
Information, a bad-tempered clerk was dealing with a

crowd of lost souls. I joined the line. Twenty minutes later I was asking for the National Theater. The man frowned, took a plan out from a drawer in his desk, studied a drawing consisting of right angles, curves, and scattered letters, and chewed his lips. "The things people ask." The crowd began to protest. "Who told you to ask here?" I pointed to the sign. "We only provide information about things we know, *señorita.*" Then, lowering his voice, he said in a whisper, "I think, though I wouldn't swear to it, that there's a theater just near here. Whether it's the National or not I couldn't say." He told me to go out into the street and look for a small door but not to ring the bell. "Knock," he said, "knock loudly." I left, all set to knock loudly. It was pouring rain by then. In the rain I looked for the little door. There was no need to knock loudly. It was open. I went in and found myself in a corridor with whitewashed walls. On the wall at the end was written in a childish hand in green paint:

WILLIAM SHAKESPEARE'S
HAMLET
LAST FEW DAYS

Beneath the sign was a desk and on the desk a young man. He was thin and dark and sat cross-legged with his chin resting on his hands, his dark, serious eyes watching me. Solitary and impassive, outlined against the whitewashed walls, he seemed like an absurd living illustration for the sign announcing *Hamlet.* But apart from his black hair and eyes there was no other suggestion of mourning about that watchman perched on top of the desk. He was wearing a violent red smock and yellow paint-stained trousers.

"Could you tell me where the Personnel Office is . . . ?"

He took out a watch from the sleeve of his smock, looked first at it, and then over my shoulder toward the door. Then, without saying a word, he lifted me up in his arms and sat me down, like a doll, on the desk.

° 13 °

AND SO Bonday ended his voluntary exile in Arroyo Manso. He'd given in, though not without a fight, to the pleas of Marga Hedelstoff.

"My sweet, I hope you won't stay stuck out there in the country forever."

"The country, as you call it, Marga, is only half an hour from the center."

"It's still awful. So far from your people, Tacho, out there in the midst of all that barbarism. I won't allow it, my sweet, I just won't allow it."

How else can an artist reintegrate himself into the society of his peers except by appearing in the flesh at the odd book launch or preview? So reflected Bonday as his attentive gray eyes calmly perused the suits in his wardrobe in search of one that would prove appropriate for his return to the world. With the exception of talking to Marga's young painters or going to hear the latest author read from his novel (events he regarded with the same trepidation a sailor does a reef of jagged rocks), these high spots in the intellectual life of the city were not unappealing. In addition to the free food and drink there was the spiritual satisfaction of knowing oneself to be one of the few, the best, the ones who counted. However resigned a face Bonday wore, he never missed one of these gatherings.

Born in a province whose only merit for Bonday was
the road connecting it to the capital, he had vigorously
expunged the melancholy truth about his origins. He
felt no nostalgia for his childhood, which he remembered as consisting of endless turns about the village
square, or for his adolescence, which he remembered
as consisting of still more endless turns around the same
square. He was saving up to come to the big city, when
a rich aunt did the decent thing and died before Bonday had succumbed to the temptation of abandoning
literature and taking up paid employment.

From the moment he arrived in the capital, he had
struggled to make a place for himself in those salons
where, despite the tiny number of guests, not another
soul could be squeezed in. Bonday's determination
helped him to rise above minor though nonetheless
vexing humiliations and to negotiate one by one the
hurdles placed in his path. He begged, demanded, flattered. Behind every article, every published story, lay a
melancholy history of telephone calls, invitations to
supper, ploys to get such invitations, feigned loves and
friendships, rejections and acceptances that, together
with his young wife, figured strongly in the debit and
credit columns of his literary career. The appearance
of his first book established him as a name; the second
won him the empty label of "avant-garde novelist"; the
third, to the amazement of both Bonday and his publisher, sold well and made money. By the fifth Bonday
was a celebrated writer and calmly set off along the path
of prizes and tributes. He'd never reread a single word
of those novels that, according to the critics, made Santiago Bonday one of the most accomplished writers of
his time. What he hated most was being unhappy, and
he vaguely understood that his books, so praised for
their originality and their mastery of narrative tech-

nique, were no more than variations on his first, rather juvenile work. And he loved his work infinitely less than he loved the city.

For he loved the city with all the sentimentality and passion of the newcomer. He loved it despite his native province and the great map of plains, deserts, and mountains that Bonday, half-proud, half-perplexed and irritated, called "this country of ours." His love of the city was born of his fear of that hostile emptiness, those vast, open spaces where being "someone" meant nothing. He gloried in the neon signs, the elegant avenues, the tall buildings, the narrow, bustling streets, the way the city, like a European capital, seemed to hold up an ornate gold-framed mirror in which one could contemplate one's own image. His decision to live in the suburbs did not come from a longing for peace. Like a man who refuses to marry his ideal mistress, Bonday maintained a joyously illicit relationship consisting of trips to the center, of carefully planned retreats followed by sorties, as on this particular Saturday night, when the skin of the city, after several weeks' absence, had all the exciting freshness of a new and desirable woman.

"Nothing's perfect in this world," he said to himself, after driving at a snail's pace along a street jammed with cars and stopping the car alongside a "No Parking" sign. "Saturday! What makes all these people leave their little homes in the suburbs? Peasants. And why on earth does Marga invite me up on a Saturday of all days, when she knows what it's like in town: just like an invasion. But, of course, Madam has her family to attend to, she gets confused, arranges things for a Saturday, and drops me in it. Sooner or later women always let you down."

He was some five blocks from the gallery. He thought with dismay of the walk ahead of him. It was an area

packed with cinemas and theaters, restaurants and cof-
feeshops, as big as warehouses into which were crammed
families, sweethearts, and groups of mature single
women scouring the passing male faces for someone to
spend their Saturday night with.

"Saturday," snarled Bonday furiously, as he pushed
and shoved his way through the crowd.

He'd just arrived at the corner when the bizarre accident happened.

· 14 ·

What would you have done in my place, Emilio? There I was, my letter in my hand, standing on a desk, late already on my first day in the job, not a policeman in sight, and that Gypsy leaping up and sitting down beside me. I wanted to get down, but I couldn't. He gripped me by the arm.

"Pas encore, chérie, c'est dangereux."

"I'm sorry?"

"Not yet. Look. I've judged the time perfectly," he said, indicating the door. I saw a long tongue of thick, muddy water licking the tiles of the entrance hall. "A minute and a half to reach the legs of the desk," he crooned, "three minutes to turn the corner of the corridor, five minutes to the auditorium . . ."

"The place is flooding!"

"Of course." The Gypsy nodded, smiling. "Past experience tells me that the water will have covered the floor of the auditorium within about ten minutes. It depends, *pourtant,* on the amount of rainfall. If the rain doesn't stop, the whole thing will last twenty-seven minutes. And then the place will be as dry as a bone again."

He looked at his watch and sighed.

"That's if the grating isn't blocked, of course. If it is,

the water reaches the stage. And then, *chérie*, it's a job for the firemen!"

I started to remove a shoe.

"Hey, where do you think you're going?"

I told him that I didn't intend dropping anchor there until the firemen rescued us; that today was my first day at work; that I had to report to the Personnel Office and . . .

He roared with laughter. "The whole place is flooded. Why get soaked for nothing?" From the sleeve of the ridiculous smock he produced a packet of cigarettes. "Let's have a quiet smoke. After all, what is life but one long wait?"

What could I do? I took the cigarette. I made an effort to seem friendly.

"Do you work here?"

He shrugged. From the other sleeve he'd produced a notebook and mechanical pencil. He said, *"Pardon,"* and started to write. Every now and then he raised his dark eyes with their long, even darker eyelashes to consult his watch or the water. I went on smoking in silence, feeling depressed.

"Boredom makes researchers of us all," he said at last, closing the notebook. "There's something I don't understand. Listen carefully."

I listened.

"When it rains, the street floods. The water comes in through that door. It goes down to the auditorium, reaches the stage, and then, pfft, it evaporates." He lifted his arms in a gesture of impotence. *"Why?* The only grating, which I've never seen, is in the auditorium. But where? And the water . . . where does it get out? *C'est drôle.* Into the river perhaps? Is there a drainpipe that goes from the theater into the river?"

The last thing I was interested in was drainpipes.

"You're foreign, aren't you? French perhaps?"

He laughed again. He had very even, white teeth. The flashing smile one associates with people of his dark complexion.

"Of course not. I'm a typical national product. You know, French grandmother, Bolivian grandfather, both parents born here. And you?"

"The same." I smiled involuntarily. "Romanian father, Italian mother. But at least I was born here."

"At least I was born here." He shook his head, amused. "That's nice, 'At least I was born here.' My name's Claude."

"You mean Claudio?"

"No, Claude." He held out his hand.

"I'm Renata."

"Enchanté."

We shook hands formally. Honestly, sitting on top of that desk like two castaways in a boat.

"I've got a job here," I said. "I have to report to the Personnel Office with my letter of appointment."

He showed no curiosity.

"Perhaps you know where the Personnel Office is."

He shook his head.

"You don't?"

"There isn't a Personnel Office," he said simply. "It's not necessary. It's always the same people here, we all know each other, so . . ."

I showed him the letter. He read it slowly.

"If I were you," he said at last, fixing me with his dark eyes, "if I were you, I'd go home and wait for more definite news."

"Oh, great," I said, irritated. "A telegram giving me the sack for not turning up for work. You know, it wasn't easy getting the job. Or finding the place, for that matter."

"Calm down."

"I'm perfectly calm. I just want to know if someone here can tell me where I have to go."

"There's me." He flashed his white teeth in a smile.

"A boss, someone in charge . . ."

He started counting on his fingers. "There's Library, Lighting, Script, Props, Stage Design . . . Look!" The water was subsiding rapidly. My strange companion took out the notebook and mechanical pencil again and once more began making notes, biting his lips. "Impossible. On the twenty-sixth of June last year it took seventeen minutes, add four, multiply by three hundred and sixty-five . . ."

"The letter says that the section I'll be in is Z-k," I said desperately.

He jumped down from the desk. "You can get down now, *chérie*."

I didn't move. "Isn't there some kind of office somewhere?"

He shook his head as if my persistence saddened him. "Be a good girl now and get down."

"Some kind of office?"

He shrugged his shoulders and indicated where the corridor curved. "Don't look for an office. Look for a clerk. They know. They'll tell you."

"Where should I look?"

He took my hand and tugged gently. "Follow the corridor around to the left."

I leaned on his arm and slid down to the floor. A moment later the red smock, the yellow trousers, and the dark head were disappearing down the corridor to the right of the "Last Few Days" notice. He didn't say good-bye, and so I set off to the left, stepping timidly along the damp floor, avoiding the puddles.

· 15 ·

"BLOODY SATURDAY NIGHT." Bonday was advancing slowly toward Marga Hedelstoff's art gallery when, a few yards from the corner, he came up against a barrier of gossiping, impassable flab. A fat woman with her hair in a bun, two girls (to judge by their build, offspring of that superabundantly fleshy back), and a tall, broad-beamed man, all four of them arm in arm. "The model family," growled Bonday to himself.

"Excuse me."

The wall of family turned their heads as one. They regarded him indignantly.

"If you don't mind." Bonday smiled in conciliatory fashion.

The woman protested, the man raised his eyebrows, and the girls nudged each other, giggling.

"Where do you think you're going?" asked the man threateningly.

"Can't you see there's no room on the pavement?" the woman added scornfully. The other pedestrians were pushing and crushing him against that solid, hostile wall. The fat woman with the bun smelled of talcum powder, the man of cheap eau de cologne, the girls of young, rarely washed sweat. There was growing pressure from those approaching from behind, a sudden swaying as if the people were getting ready to break down the obstacle standing in their way, like a wave on the crest of which Bonday, losing his balance, raised his hands as a buffer against the coming collision with the family. Unexpectedly, the family gave way. Bonday stumbled into a sudden clearing on the pavement and stood there a moment, feeling dizzy.

Then he heard the intake of breath.

"Aaaah . . ."

He was alone on a miraculously clear pavement, mopping the sweat from his brow. And because the people nearest him were looking up at the sky, Bonday did the same. He couldn't see anything. The people weren't looking at the sky but at the building to his left. He shifted his gaze.

"Aaaah . . ."

On the ledge of a second-floor window swayed a glass-fronted sideboard.

Surprise paralyzed Bonday. The following day he wrote in his diary, *Scenes from my past life flashed before me like scenes in a film.* But at that moment he didn't remember or feel anything. Rigid with fear and amazement, his mind a blank, he stood pinned to a paving stone, watching the sideboard falling. Just a few paces away from him it shattered into fragments of wood and glass. Bonday closed his eyes. A second later he heard a concerned voice say, "Do you think he's hurt?"

He opened his eyes. The face of a plump woman smelling of talcum powder was very close to his.

"Don't just stand there with your mouth open, sir. We're taking you to the hospital."

The broad-beamed man took her by the arm. "Are you crazy? Then the police will come, we'll have to make a statement, and that'll be our Saturday up the creek."

One of the girls was brushing down the lapels of his

jacket. "Poor thing, look at you, you're all covered with broken glass."

Still trembling, Bonday just let them get on with it. His legs felt weak; unsteady with terror, they scarcely held him up. Because he was blocking their view of that wrecked carcass with its wrenched-off doors and viscera of china and glass scattered in brilliant fragments over the pavement, unknown hands pulled him away. Bonday felt sick and dizzy; he took a few steps and slowly moved away from the scene.

He was only half a block from the gallery. He covered the distance like an automaton, zigzagging like a drunkard. *I could have been killed. Good God, I could have been killed.* He'd been only a step away from losing his life, he thought with a shudder, taking in a great gulp of cool night air. *On the point of death.* He touched his face. *But I'm alive.* Safe and sound. *The literary world would have lost its most eminent figure, in the prime of life, in a period of intense creativity . . .* He imagined the comments of his admirers, anticipated the pleasure of retelling the incident, the satisfaction of calming his friends' worries. "It would have been just dreadful to have lost you, Tacho. It's dangerous having madmen like that loose in the city. A sideboard full of plates? That's incredible. I don't know what the world's coming to." He was smiling his melancholy smile; he could see himself lighting his pipe with steady hands, recounting the incident with an indifferent calm to a terrified audience.

By the time he reached the art gallery, he'd quite recovered his firmness of step.

"At last, my love! At last!" Marga ran to embrace him and wrapped him in a cloud of sky-blue gauze and L'Air du Temps.

Bonday pushed her gently away and in his clear, beautiful voice recited:

"One day went by and then another
another day and still another
and he did not return from Flanders shore
Don Juan who to Flanders will go no more."

"Ah, Neruda!" said Marga, half-closing her eyes. "My favorite poet, absolutely divine, I adore him."

"Zorrilla, actually, but you know, my dear, I very nearly didn't come back from Flanders," Bonday said, giving her a long, serious look.

"It doesn't matter. You're here now. Everyone is asking for the Master, my love. Just as well the photographers haven't gone."

"When you know why I was delayed—"

"Don't apologize. You're here and I adore you. . . ."

"Marga, I was on the point of—"

"On the point of ordering a drink. Waiter!"

"Because death awaits us at every corner—"

"Ice or water, Tacho?"

"You look so lovely that past fears . . ."

She opened her eyes wide and smiled. "Tacho . . ."

"Not even death . . ."

"All right." She put her face close to his and whispered in his ear, "Let's say *Monday* then."

Oh God, no. It didn't pain Bonday (on the contrary it cheered him up) to watch his men friends aging, but it was hard to see it happen to women. Marga had been lovely once.

"No, I didn't mean . . ." he tried to say, looking away from that face plowed and furrowed, like a field ripe for sowing, by the unforgiving hand of time.

"See you here on Monday, my love. I'll close the gallery, there'll be just the two of us. Can you wait until then?" She gave him a conspiratorial wink. "Don't embarrass me in public. I'll leave you to your admirers.

There are some very important people here. Monday at five."

Feeling deeply depressed at the prospect of that un-expected rendezvous on Monday at five, Bonday glanced about him. The whole city was there. Anyone who was anyone in the world of culture and art. The presence there of friends and enemies, of familiar faces and voices, soon cheered him up. Happy to be back among his own people, he prepared himself to tell his story. "The most terrible of fates may await us on any corner—"

"Talking of terrible fates, have you heard about Luis-ita? She put up with that awful Marco for three years, and now he's upped and left. And with no pension, Tacho, can you imagine?"

"Death is the measure of our time on earth, and al-though it may seem ridiculous that a sideboard—"

"Yes, the publisher wants me to be my own censor, in the scene in the lesbian brothel in chapter ninety-three. . . ."

"Just minutes ago I faced death."

"Really, Tacho? So did I. My analyst says I should learn to accept it. I should avoid the crisis. I've gone from three sessions to five, and he's leaving in Febru-ary, he's really going, I swear I'll kill myself. . . ."

Bonday had, without success, exhausted the pool of potential listeners when he saw Captain Beh. He didn't recognize him at first. He was out of uniform and was standing staring at a picture.

Bonday was not so much surprised as overjoyed at being able to tell him about the accident. He rushed up to greet him. "I see you're interested in the work of our young creative artists, Captain."

The captain turned to look at him. "Oh, it's you," he said coldly.

Bonday pointed at the picture with his pipe. "There's a lot of vitality in the shapes, don't you think? A vigor in what it sets out to do, a break with traditional norms."

"It's called 'Death,' " replied the captain, brandishing the crumpled catalog in his chubby, freckled hand.

"How fitting." Bonday smiled. "Imagine, just a few minutes ago, on my way here—"

"And is this the kind of art they're trying to sell us?"

"Death, Captain, goes beyond art. By the way, I'd like to talk to you about an experience that—"

"And I," roared the captain, "would like to know if they expect one to hang this rubbish in one's living room for all the family to see!"

Bonday looked at the picture for the first time. It was a large blue stain, the color of watered-down ink, and on it were pasted cuttings from magazines, newspapers, and little pieces of twine and buttons, quite tastefully done.

"Answer me, Bonday, you can be frank with me."

"Well, on second thoughts—"

"Do they expect this obscenity to adorn the walls of a decent home?"

"I don't know if—"

"Oh, yes you do. You're just afraid to say it. You're a coward." Bonday nodded as ambiguously as he could, already looking for a means of escaping from that awkward dialogue. But the captain took his arm. "Look, Bonday, take a good look at those people. It's the decadence of Imperial Rome all over again."

Bonday looked. The captain and he were alone, miles away, within a suffocating magic circle, terrifyingly far from the others, who were happy in their decadence, endlessly chatting, laughing, drinking, and greeting one another.

"Sophisticated society, Captain, does have its faults. For example, this accident tonight—"

"To use a theater of this magnitude to corrupt our traditional way of life!"

"Well I wouldn't go so far as to call it theater. . . ." Bonday protested weakly, thinking with belated loyalty of Marga and her friends.

The captain's red hand rested heavily on his shoulder. "Bonday, we're going to have to make some very important decisions."

We? wondered Bonday, perplexed.

"A theater is above all else a theater, all the more when it's a national theater. It cannot, it must not merely answer to the caprices of a few madmen. Make a note in your diary, Bonday."

"He has no right to impose his authority on me," Bonday said to himself, "and anyway the commission has done what it set out to do."

"Ready when you are, Captain," he said docilely, just in case.

"Interview with Captain Beh. Advisers' Meeting. The management have already been informed. Got that?"

A short, fat man with oily gray hair approached them. "The car's here, Captain."

It was the smile Bonday remembered, rather than the face. The servile smile of Hugo Pantaenius, who was standing in for Castro Miranda while he was away at conference in Las Vegas.

And then, and only then, did Bonday realize that Marga Hedelstoff's art gallery was in the same building as the National Theater, just yards from the place where William Shakespeare's heart lay beating. And only then did he understand Captain Beh's presence at the exhibition.

Suddenly vigorous and very serious, he shook the captain's hand. "I'll be there, Captain, you can rely on me."

· 16 ·

When one looks back in time, it doesn't matter how many days, weeks, or months have passed: Every fact becomes a fiction, every person a character, every place a scene on a stage. The Gypsy in the red shirt measuring the water level of a flood has disappeared forever from reality and today is replaced by a friend, Claude. My anxious search for an office and a boss is no longer mine; it belongs to the Renata telling the story of my first hours at the theater. I call up my memories and see myself, from the outside, walking down that corridor, skirting puddles, finding a second office and in it a clerk.

He was wearing a blue jacket and cap, had a coffee-pot in one hand, and a plate of sandwiches in front of him: He was having lunch. He continued eating while he listened to me. Then he carefully wiped his fingers on his sleeve, opened a desk drawer, and took out a plan. With relief I saw that my name was there, scrawled crazily in red ink under the letters Z-k. With a pencil he indicated the route to take: down the corridor, turn left, and down another corridor. My destination was a door. He drew the door and wrote a word: *Wardrobe.*

I no longer felt cold or tired. I set off. I was thinking, How nice, the Wardrobe Department of a theater. No more invoices, or phrases in technical English for my fingers to stumble over on the typewriter keyboard. The Wardrobe Department.

The door was easy to find. It had a bronze plaque on it. *President Herrero National Theater. Wardrobe. Head Office.* I knocked. No one answered. The silence began to worry me as it threatened to become as long as those endless corridors I had just walked. "I must be late," I said to myself. My feet were aching. When I leaned against the door, it opened. I went in with ridiculous stealth. It was a large room. There was a window that looked onto the river. But apart from an old desk and on the desk an inkstand made out of badly stained mica, a folder with oilcloth covers, and a battered kerosene lamp, there was no other sign of human habitation. There were no chairs. I stood leaning out of the window, waiting for the head of the department indicated on the plaque on the door.

It was a melancholy view (muddy waters, gray shores, dim scrublands in the distance among blackish rocks) but at least it gave an illusion of open countryside, the freedom of an expanse of water, the river. I stood looking at the landscape for fifteen minutes, twenty. I couldn't leave. I would wait for the head of the department, unto death if necessary. But sitting down. I went out into the corridor in the unlikely hope of finding a chair. I came back in. In the office of the Wardrobe Department I noticed a door that obviously communicated with a side office. I turned the handle. It wasn't locked, so I went in. From the heavy penumbra came the smell of dust and dampness that abandoned rooms retain. I felt along the wall and the doorframe and found the light switch.

Dozens of small spotlights lit up like sudden stars in an empty sky. I smothered a gasp, almost a shout, of surprise. A faceless throng hung from the wall-to-wall transverse rails in swathes of velvet and brocade, satin, and silk: All the boots, clogs, and buskins stood there empty. I laughed (nervously) when I realized that this fantastic crowd was the Wardrobe Department.

Feeling all the delight and enchantment of childhood carnivals, I plunged into the sumptuous but shabby world of disguises and masks. I touched, tried things on, tested the shapes, textures, and sizes of those amiable phantoms. I lifted the lids of the many boxes piled on the shelves and, so I could see them in the light, took out scepters, swords, crowns, hats, bonnets with incredibly fine feathers, and jewels. The fictional gems gleamed (falsely—but they still gleamed), craftsmen's inventions in gold and silver.

"Eureka!" I heard a voice say behind me.

I turned around, my heart in my mouth and a paste tiara in my hand. There in the doorway stood the head of the department. He was tall, very thin, of uncertain age (that period of maturity when health can tip the balance favorably or unfavorably); the sunken chest beneath a suit that hung loosely off a bony skeleton; the sparse, fine gray hair that hung down to his drooping shoulders; deep lines on his high poet's forehead; gentle eyes, moist and sad; and a very soft voice. "It's time for tea," he said from the door.

Time for tea? He'd surprised me rummaging around in the Wardrobe Department like a thief. My nervousness got the better of me, and I let the tiara fall to the floor where it rolled with a bell-like tinkle.

I blushed. The head of the department laughed very softly.

"Aha, the jewels of our Wardrobe Department! Renata's treasure."

He knew my name! So he was expecting me. Once

more I held out the letter. "This is my letter of appointment, sir."

He took the letter and read it unhurriedly. "Aha," he said, and gave it back to me.

"I came early, but I couldn't find . . ."

"Find who?"

"You, of course."

He raised his eyebrows. "Me?"

"Aren't you the person in charge of Wardrobe?"

He shook his head as if marveling at this suggestion. "I'm just here to tell you it's time for tea."

I felt tears beginning to burn my eyes. I said nothing.

"How could we leave you all alone, poor thing, when it's so cold and it's your first day at work?"

"I have to see the head of the department," I said tearfully. "They'll fire me if I don't see the head of my section."

Then that long, thin, sad face lit up. "But, my dear child, you don't need to see any head of any department."

I'm going as mad as the rest of them in this madhouse, I thought.

"Because *you're* the head of the department, my dear," he said with a kind smile. "You've joined Z-k. Z-k is the Creative Section, and in the Creative Section, my dear Renata, everyone's a head of a department."

"But the office," I stuttered, "this office . . . it's empty."

Again came that velvety laugh. "This office is empty because it's waiting for you to occupy it. No one's been given it because you weren't here."

"And the director?" I begged. "Couldn't I see the director?"

He gave a deep sigh. "A vain hope, my dear, although there is a certain logic to it. If there were a director. But the last one we had was relieved of his post, oh, ages and ages ago. . . . Did you speak to the clerk at the entrance? Good. Everything's in order then. The clerk is an M-b. He belongs to the Administrative Section. He'll fill in your form and register you." He held out to me his long hand with its thin fingers. "My name, dear Renata, is Burgossi."

I shook his hand.

"What should I do now?" I asked stubbornly. "What does my job consist of?"

"Dear child, you just have to carry out your set tasks."

Exhausted, I murmured, "And what are my set tasks?"

Languidly his hand sketched a parabola in the air, taking in the fantastic throng, the opened boxes, the jewels, and the smell of dust and damp. Without hesitation and with the most amiable of smiles, he said, "Why, these are."

· 17 ·

"You're probably wondering why I've come to see you," Bonday said to the other man, who was watching him in silence.

Bonday had always found it difficult to remain silent, and he now discovered that talking to oneself (the man lounging in the armchair smoking a cigar had still not said a single word) was equally maddening. He paused and waited for the other man to ask him something. He didn't. Bonday pretended to be interested in the picture adorning one wall of the luxurious consulting room. *The Parable of the Blind, 1586, Brueghel,* it said on the small gilt plaque. "A great artist, Brueghel," he said emphatically.

There was another, even longer and heavier, silence. Mentally Bonday rolled up his sleeves. "Yes, Doctor, here I am. A writer of my temperament, used to the lively dialogue between reality and unreality, seeking help in psychoanalysis."

Dr. Ranisky took another cigar from the box, chewed the end, carefully licked the edges, and lit it with a lighter in the shape of an hourglass. There was sand in the lower part of the lighter.

Feeling intensely irritated now, Bonday thought how different this man was from the sage Marga Hedelstoff

had described so admiringly to him on that fateful
Monday at five. He had an enormous bald head and
prominent ears above which a few fair curls bloomed,
and his eyes were very round and heavy-lidded. He
looked as if he had slept in his clothes: The striped suit
and the shirt, unbuttoned at the neck, were all crying
out for an iron.

The evident gap between how much the sessions cost
and Dr. Ranisky's appearance annoyed Bonday. He de-
clared disdainfully, "Forgive my frankness, but I really
don't believe in psychoanalysis."

The doctor nodded and shifted the cigar around in
his mouth, but still said not a word. Bonday sought refuge again in Brueghel.

"But a perfectly ordinary sideboard has made of me
one of those blind men frisking about on the edge of
the abyss. So I . . ."

Now those were real painters, he thought distractedly, mentally continuing his eternal argument with
Marga about nonfigurative art.

". . . You'll probably say that I'm putting up de-
fenses, that there's no cure without faith. You'll say I'm
resisting, erecting barriers."

Dr. Ranisky said nothing. As discreetly as he could,
Bonday looked at his watch. Fifteen minutes of his session had gone already!

"You'll say my obsession comes from feelings of guilt.
Maybe. None of us is short on guilt."

He'd felt very guilty in the gallery, which Marga had
closed especially, in expectation of an afternoon of
lovemaking. It had never happened to him before. Good
grief. Marga had been the soul of kindness and generosity and had simply put her clothes back on, all the
time cooing to him, consoling him. Bonday had thought,
Women are always mothers, even when they don't have

children. But that afternoon he hated her. He swore never to see her again. He swore he wouldn't go to the psychoanalyst. He swore he'd forget. But here he was, obeying his friend's advice.

"My childhood was, like everyone's, sad. . . ."

Twenty minutes gone. He converted them into cash.

"Doctor, I'll come straight to the point. Two weeks ago I was involved in a serious accident." He cleared his throat. "With a sideboard. Since then I haven't slept. I wake up in the middle of the night drenched in sweat, seeing that piece of furniture full of plates and glasses coming straight for me."

He couldn't tell him about his bitter experience at the gallery; he could never confess his intimate secrets to a stranger. Instead he described the scene on that Saturday night, the sideboard at the window, the crash at his feet, how death had been only inches away. The memory made him shudder.

"One goes confidently about the world," he said, genuinely sad now, "and suddenly there's this sideboard."

Unperturbed, Dr. Ranisky inhaled the blue smoke of his cigar.

"Of course," sighed Bonday, "every artist is always exposed to the torture of his dreams. The writer and his ghosts and all that. But this is different." He shook his head. "If I dream about something once, well, I just let it pass. Twice, then I make a note of the symbolism, on the typewriter. Three times, I just correct the original and send it to press. But days and days with this blessed sideboard and me unable to sleep, going to the kitchen for consolation, a glass of milk, a mouthful of something to calm me down, that's quite another matter." He was almost begging now. "If it's something to do with the subconscious, a mechanism we can only master when inspired, then, Doctor, I offer it up to the experts."

Having resigned himself to being the only one to talk, the sharp voice startled him.

"I understand, Señor Bonday. And it's a shame that I won't be able to take you on."

"But . . . Marga Hedelstoff told me that . . ."

"A marvelous woman but with very little imagination."

"What are you trying to say?"

Dr. Ranisky pointed at him with the cigar. "Let me put it this way: A sideboard keeps falling on you. Is that right?"

"That's right."

"Marga, for whom I have the greatest respect, gives you my telephone number. For her sake, you understand, I waste my time when I should be loading my suitcases into the car. You install yourself in here and tell me the dream. Am I right?"

"Quite right."

"Then you expect me to treat you, to cure you, yes?"

"Yes," said Bonday, his throat tight.

"Then I tell you I can't treat you."

"That's what you said."

"And you were shocked rigid by the news."

Bonday did not reply.

"Learn to accept it. You still haven't, have you? And what if now I add that I can't even recommend a colleague?"

"I suppose I'll just have to try and live with it," said Bonday with a contorted smile.

"Look, for Marga's sake, I'll ignore your sarcasm. And as I'm a generous man, I'll pass on some information to you. A scoop. Our mission in this country is over." He sucked the end of his cigar and added, "We're leaving."

Bonday looked back at the Brueghel. "I see," he said

hoarsely. "The mission's over. The doctors are leaving, and one just has to put up with the sideboard."

Dr. Ranisky stood up and stubbed out the cigar in the ashtray. "No, I don't think you do see. You laymen don't understand that the sick of this country, of whose vast range of neuroses our profession is justly proud, are now in a state of complete decadence."

"You don't say."

"I do. And I say this with real sorrow: There are already analysts who allow their patients to get scandalously behind with the payments for their treatment. Others, and I assure you I would never sink so low, go so far as not bothering to take their debtors to court."

"Incredible."

Dr. Ranisky raised his voice. "When they imperil the very basis of a science we've built up with our blood, sweat, and tears, the only option left to us is to withdraw. The only way out is to practice our profession, with our heads held high, in more developed countries than our own."

"I see."

"I'll give you some advice, Bonday." Dr. Ranisky smiled. "Your health is the most important thing. Rather than taking the obvious step of booking yourself on a Caribbean cruise, invest in a trip to Barcelona. Here's my address. I'll keep an opening for you in my diary from now on."

"Thank you."

"It's not thanks I want from a compatriot, a sick one to boot. Just pay me, I'll give you a receipt, and I'll look forward to seeing you in my new consulting rooms. Oh, and keep an eye on that sideboard. It's very interesting, Bonday, I find your case most interesting."

· 18 ·

Dear Emilio,

This morning I went to the Main Post Office.
The strike is over. My letters (so they told me)
are still here, but letters from abroad have all
been delivered. You haven't written to me.

Is it because there's so much written about the
sorrows of love that when friendship demands
that its quota of unhappiness be heard, one
throws up one's hands in censorious horror? I
reproach myself for feeling this iniquitous anxiety, this unjustifiable impatience. Ah, how
quickly you've forgotten me! While I, with
shameless egotism, miss you madly. I miss your
intelligence, which used to nourish my intelligence (a fragile plant requiring regular watering and constant attention). I miss the way you
could smile at the craziness of the world and
the imbecility of the species. I don't have that
kind of courage. At the first hesitation, I lose
heart. I fall into superstition, I imagine that I,
with my little ambitions, my little griefs, carry
the weight of the world on my shoulders, that
I'm the stem holding up the flower. I can't accept that people forget about me, that they don't

care, neither applauding nor criticizing the modest course of my life. And you went away and couldn't even be bothered to send me a postcard. You're too immersed in your journeys and your books. I have no place in that world I thought I shared, and your betrayal . . .

Dear Emilio,

This morning I went to the Main Post Office. The strike is over. My letters (so they told me) are still here, but letters from abroad have already been delivered. I understand why you don't write. Do you have a lot of work? Is your book going well? I miss our conversations. I don't normally know what to say to people, but with you, how I talked! Our friendship was like having a home. What did it matter if I had to take temporary lodgings in other houses if, whenever I wished, I had only to open a door to find the easy familiarity of brother and sister?

Although it may seem childish, your silence worries me. Is it fear of losing the little good there was in me? Or fear of being cut off from a past that included you?

Do drop me a line when you have time.

Love,
Renata

P.S. I've abandoned the novel. It was dreadful. I'm trying the diary though. You see how obediently I follow good advice. Of course, if you were here, we'd talk about the novel. . . . But that's by the by.

Good and bad always arrive together. For a long time two dreams kept me going; escaping from the agricultural-machinery office, and escaping from the Pension Stella Maris. How I nurtured that double dream! Tonight, living it, I still can't believe it.

Two weeks after starting work at the theater, the staff in section Z-k got a salary increase, paid retroactively. I went to the accounts window to clear up the mistake. The clerk (one of the M-bs, by nature a very irritable race) was furious. What did I want? To protest to the ministry? Wasn't it bad enough having to find my complicated name in a sheaf of lists? I timidly pronounced the word *swindle*. He roared with laughter. "Oh, so you're one of the people who believes this theater exists!"

There was enough money to pay the deposit and the first month's rent on this small apartment. It's in a nice, though modest area and has one bedroom, with living room, kitchen, bathroom, and a balcony. It's such a luxury to be able to have some potted plants. I always wanted to have a jasmine plant. I don't have to worry about furniture. There's everything I need: bed, wardrobe, table, chair. But no bookshelves. The books await their place (as I await mine) piled up on the hideous old carpet covered in once-yellow chrysanthemums turning brown beneath the ingrained dirt.

Today I said good-bye to the Pension Stella Maris. Or rather, they held a farewell party for me. And who was in charge of it? Who else but my big-boned, tyrannical Gertrudis.

I didn't want to take the bus to the part of town where the Pension Stella Maris, that star of the sea, had held me submerged beneath the waters of promiscuous coexistence for nearly four years. I walked there, slowly, to savor the sweetness of farewell.

Farewell to the Virgin of Casamanta, to the lime-flower tea and the felt slippers. Never again. No more Gertrudis. No more sudden awakenings to hear sobs coming from the other side of the partition wall. Never again that nocturnal weeping, the spilling into the shadows of those long-repressed tears, the anonymous weeping—though there was never any need to put a name or a face to them, it was all the same, for each of the twelve women in that circle of bodies would have something to cry about some night.

Farewell to those terrible Sundays, the low point of the week. Never again that false Sunday cheerfulness, the sadness of female rituals, wet hair drying in the sun, bunches of heads craning over balconies to look down onto the street, the awful smell of homemade unguents intended to smooth complexions, the filing and polishing of nails ruined by the detergent used in the kitchens of bars, or of long, feline nails ready with the professional caress, the short, clean, humble nails of hands repeating automatonlike movements in the factory, pulling levers, wielding dusters, answering telephones, and making hotel beds.

Farewell to the laughter. Never again that loud, saucy screech of laughter over stupid pranks and dirty jokes. Farewell to the cheap music and the hit songs with easy-to-remember words. They used to sing a lot. I didn't. I read. I didn't know any jokes. I wrote. And when I cried at night, it was simply because it was my turn.

No, I had nothing in common with those women. Like the bewitched princesses in fairy tales, I waited in poverty and solitude for the moment I would be rescued by my noble equals, waited for an end to days turned to stone by a witch's spell, waited for the open doors of the palace and my return there to a fanfare of brass trumpets.

Farewell. I found I was smiling. But at the door I composed myself. I didn't want to offend them. They were all there. There was even a cloth on the kitchen table. There were plates with salami and cheese, olives bristling with toothpicks, and a bottle of vermouth. At the head of the table the Catalan landlord was beaming like a saint (less out of love than relief to be free of a bad payer). Got up in all her finery, Gertrudis trembled with emotion; her embrace left me breathless. While the others lost no time in advising me on the potential of the apartment for amorous exploits, Gertrudis took a hanky from her cleavage and dabbed at her streaming tears. "I swear she's like a daughter to me, girls. Even though we're the same age, well, more or less, I still feel like a mother to her. My Renata, oh my poor little lamb, all alone in the world!" The little lamb was shaking with terror at the idea that Gertrudis's horrifying maternal instinct would lead her to my apartment that night. Fortunately she just screwed up her hanky and cried. But when I finally turned my back on the Pension Stella Maris, Gertrudis let out a terrible moan, and the others had to hold her down to stop her running after me. Forgetting about the elevator, I ran down the four flights of stairs as fast as my legs could carry me and took the first taxi that appeared as if the Devil himself were after me.

It's three in the morning. I'm here in my own room, and I can't sleep. My head aches, and my eyes are burning with so much crying. The tears I didn't cry when Gertrudis brought the cake to the table (a cake made by hands with so little practice in the kitchen) and I saw my name written on it in chocolate. The tears I didn't cry when, surrounded by those faces coarsened by prostitution and hearing that familiar laughter, high-pitched, vulgar, saucy, I knew that I wasn't the princess in the fairy tale, that I was one of them, the same only different, and a rush of compassion for all of us made me bow my head over the already empty plates, over the darned tablecloth, and say, "I'll really miss you all."

To my misfortune, to my humiliation, in my solitude, it's true.

· 19 ·

BONDAY WAS ROUSED by a warm ray of sunlight and a hand shaking him. "You're going to be late, Tacho. Tacho!"

He stretched lazily. Bonday was by nature contradictory, and although he believed absolutely in the healthy custom of early rising (he knew of many great literary names who were up and writing at the crack of dawn), he himself hated it. The agreeable knowledge that he belonged to a race whose work took its power from the first light of day collided with the no less intense attraction of his bed, where he could lie and reflect in comfort, where he could, effortlessly and without compunction, drift off to sleep again.

He opened his eyes. Framed by the window was a glorious world: blue sky, a lawn shining with dew, leaves turning golden in the first weeks of autumn. As usual, he congratulated himself on living in the country.

"Clean air encourages good circulation and stimulates the brain." He yawned, put on his slippers, went over to the window, opened it, and took a deep breath. An icy blast struck him full in the face. "Bloody hell!" He shut the window violently and clutched his dressing gown about him. Once more he had fallen into the usual outrageous meteorological trap. Yesterday it had been as warm as spring, today it was like winter. "This country," he said bitterly, "this dreadful country!" He studied the clear sky with the expert eye of a soldier accustomed to doing constant battle with the weather, and spotted a cloud. "If I wear my overcoat, I'll melt in the heat. If I don't wear it, I'm certain to catch flu. And I wouldn't be in the least surprised if it started to rain."

It took him so long deciding what to wear that he had to bolt his breakfast, had no time to read the newspaper and barely time to say good-bye to his wife. He reached the station out of breath and flustered. Despite his haste, he had stuck by his original decision to take the train. He couldn't drive and think at the same time. And on today's journey he needed to think. He wanted to prove to Captain Beh that the committed writer was as capable as any Greek philosopher of intelligent action in the real world. The 9:15 express arrived punctually at 9:40. Bonday chose a window seat, stretched out his legs, took out his pipe, and opened his book. It was a much-thumbed *Divine Comedy,* a 1929 edition by Ulrich Hoepli. The margins were heavily marked with penciled notes in Bonday's fine English calligraphy, which traced garlands of words around the six cantos of the *Inferno* that he had managed to decipher during the course of innumerable train journeys. In winter he chose Dante as his companion; in summer, Shakespeare. Both fitted his image as a man of letters, but above all they helped him to believe in his passion for the classics, a passion that deep down, in moments of uncertainty, he doubted. It was rare to find Bonday traveling on the Southern Railway without one of his classics.

He didn't often actually read the book. With his pipe in his mouth and an air of solemn concentration, he would open the book, glance over the page (this took one or two minutes), then turn to the window. But he didn't look at the landscape (he found it painfully boring); he would look at his own reflection in the glass: the melancholy face, the book by Shakespeare or Dante, the pipe. This morning, however, on his way to the interview with Captain Beh, he recited to himself:

> *Nel mezzo del cammin di nostra vita*
> *mi ritrovai per una selva oscura*

Selva oscura. He wondered what it was that was bothering him. The cold? Bonday was a tropical animal, and cold had the same stupefying effect on him as it had on flies. The fact that the train was late? Not at all. The train had arrived, as it always did, exactly twenty-five minutes behind schedule. Was it Captain Beh's dawn phone call? The phone had rung at two in the morning.

"Bonday? Captain Beh here. You haven't forgotten our appointment, have you?"

Half-asleep, he answered, "Our appointment, no, of course not."

"Because at this grave juncture in our history, the support of the intelligentsia is vital."

"Yes, Captain, this grave juncture, of course."

"A man of your special character, recognized abroad for his literary work, cannot remain on the sidelines of history. . . ."

"Yes, I see, history . . ."

"You know, of course, that although we are far from seeking the gratitude of our country, its greatness remains our aim."

"Who can doubt it, Captain."

Bonday was beginning to wake up. Disconcerted, he wondered why the captain was phoning him. As if he had guessed the question, the captain barked, "Have you got the address I gave you?"

"Of course."

"Well, cross it out. I'm going to give you another one. Don't show it to anyone."

On the train, Bonday closed his book, took out his diary, and looked up the address. He'd always thought he knew the city like the back of his hand, but there was nothing on the back of his hand called Calle Flechas de San Esteban. "Flechas de San Esteban," he said to the cabdriver at the taxi stand outside the station.

"Flechas de San Esteban?" asked the driver, shaking his dark, leonine head, then exclaimed scornfully, "Oh, Flechas de San Esteban!"

"Do you know it?"

The lion held up a paw with long black nails. "I know this city like the back of my hand." Ten minutes later, there was still no sign of the street, but the driver kept waving his black hand at him. Bonday insisted they consult a map. Furious, the driver stopped the car and got out. Bonday saw him go over and question a street seller. The seller put his basket down on the ground, and the driver showed him his hand. They were arguing. Bonday looked desperately at his watch. The driver was taking his time. He chose a cake from the basket. The seller offered him another. At some point they seemed to come to an agreement; both of them looked down to the far end of the road, nodding. The driver returned to the car, munching his cake.

"What did he say?" asked Bonday.

"You might have told me, sir," said the driver with his mouth full, "that it was Flechas de San Esteban *Mártir* you wanted. If the passenger doesn't give us the right information . . ."

He accelerated sharply. Convinced that at any instant

they would crash, and that at any given moment they
were only inches away from (at best) the hospital or (at
worst) death itself, Bonday asked no further questions.
He just let himself be carried along, terrified, through
a nightmare of speed and near-catastrophe.

"Flechas de San Esteban," said the driver, screeching
to a halt.

Bonday's head was spinning. He got out of the taxi
on shaky legs. There was only one house on the block.
It had an iron gate, and on the gate was a silk banner
embroidered in gold letters:

FLECHAS DE SAN ESTEBAN
SPORTS AND SOCIAL CLUB
*For the Defense of the Fatherland, Property, and the
Family*

"Are you going to pay me, boss? Or don't you believe
in it?"

Bonday paid, and the taxi roared off.

The house had the look of one of those pretentious
abodes slowly sinking into disrepair beneath the weight
of taxes. Bonday rang the bell. A maid in a black uniform with a white collar came out of the house, crossed
the small garden, and approached the gate.

"Your name, please."

She looked for Bonday's name on a piece of paper,
then nodded. Taking a bunch of keys from her apron
pocket, she opened the iron gate and led him into the
house.

He waited alone in a dark, sparsely furnished room.
There was a disagreeable smell of wilting flowers. "Nar-
cissi," Bonday said to himself with repugnance when
he finally tracked them down in a corner. "Cemetery
flowers."

"Bonday, my friend!" The door opened, and there with his cloying smile was Hugo Pantaenius. "Personally, I find nothing blameworthy in your lack of punctuality, Master," said Pantaenius as he led him into the next room, "because I think artists should be permitted a few vices, but the captain is furious." In the room was a platform and an audience. The audience, not more than thirty in all and mostly men, had occupied every seat. At the microphone on the distant platform stood the imposing figure of Captain Beh.

"Santiago Bonday!" shouted the captain. "Welcome!"

The military life certainly develops the muscles, thought Bonday when he saw the massive arm raised in rigid welcome.

"Sit down, Bonday!" bellowed the captain, forgetting the microphone was on. Bonday looked around him. There wasn't a single free chair.

"I'm fine here," he said bitterly.

The captain shrugged. "As you wish. Here, we don't force anyone to do anything. This, my friends, is a democracy."

Democracy or not, Bonday felt like asking for at least a bench to sit on, but he didn't have the nerve. He folded his arms and held his head high. The committed writer, he thought heroically, renounces frivolity and refuses to take the easy way out.

He couldn't have arrived that late, because the captain was announcing to the audience, "And we have gathered here with but a single aim: the promotion of our great culture."

Murmurs of approval.

"A single end draws us on. And the end, my friends, justifies the means. And what are our means? Culture. And what is culture? The very basis of a free and sovereign people."

Applause and shouts of approval.

"Yet I ask you, my friends. Does the culture we see around us today deserve to be placed on a pedestal, as all the developed countries claim? I say no. For what is the reality of this so-called culture? The loss of our traditional values."

A pause. He's really impressive, thought Bonday admiringly. The captain's a born orator.

The captain raised his arms to the heavens. Bonday had a clear view of those disconcertingly chubby, freckled hands.

"One cannot be," the captain was saying, solemnly and sententiously, "other than what one has been. We can only truly live by being ourselves. One cannot be other than what one is."

The applause deafened Bonday, already quite dizzy on the captain's dialectic.

"González!" shouted the captain, skillfully bringing the speech to a close. A diminutive man with a gleaming pate climbed on to the platform. Under his arm he was carrying a notebook with a blue cover.

"González, read out the curriculum of our eminent cultural representative."

González asked, "What's his name?"

"Santiago Bonday," said the captain.

Bonday jumped. *Representative?*

"He's not in here," said González, running his finger down a page of the book.

"The curriculum's separate, González," the captain explained patiently.

"Ah," said González.

"Read it."

"Santiago Bonday passed his secondary school exams . . ."

"Further on, González, further on. Where it says 'Published Works.' "

"Ah. Published works, colon, new paragraph, *The Soul and Other Vagaries,* National Prize for Literature, semicolon, *The House of the*—"

"That's enough, González. Friends," shouted the captain in vibrant voice, "this genius, this intellectual, this creative artist, does not shut himself up in an ivory tower as others do. He supports our goal and is ready to fight for it, for the salvation of our culture. For our dishonored National Theater. For a great destiny. Bonday, the floor is yours."

A sea of heads turned to look at Bonday. Startled, Bonday hesitated. *Do I quote Shakespeare? Dante?* He cleared his throat.

"Culture, as everyone knows, is that which—"

"Thank you, Bonday. González, add the gentleman to the list."

Another burst of applause. A man leaned forward in his chair and held out his hand to the writer.

"Master, I don't know how to thank you for throwing in your lot with us."

Bonday smiled hesitantly and shook his hand.

"The notebook's full, Captain," said González, his voice amplified by the microphone.

The captain tried to ignore him. "We who are gathered here, as members of this club, we know that no bed of roses awaits us. But could we stand by, arms folded, and watch the murder, the violation, the slide into oblivion, of our national culture?"

A chorus of voices roared, "Never!"

"Can you just tell me where I should put the writer's name, Captain?" insisted González.

"There, González, there. What matters is that we have a sense of national identity. We must wrench our eyes away from Europe."

"Don't come complaining to me later about there being too much detail, Captain."

"Liberation through culture. Let's educate the people. For what happens to the people when they are not educated? Their very souls become corrupted, my friends."

"Is Bonday written with an *i* or a *y* at the end, Captain?"

"Ask the gentleman, González. What does the lost sheep seek? If he's one of the poor in spirit, he'll trot off after food and, if you'll pardon the word, sex. If he's one of those who would never pass through the eye of the needle, he'll apply himself perversely to the study of mathematics, astronomy, art, and even try to learn foreign languages—"

"Excuse me, sir, you, the one with the pipe. Is Bonday written with an *i* or a *y*?"

Hunched at the back of the room, Bonday first nodded, then shook his head.

"We love this land unto death. We can't let it be all bread and circuses. The spearhead of our Campaign for Cultural Reconstruction will be the President Herrero National Theater."

"Christian name?" asked González on tiptoe by the microphone.

"Santiago," shouted Bonday, reddening.

"Heads held high, indifferent to tittle-tattle and calumnies, we will set to work."

González shook his bald head. "I can't fit Santiago in the book. Would you mind very much if I put you down as Juan?"

"Don't write anything," shouted Bonday.

"The captain would kill me! Listen, sir, what if we leave it as *St.*? What do you think?"

Bonday, furious with González, applauded too; Pantaenius was clapping him on the shoulder, and González, brandishing his notebook, was yelling to him from the platform, "Look at that? You're the last entry in the book, St. *Bonday!*"

· 20 ·

Dear Emilio,

I'm beginning to suspect that the postal strike, although officially at an end, is still continuing in some way. They tell me that our letters are now leaving the country, but it's rumored that a lot are not being let in. But we've got used to it, living in this city. After a while the flow of correspondence will return to normal, no one will give us any explanation, and we'll forget about our lost letters, the wasted stamps, the frustrated love affairs, the anger of parents and children, we'll forget everything and doubtless one day soon, either out of lethargy or implacable faith, we'll start posting our letters in the mailboxes again.

Perhaps my news will reach you. It's good news. I like the theater, and I like my work. Well, to be honest, I don't work. I spend the morning in the office of the Wardrobe Department and a good part of the afternoon in the pompously named "Salon de Thé," an enormous room with peeling walls where my colleagues gather to rest from the fatigue of doing nothing for eight hours in a row.

I do a lot of reading and writing. I've abandoned the novel because I didn't feel comfortable with the genre; I keep a diary but I'm equally unhappy with that genre, and I write you letters that aren't real letters. Was I born out of sympathy with genres in general, or is it just incompetence? Don't tell me, I know. It's incompetence, pure and simple. When I find the novel is degenerating into rather inferior autobiography, I turn to my diary. When I find the diary is bordering on becoming a novel, I turn to letters. When I find narrative and dialogue appearing in my letters, I get up from my desk, grab the broom and duster, and vent my anger, ridding the Wardrobe Department of dust and cobwebs. . . .

The costumes for *Hamlet* are not kept in the Wardrobe Department. They're kept downstairs in a small room near the stage. I still don't know the actors well. Without their makeup on, without their masks, they all look the same to me. The only one I recognize is Juan Martínez Tormi. He plays the Prince of Denmark, the aging hero of doubt. Poor man. He pays the tailor out of his own pocket. Each season he buys a new costume. Always the same black clothes, the short cloak with its silver clasp. Juan has grown old with the play, has grown old in his dream come true, the dream of all the actors in the world. His pallor, tinged yellow with old age, shines out amid the silk and black velvet. I find it touching, the contrast between that fading elegance and the rest of the cast, his ragged court. He's slim and proud. Behind his back (the actors fear the authority that comes with being a

survivor), everyone laughs at him. They call him
Sir Larry.

Have I already told you about my colleagues
in the Creative Section? Claude, the Gypsy, is
not an expert in hydraulics but a painter. Having no eye for painting, I couldn't say if he has
talent or not. His paintings, which he paints and
exhibits in the Salon de Thé, are vast blotches
of color that are echoed on the artist's clothing.
I think they're awful. If he is a genius, he'll die
bereft of my admiration. Burgossi, the man I
took for the head of Wardrobe, is head of the
Script Department and a teacher of literature.
Have I mentioned Clarita before? Clear by name
and clear by nature: I never saw a more transparent woman. She's perhaps forty years old.
I'm not tall, but she only comes up to my shoulder. She's as plump and ineffectual as a single
teardrop. The slightest thing sets her quivering.
The noise of a window shaken by the wind, some
spilled tea, a fight between Ariadna and the Kid.
Clarita is in charge of Functions, but as there
never are any functions because there's no budget for them, Clara knits. She crochets handbags and sells them in the theater. She writes
poetry: all nightingales, stars, and soft breezes.
She sells them in the theater too. We all buy
one of her handbags and a little book printed
on the old copying machine lent her by the Tax
Returns Office. We artists support each other.
I've already bought my quota. . . .

FIRST CONTACTS WITH THE CREATIVE SECTION Z-K. THIS AFTERNOON'S DIALOGUE.

"I find homosexuals fascinating. They have a natural feeling for art, don't you think? Richard, for example . . . don't look like that, yes, I do mean that Richard, he's gay too. We're very close friends. He tells me everything. It's only natural. They feel they can trust women more. I'm his friend and confidante. We're inseparable."

She gives me an intense look. I'm a new and untried conversational partner. She wants to impress me, and she succeeds. I hear Claude laughing at his easel.

"God help anyone you become friends with, *chérie.*"

Ariadna shrugs and lights a cigarette. Looking at me, she continues.

"Because, despite being the golden boy and famous and all that, Richard has his problems too. He turns up at my house in tears and says, 'Ariadna, I'm going to kill myself. . . .' "

"Oh, don't let's have any talk of suicide," says Clarita, in her little trembly voice. "Or death."

"He was going to kill himself. And why? One of those complicated situations these gays get themselves into." Ariadna taps the ash from her cigarette and crosses her long legs. She's sitting on a desk, and as she wears very short skirts, I can see the tops of her black stockings and the lace on her frilly garter belt. She makes no attempt to pull her skirt down, and no one looks at her. "Poor Richard, you see, was madly in love. I know his boyfriend. Only seventeen! A horrible snotty little madam. What Richard told me would have made me throw up if I wasn't so used to hearing about that kind of thing. And after all I am his best friend. . . ."

There's a loud banging: Klappenbach, known as the Kid, is kicking a cupboard. The soft, soft voice of Burgossi says, "My dear boy, you're going to ruin the bookcase."

"Shut up, you old fool! It's my bookcase. I'm in charge of the library, aren't I?"

"You are. But insults aren't going to help you open those venerable doors, my young friend," says Burgossi with a faint laugh. "Allow a possibly foolish old man to make a not entirely impractical suggestion. You'd be far better off looking for the keys rather than breaking down the doors."

The Kid is letting his beard grow. Where the sparse, dark hair still refuses to appear, you can see his round cheeks, the last trace of babyish skin.

"What keys, old man? This cupboard's about a hundred years old, like you, and only works if you kick it."

"And what if you went down the great marble staircase in search of an M-b with some knowledge on the subject, or, failing him, a locksmith . . . ?"

"And what if I came over there and kicked you instead, or failing that . . . ?"

From Claude's corner comes a tinkling noise followed by laughter. The boy, red-faced, looks over at the painter, who emerges from behind his easel shaking a key ring.

Silence.

"Oh dear, oh dear," says Clara, holding up her knitting like a shield.

"*Alors,* thank me then, Chief Librarian." Claude throws him the key ring.

The Kid bites his lip, but then, still red in the

face, bends down to pick up the keys from the floor. In sulky silence he opens the doors of the cupboard and takes out a packet. It contains a couple of sandwiches. He goes to his desk and without looking at anyone starts to eat.

Burgossi goes back to his book, Clara knits, Claude paints, the Kid munches his sandwiches, and I listen.

"Poor Richard. He was devastated. His boy-friend was leaving him. Suddenly, screaming like a madman, he grabs a knife from the table and tries to slash his wrists. Just as well I'm strong, otherwise he'd have bled all over the table-cloth. . . ."

Ariadna certainly is strong. Her back is immensely broad, her hands and feet huge. None of the feminine artifices she affects (permed hair with a copper rinse, low-cut blouses in flimsy material, tiny skirts, stiletto heels) diminishes the very masculine stature of this woman. She's in her thirties, and looks as if she always has been. It's impossible to imagine her as a teenager, let alone a child.

"I took the knife off him," she says in her fe-line voice, like a cat shut up in that great cage of a body. "If it hadn't been for me, the famous Richard, prizewinning artist and genius, would have killed himself."

The end. But not quite. A voice, grave and intense as organ music, crosses the Salon de Thé.

"In the Age of the Fleur-de-Lis, there will be no suicides." Isolated in his corner like a pariah, Fortunato Candini, our mystic, street-corner preacher, and astrologer, speaks. His mysterious prophecy is greeted with an explosion of laughter. I'm the only one who doesn't laugh.

In every group such as ours, brought together willy-nilly by work, there is always someone like Candini. An idiot, a madman, a poor
fool with some mania slightly more bizarre than
our own, but who draws down scorn and per-
secution on himself as surely as honey attracts
flies. I don't like being a fly. So I don't laugh,
and I win from him a smile, which reveals long
teeth, yellow against his sallow skin, a grateful
nod, and a conspiratorial look.

No, I don't like being a fly. But I don't like
Candini's eyes either. The fire in them belies his
humble behavior. There's something sly about
the respectful way he treats his cruel colleagues.
Is Candini in his corner just biding his time?

. . . And though at first I felt a bit odd among
my colleagues, Emilio, now that I know them a
little, they amuse me. What have I got to complain about? They're nice to me. At six I punch
a card at the control board in the foyer, and I
come home.

I think I'm happy. I have my own room, and
I've bought a jasmine plant for the balcony.

I count the days until your return. I'm dying
to hear all the stories you'll have to tell, but I
won't be able to reciprocate. Nothing much has
been happening here.

Love,
Renata

· 21 ·

THE FOUNTAIN in the Jardin des Plantes (the official name of the city's botanical gardens) was a slim, rather shallow rectangle. In the center a bronze nymph held a pitcher in her arms, her lovely Greek head to one side, a half-smile playing on her delicate, grubby lips. Doubtless long ago a stream of clear water would have flowed from the pitcher; her half-smile, which at present gave her a look of pathetic expectation, would have been part of a single graceful gesture captured in a moment of playful mischief, and her blank eyes would have watched red fish darting, crisscrossing a web of water-weeds. But that must have been a long time back, because the moss growing around the nymph's feet was brown and dying for lack of rain and beginning to break off like a dry husk, soon to join the screws of paper, fragments of glass, and remains of food that formed an amorphous, sordid lining round the basin of broken tiles.

Seated on the only wooden bench near the fountain, Bonday yawned. The little nymph, who stood on a sort of stony island (the small gravel square, exposed, and arid amid an ocean of tropical vegetation), was beginning to depress him. "If I look at her much longer," he said to himself, "I'll fall in love with her."

It was seven o'clock in the morning, and he was finding it hard to stay awake. He lit his pipe. Why had Captain Beh arranged to meet him here? Of all the possible
places in the city, this seemed to him the least appropriate for a working meeting, particularly one at this
hour! Once again he yawned and looked at the landscape around him.

Despite his having lived in the city for thirty years,
this was the first time he'd visited the Jardin des Plantes.
Never having been one of those lovers forced to hide
their ardor among the vegetation of the garden, never
having felt any interest in plants other than those in his
own garden at Arroyo Manso, and having no children
or dog to take for walks on the grass, that was perhaps
not so surprising. However, he had written a description of the garden in his best-known novel, and com-
paring that much-praised literary landscape with what
he saw before him now, he was astonished at the difference. It was far lusher than the backdrop of willows,
roses, pergola, and English-style lawns across which his
characters had wandered. From the small square with
its fountain and nymph down to a far-off street below,
the garden flowed with deep rivers of plants. Gigantic
trees, fleshy-leaved plants, ferns, creepers, and para-
sites made of the garden a compact universe, silent and
mysterious in the morning mists, a damp, green, uncertain world in which red bougainvilleas in flower glowed
and fluttered.

Well, thought Bonday, recalling the passage in his
novel with some embarrassment, who knows what might
be hidden here among all this vegetation? Why not a
few willows and a pergola? He looked at his watch, then
at the heavy iron gates through which he had entered.
Still no sign of Captain Beh. He felt like leaving. Despite the few warm rays of sun beginning to fall on the

square and on his bench, he was feeling cold. "I'll give him two more minutes then I'm leaving." What kept him there was the memory of his telephone conversation with Captain Beh the previous night, or rather that morning.

"We must return to the fountainhead," the captain had said to Bonday, who was still half-asleep and entangled in the telephone cord.

"Is that you, Captain?" asked Bonday as he struggled to free the receiver from a tangle of wires. The phone, which was always on his wife's side of the bed, had fallen on the floor.

"Is that you, Captain?" he asked again, lying across Elsa's prone body.

"We've taken our first step toward Cultural Reconstruction, and we have a platform from which to launch the process. Now what we need to find is a charismatic figure, a central focus for all the main currents of opinion. Are you listening, Bonday?"

At half-past two in the morning Bonday was not in full possession of all his faculties, but his ear picked up the pleasant hint. Feeling around in the dark, he managed to switch on the lamp.

"Ah, yes, a charismatic figure. I understand, Captain."

"We know what our objective is, we have a strategy and a platform or forum, but without someone up front, to welcome people and explain, to talk to journalists, someone photogenic, we're lost."

"Very true, Captain. My sincere thanks for having thought of one who, always ready to take up his public responsibilities, with no other thought in mind than—"

"Don't thank me, Bonday. Tomorrow at seven in the Jardin des Plantes."

"Tomorrow evening at seven, fine."

"Seven in the morning, Bonday. By the fountain."

And so, seated on the hard wooden bench, numb with cold, Bonday waited by the fountain, smoking his pipe. The mist was beginning to lift, laying bare the dirt tracks that crossed between the trees, revealing to Bonday a small stone bridge and old lamps with broken shades. "Lack of punctuality is unforgivable!" he grunted and stood up, almost relieved by the certainty that the captain would not turn up. As he did so the captain appeared through the iron gates.

He wasn't alone. Although he was in plain clothes, his height, build, and severity of expression distinguished him from his companions like a uniform.

"My dear Bonday," said the captain with unexpected warmth.

"Captain," smiled Bonday, and nodded politely to the others.

"No introductions," said the captain when Bonday went to hold out his hand. "Time is of the essence."

With the captain at their head, the group set off again.

"Where are we going?" asked Bonday. No one answered. For a moment Bonday considered taking offense and continuing his retreat toward the gates. The captain and his companions were fast disappearing from view down a slope. Incapable of letting anyone have the last word and drawn on by curiosity, Bonday followed them.

The garden, which before had seemed dense and impenetrable, opened out suddenly into narrow, shady paths. They marched on in silence. The captain went on ahead with the other men a little behind him and, bringing up the rear, Bonday. On a curve in the path one of the men turned his head and smiled at him. Bonday, left breathless by the brisk pace, recognized the smile. It was Hugo Pantaenius, the man standing in for Castro Miranda while the latter was abroad at a conference. Bonday's irritation grew as he stumbled over tree roots, pushed branches out of his face, and dodged puddles. He felt thoroughly fed up with the interminable vegetable kingdom and was once again seriously considering flight when, halfway down the slope, Captain Beh stopped and announced, "We've reached the fountainhead."

· 22 ·

Dear Emilio,

Today, while I was arranging my books on
my brand-new bookshelf (I got it very cheaply
at an auction), I found the photograph we had
taken in the Jardin des Plantes, two days before
your trip. Do you remember? The fountain with
the nymph, the little square, the sun. I look ri-
diculously solemn, hard, sad, because cameras
always make me nervous. You're at my side,
smiling. You have one hand raised. What were
you pointing at? The nymph? The photogra-
pher? Or were you just saying good-bye? You're
definitely saying something. On your lips I can
see the trace of some indecipherable word. That
was the last time we spoke. Still no letters from
you . . .

I've put all my books on the shelves, and I've framed
the photo of Emilio and me in the Jardin des Plantes.
Why did we choose the garden, of all places, as if we
were lovers or tourists up from the provinces? And why
have I placed that photo on the middle shelf, where I
can see it best? Fetishism! And to think I made fun of
Gertrudis and her devotion for the Virgin of Casa-

manta and Tyrone Power. The Virgin had a body like
Venus, spiky tufts of dead hair, and glass eyes whose
terrible gaze dominated the narrow landscape of our
shared room. I couldn't bring myself to be very rude
about the Virgin; there's always something about other
people's superstitions that brings me up short. But I
had to laugh when Gertrudis, all dressed up and
drenched in perfume, ready to go down to the police
station, kissed the paper face of Tyrone Power. "Oh
come on, Gertrudis, he's only an actor and not even a
live one at that!" I can see her as she was then, serious,
her face a mask, saying categorically, "The only good
Indian's a dead Indian."

Gertrudis would go then, leaving me alone with the
unpleasant feeling that her idols were watching over
me for her. Sometimes I get the same feeling in the
Salon de Thé, where each person, within the individual
constraints of office and wall, constructs his own little
house, his temple. Like stilts holding up a village built
on water, idolatry sustains our desire to survive the dis-
illusionments and dangers of this world.

In Clara's corner there's the almanac with a Japanese
print; the Parthenon at dawn and a spotlit Eiffel Tower
belong to Ariadna, the Chagal reproduction to Claude;
on Burgossi's desk there's a bust of a disheveled
Nietzsche. The Kid is a more fickle idolater: today a
wild-eyed musician, tomorrow a photo of beggars dying
in a ditch; if it's not a half-naked chorus girl, it's a poem
written by himself, and so his ever-changing corner is
born and dies with each new day.

Poor old Candini has his fleur-de-lis. He drew it himself, rather badly, in Indian ink on a piece of white
card. The fleur-de-lis makes me think of France, and
of Emilio, who still hasn't written. Why has Candini made
a religion of that flower that isn't a flower? If I remem-

ber rightly, the fleur-de-lis represented three crossed halberds. Weapons of war. Candini, of course, doesn't know that. He talks of love, of the spirit, of faith in a time when there will be no suicides, no death, no pain. Nor, of course, any pariahs like Candini himself.

Dear Emilio,

At last I've got a splendid plot for another novel. I'm not going to tell you about it in a letter. I'll save it for when you get back. I want to see your face on the other side of a table in our café on the south side. I know you'll like it. Can you believe it? I don't feel alone now, or ugly or stupid. I've got a story! Ah, if only you were here!

My colleagues claim they love literature. But they read and write a different kind of book. The nicest, most intelligent one is Claude. But he, alas, belongs to another world, the world of painting. And it irritates me that he lards his conversation with French words. Burgossi, who's a dear man, has yet to scale the slopes of Miguel de Cervantes Saavedra. To make matters worse, we've entered a new stage with *Hamlet.* Wait for it, Emilio; now we're doing *Hamlet* in English! I swear it's true. *Shakespeare in the language of Shakespeare.* The decision of some unknown official. If this is life, how can one possibly take it seriously? The worst of it is that they force you to. Yesterday I was reminded (they reminded me) that I'm in charge of Wardrobe. I was not amused. Not at all.

"We have a problem, *señorita,*" Candini says respectfully, handing me a sealed envelope. I give him an un-

necessarily friendly smile. We're all so superior here. I
immediately regret my smile. I don't like his eyes, like
two burning coals, or that wide, loose mouth of his, like
a fifth-rate actor's, or the grave voice in which he in-
tones his ridiculous prophecies. I read the name on the
envelope. It's mine. And underneath it says: Head of
Wardrobe.

"Ah, news," purrs Ariadna, and comes clicking over
to sit on the edge of my desk.

"It's addressed to Wardrobe," I say, irritated.

"So what? Everyone's dying for a bit of news."

"Not me, *chérie*," shouts Claude from behind his easel.

Burgossi gives me a feeble smile. "Read your letter
in peace, dear child."

"Oh, please don't argue," begs Clara, "my head's
throbbing."

The enormous cat sitting on my desk lets out a ti-
gerish laugh. "Hypocrites! You all know perfectly well
what a letter means. A letter, sister, means you've been
given your notice. And that means dismissal. Which in
turn means tomorrow you'll be reading the classified
ads in the newspaper."

There's a heavy silence: Again Ariadna is the one who
breaks it, while I open the letter.

"Very well, colleagues. I can tell you're thinking about
it. We're hanging on to our jobs in the theater by the
skin of our teeth. And the theater itself, Miss Head of
Wardrobe, is hanging by a thread."

Another silence. The Creative Section is fertile soil
for sowing and harvesting rumors about the fate of the
theater. One day it's being demolished, the next converted into a national monument, the day after it's to
be "the great theater of the world." Behind all these
false rumors, delivered with paradoxical delight, lurks
the fear, but also the conviction, that nothing of value

or interest exists outside the theater, that the only true reality is enclosed within these old, dilapidated walls. At least we're united in our passion for the here and now.

"Are you going to read it or not?"

I may be a coward, but I'm stubborn too. I raise my head and look her straight in the eye.

"No," I say.

· 23 ·

"WE'VE REACHED the fountainhead," said Captain Beh, indicating a long arbor, a tunnel of ferns and creepers.

"And not before time," said Bonday under his breath, as he bowed his head and followed the captain and the others into what seemed like a shadowy green cave.

It took them a few minutes to get through it. Bonday kept his eyes on the fleshy neck and back of the man immediately ahead of him: Pantaenius. By the time the roof of the tunnel got higher and they could stand up straight, they were already nearing the end. Bonday, who had imagined that the captain's "fountainhead" would be a replica of the fountain with the nymph, blinked in astonishment. They emerged onto a broad terrace, a clearing in the dense growth of the garden, still shady and swathed in morning mist. Thick and tinged with blue, the mist made the terrace look like a lagoon on which floated round tables, circular benches, and odd human silhouettes linked by vaporous ribbons. He grabbed Pantaenius's arm.

"Where are we?" His voice boomed out like thunder in that aquatic silence. Pantaenius's mocking laugh and the calls for silence that sprang from the ghostly gathering were followed by a reproach from the captain— "Don't disturb the people, Bonday"—and with his chubby, freckled hand he pointed to a sign.

On the sign, which hung from a branch, Bonday read:

XVI ANNUAL AMATEUR CHESS TOURNAMENT

Captain Beh looked at his watch. "We're early. Just as well. We can have a good look at the terrain."

Bonday felt ridiculous tiptoeing round the terrace looking at the players. They were all male and of varying ages; there was even a boy who couldn't have been much more than ten. This boy in particular attracted his attention. The son of one of these madmen, no doubt. The boy was small and blond, with an extraordinarily dirty face in which shone a pair of sky-blue eyes.

"The people are early risers," commented the captain.

"The sign of a healthy race," agreed Bonday.

"Oh no, don't be taken in. They're a slovenly, lazy people. They'll get up early to enjoy themselves, but they don't leap out of bed to go to work. No one works in this country."

Bonday thought of the trains at Arroyo Manso early in the morning when he'd happened to be there on his way back from the center; he recalled his horror at the way the crowd pushed to get on to the train and his human relief at being able to escape to his cozy house and his warm bed. Where were those people going? To a chess tournament in the Jardin des Plantes?

". . . and that's why, Bonday, that's why . . ." The captain was continuing a sentence the beginning of which Bonday had not heard, "we've come here to seek out our charismatic figure. Here, at the very fountainhead."

"I don't understand. . . ."

The captain patted his shoulder affectionately. "Don't pretend now. You knew all along. A man of genius like yourself, an honored man of letters, with all those famous books to your name, you knew what I meant at once. You didn't make the mistake of thinking that you, or I, or Pantaenius, or any of our loyal friends, could occupy that key post. We don't want old faces," he sighed, "because the public has had enough of them. We had no option but to come back to the fountainhead."

Bonday took his pipe out of his pocket, put it in his mouth, and chewed it furiously. *If I speak, my voice will give me away.*

"What do you think of the one in the checked scarf?" whispered the captain. "Have you noticed how respectful the other players are toward him? He seems nice."

"The one with the scarf?" asked Bonday in a reedy voice. He needed time, time to understand, to recover from the blow.

"With the blue-and-yellow checked scarf. At the table in the middle."

"Ah, yes."

"But Pantaenius isn't convinced; too old, he says. Frankly I think he's perfect. Come on, let's walk around again."

Slowly Bonday and Captain Beh went around the terrace again. Suddenly the captain stopped dead. "Where's Pantaenius?" His narrow eyes searched anxiously through the group of men following a few yards behind. "He's gone," he said querulously, "just when I most needed him. But you've got something to write this down on. Make a note."

"A note of what?"

"Of the candidates, Bonday. Let's see."

As potential charismatic figures, as well as the man with the scarf, there was the man in the leather jacket, the one in a beret, the one with a ring on his left hand, and the thin one wearing a poncho. "All we need now to complete the whole lunatic exercise," a flustered Bonday said to himself, "is the little blond-haired boy."

The captain smiled, pleased. Bonday screwed up his

courage and asked, "Do you think it's practicable to involve one of these chess players in the Campaign? He'll have to be given a job, a salary. . . ."

"The job's already there. Or didn't you realize?" The captain lowered his voice. "Director of the National Theater. It's clearly laid out in the organization chart Pantaenius prepared for me." The captain rested his hand on Bonday's shoulder again. He spoke to him now like a father touched by a favorite son's ingenuousness. "We have to save that theater. Prove to the world out there watching us that we're not savages, that we're ready to fight tooth and nail to defend our sacred cultural heritage."

The captain half-closed his eyes. "Future generations," he said in a voice trembling with emotion, "are watching us. We don't want them to reproach us with having stood by and allowed the plays of William Shakespeare to appear on the stage of our National Theater for almost a century. That's why we've come back to the fountainhead."

"Ah," said Bonday.

"It doesn't matter which play they put on, Bonday. It's the theater that matters and the audience. We'll remodel the theater, extend it. As for the audience, we'll have a man in charge of the theater who'll be in direct contact with the audience from the stage, who'll be able to answer any questions they want to ask him."

"I thought that . . ." The captain wasn't listening to him. He was looking questioningly at Pantaenius, who came running up, his smile more unctuous than ever. "Ready when you are, Captain. We've struck gold."

The captain pointed to the tables.

"The one with the scarf, right?"

Pantaenius shook his head. "No, you're wasting your time there."

"Don't you like them, Hugo?" asked the captain with

a disappointment that bordered so nearly on submis-
siveness Bonday felt surprised.

Pantaenius shook his brilliantined head. "The chess
players were a good idea, Captain, but it just won't work.
Some of them are too old, others too young, and a lot
simply want nothing to do with the whole business."

The captain gave a melancholy glance at the tables
where the men continued their silent game. "Are you
sure, Pantaenius? Such calm, simple people, so involved in what they're doing. Remember the last Chess
Masters' Tournament? No, I can't give up just like that."

"What's past is past," interrupted Pantaenius, smiling. "Remember, it's risky betting on the same number
twice."

"But you yourself suggested . . ."

"We live and learn." Pantaenius shrugged. "Believe
me, Captain, the man we want is on the other side of
the park."

When he heard mention of the other side of the park,
Bonday's head spun and he felt a sharp pain in the pit
of his stomach. He was hungry now as well as tired,
and there was that idiot suggesting another trek through
the jungle and without even a café in sight. But he said
nothing. Resignedly he rejoined the captain and his
retinue. They crossed the terrace and jumped over a
low privet hedge. Less than a hundred paces from the
chess players was another terrace. The sun was dazzling there.

"Here we are," said Pantaenius.

Blinded by the sun, Bonday couldn't see anything.
But something odd happened to him: His body refused
to go forward. He was helpless to resist. He turned on
his heels, jumped back over the privet hedge, and,
without really knowing what he was doing, looked for
the tunnel and went down it.

He walked blindly on, aflame with indignation (after all the talk of an interminable walk to the other side of the park, it had turned out to be only a few short steps), indifferent to the captain's annoyance, and sure that they would drop him from the campaign. Minutes later he stopped. Darkness closed around him in the tunnel. Alarmed, he reached out to touch the walls that seemed to press in on him.

"You're lost," said a small voice.

Bonday caught his breath.

"Don't be afraid, sir, open your eyes."

He opened his eyes. *Did I really have them closed?* he thought, blinking in astonishment. Among the green shadows and from his adult perspective, he could just make out a yellow head. It was a boy.

"Ah."

"Are you ill, sir?"

Bonday cleared his throat. "It's very dark in here, sonny."

A small, rough hand took his. "Come on, I'll get you out."

The hand pulled Bonday along, the small voice giving him instructions. "Put your foot here, watch out for that branch, lower your head, there's a puddle there."

Once out of the tunnel Bonday mopped the sweat from his face.

"Thank you."

Two sparkling blue eyes looked up at him. It was the boy from the chess tournament.

"You're welcome."

Bonday started walking down the path. The boy trotted along after him. *There's nothing for it, I'll have to talk to him.* Bored and irritated, he asked as amiably as he could, "Do you go to school then? What year are you in?"

"Did you come with the captain? I heard them call him Captain. Or was it General?"

"Was your father playing in the tournament?"

"The captain stayed with the other gentlemen. Why did you leave?"

"Which one is your father? The one with the checked scarf?"

"The captain went to see the fleur-de-lis."

Bonday stopped. "What fleur-de-lis?"

The blue eyes shone in the dirty face. "My grandmother comes here every Sunday. She says people have to believe in something. Perhaps you know . . ."

"Who, your grandmother?"

"No, not my grandmother, the fleur-de-lis. Before, she used to look for them in the garden. I can't find any fleur-de-lis, she used to say. Now she says it doesn't matter, that she likes the gentleman, the way he talks and all that. He speaks here every Sunday. Now the captain and those other gentleman know him too. You missed him."

They were back in the small square with its fountain and nymph. The fleur-de-lis! thought Bonday. Is that what Pantaenius meant when he said they'd struck gold? Relieved, he walked toward the iron gates. "Good-bye, sonny," he smiled, patting the blond head. "No doubt your father will teach you to play chess, and then one day you'll win the tournament."

The blue eyes shone. "Look."

Bonday looked at the hand he held out. "What is it, a coin?"

The boy shook his bright, grubby head. "It's the medal, sir. The winner's medal. I win all the tournaments. My father hasn't played for ages. I'm the one who plays."

· 24 ·

My bangs need cutting. What's the use of having my own room if all I do is look in the mirror and go over the same scene again and again in my mind? I search my face for the feeling of pride I had when I stood up to Ariadna, and all I see is the sense of guilt I felt when I went down to the hall. Guilt about what? I really should cut my bangs.

"No," I said.

In my memory Ariadna is still looking at the envelope addressed to the Head of Wardrobe. Bangs or not, I am the head of Wardrobe.

"No," I repeat.

"Bravo," says Claude approvingly.

"Giving in to one's own or to other people's curiosity was not one of the virtues admired by the Stoics," says Burgossi quietly.

"You've met your match, Ariadna," laughs the Kid.

"Please, don't make so much noise, my head's pounding," moans Clara. Tonight, in my room, in front of the mirror, I can still hear them, they're all around me. I was glad to have their support. But I can still hear Ariadna's words to me. "Don't kid yourself. It's not you they're supporting. They just want to get at me." But then when Ariadna left, slamming the door, I turned

to my colleagues, and I read them the letter. It didn't
in fact say very much.

"With regard to the changes to be made to the present season, in your capacity as the head of Wardrobe
you will be expected to assist the consultant."

I looked up and shrugged.

"It doesn't say when the consultant will be coming."

"He's already been, *señorita*," said Candini, who stood
waiting by my desk.

"When? Is he here?"

Candini shook his head. I thought I saw a shadow of
a smile on his wide, pale mouth. "The consultant un-
loaded the parcels from the truck and left."

"What parcels?" I looked at my colleagues. Their interest, support, enthusiasm, had rapidly extinguished,
like a bonfire of paper; all that was left was a thin layer
of black ash on the floor of the Salon de Thé. The letter had brought no news of dismissals or promotions.
Claude was painting, Burgossi was reading, Clara was
counting the stitches on her needle, the Kid was biting
into an apple. Just another visit from the consultant,
the same old story, nothing new, nothing that would
make any difference. I wanted to grow up there and
then, and cut off my bangs. With brusque authority I
said to Candini, "Get an M-b to bring the parcels up to
the Wardrobe Department. I'll deal with it tomorrow."
I didn't ask what was in the parcels. With the fluency
of an old hand I gave my orders to my inferior, to the
pariah. You learn fast in the Creative Section. But only
seconds later, with an equally sudden onrush of shame,
I was humbly excusing myself. *"Please,* Candini. If you
wouldn't mind . . ."

"It's not the parcels that are the problem, Señorita
Renata," he said with an unpleasantly malicious smile.
"It's Señor Martínez Tormi who's the problem."

The black ashes stirred, throwing out a few sparks.

"It's his nerves again."

"Don't forget, dear child, Juan is a very sensitive man."

"Be firm with the old hysteric, Renata."

"Ah, *chérie*, what I'd give to see this!"

"You'll have to talk to him, Señorita Renata. He's waiting for you downstairs."

I went slowly down the marble staircase.

"Oh God, oh God!"

I looked cautiously over the banisters. Down below, surrounded by dark shapes, our Hamlet was tearing at his silver hair. However much I admire his odd pride in eternally playing the Prince of Denmark in this abandoned theater, his temper terrifies me.

"Renata!" Hands on hips, brows furrowed, a threatening Hamlet glowered up at me from among the circle of parcels.

"What is all this, Juan?" I asked from the stairs.

"That is the question."

I was on the last step. I looked at the parcels and said, "They're furs."

His shouted reply almost bowled me over. *"Yes, I can see they're furs!"* I retreated a step. "Come back here, my girl, and have a good look. Yes, they're furs. Now don't you run away." His voice dropped to one of those stage whispers that could be heard at the back of the stalls. "And do you know what these furs are for?" I shook my head. "They're for Hamlet. Fur cloaks. They're our new costumes!"

Candini smiled his unpleasant smile and raised a finger to his lips. The old actor had collapsed onto a carpet of piled-up furs, his face buried in his arms. I didn't know what to do. "It's a mistake," I stuttered. "It must be a mistake."

Juan's voice, still young and beautiful, rang out in the empty hall.

"A mistake? Don't be ridiculous, girl. Read this."

To the Principal Actor, Don Juan Martínez Tormi:
After prolonged research into the climate at the
Danish court during the period in which the
events described by the playwright William
Shakespeare take place and in conformity with
our belief that contemporary theater should at
all costs be built on a solid sense of realism, the
Special Advisory Board of the President Herrero National Theater orders as follows:

1. A change in the costumes hitherto used.
2. The replacement of all silks, velvets, and other
    materials by fur cloaks, which will be duly
    delivered to the head of Wardrobe of this
    theater.
3. The use of the attached consignment given
    in lieu of tax by Digazola Ltd.

> Your humble servant,
> Hugo Pantaenius

I raised my eyes from the letter.

"Good God!" Before me was a sort of rampant beast,
a parodic synthesis of Jekyll and Hyde. I saw a noble
head of silver hair, a delicate, angular face, sad eyes, a
bitter smile, and below that a grotesque hairy body,
broad and amorphous. "The slings and arrows of outrageous fortune," said the beautiful voice of my sad
Hamlet, his appearance disfigured by the vast fur coat.
"To be or not to be: That is the question."

"Juan—"

"I've no intention of disguising myself like this! I refuse to ruin my career! I won't go on!"

"Of course, Juan, we won't allow it."

"Señorita Renata."

I turned to Candini, startled. I'd forgotten he
was there.

"You're new here, *señorita*. You're young and inexperienced. But, with respect, believe me, there's nothing we can do." He fixed his burning eyes on Juan. "Señor Martínez Tormi knows it. He's worked here a long time."

I waited for the leading actor to explode. He said nothing.

"Señor Martínez Tormi knows"—there was a murky sediment of pleasure in Candini's voice—"that if they fire him from the theater, no one else will give him a part."

Juan slowly pulled himself together. He clumsily removed the monstrous fur coat. First one sleeve, then the other. He was wearing the silk and velvet costume that he wears at all the rehearsals. I didn't find him ridiculous standing there, a faded, once-glorious Hamlet; he just seemed a fragile, vulnerable old man, trying to be true to his youthful ambitions.

Candini, suddenly fierce, was saying, "Señor Martínez Tormi also knows that if you take his side, you'll be dismissed from the theater with him, the same day."

"Leave him alone," I shouted.

Candini bowed his head. "You're wrong, sister. You don't have strength enough to control the forces of evil. Only in the Fleur-de-Lis will you find protection and support for your desire for justice."

I watched him leave. "We're all mad," I said to myself. And yet it wasn't the old actor's eccentricity that alarmed me. That I could understand.

"Take no notice of him, Juan. There must be a way around this."

I saw the almost imperceptible glimmer of tears in eyes that still retained a trace of their past beauty. "That worm's right. There's nothing we can do."

Impulsively I took his hand. He did not withdraw it. "Juan, let's hide the furs."

He looked down at me in astonishment from the lofty heights of his inviolate dignity, and arched his eyebrows as if he were seeing me for the first time. Then, with a forced smile on his thin, ivory lips, he said haughtily, "There are more inspectors here, young lady, than are dreamed of in your philosophy."

I laughed.

"You don't seriously mean we should pay attention to what that poor idiot of an astrologer says! The world's full of idiots like him. Come on, let's hide the furs. No one will notice."

The old actor smiled, a sad, utterly unspontaneous smile. "How young you are, Renata. You haven't yet learned to fear stupid people." He gently withdrew his hand from mine and with the same delicacy picked up Hamlet's cape with its silver clasp from the floor. "I won't be able to use it anymore. You have it. Keep it in a safe place. I wouldn't want the consultant to have it. After all, I paid for it. It belongs to me." Again he looked into my eyes. "I know I can trust you, my dear."

I had a lump in my throat. I couldn't protest or thank him for his trust. I just stood there, silent and unmoving, and let him go. But before he disappeared along one of the theater's corridors, humbled, defeated, stripped of his madness, he turned a moment and said to me, "Candini is worse than stupid, he's a fanatic."

And I look in the mirror and I see myself, the head of Wardrobe, an impotent coward. I really should cut my bangs.

· 25 ·

The Editor
People magazine
Sir,

In the last issue of your excellent magazine I
read an article that referred to my short work
Europe Is Watching Us, and I feel obliged to answer the author's libelous description of me as
an "artist who has sold himself cheap on the
European cultural market."

I do not answer him as Santiago Bonday the
writer, but as Santiago Bonday the man.

After a lifetime dedicated to art for art's sake,
I feel it unnecessary to justify a body of work
translated into more than fifteen foreign languages, which, over the past decades, has won
every major national literary prize and even the
congratulations, conveyed either in person or by
telegram, of our country's presidents. However,
I wish to correct your critic's crude interpreta-
tion. It was never the intention of *Europe Is
Watching Us* to encourage the tendency so common in beginners to admire the great creative
artists in a spirit of excessive servility, in short,
the tendency to believe that this painful humil-

iation is an essential part of the learning process. Speaking as one who himself came up the hard way, nothing could be further from my intention.

My aim in *Europe Is Watching Us* is altogether worthier and, if you like, more patriotic: to create an immediate and necessary awareness that our national culture has its spectators and judges. Briefly, what it seeks to do is to establish what our image in the Old World should be and to win the plaudits our national achievements deserve.

But it is not anger alone that prompts me to write these lines. Putting modesty aside, I feel I must openly confess my feelings at this grave juncture in our history. This is not the time for reasoning. One must give up one's privileged and elitist position in favor of pure action. The writer of that vile article should know that Santiago Bonday is abandoning the hedonistic pleasures of literature to join a Cultural Campaign that will once and for all wrench our obsessive gaze away from Europe.

I am not a man to bear grudges, and I am happy that your publication should be the first with this news. There is a popular cult (your critic appears to have forgotten it, for he does not mention it once in his notes) whose symbol, the Fleur-de-Lis, will shield this "artist who has sold himself cheap on the European cultural market." The people, and Santiago Bonday puts his people before his art, know how to preserve their roots with dignity. The Fleur-de-Lis, the flag of this Campaign of Cultural Reconstruction, will teach a lesson to this world that dares to label us "savages."

Santiago Bonday is breaking down the walls
of the ivory tower, he takes up his orders and
commits himself to the struggle, he accepts the
challenge.

Yours,
Santiago Bonday

Dear Emilio,

Marga Hedelstoff is leaving for France today
and will deliver this letter personally because
there are problems here with the mail. I'm writing this by candlelight (there's a power cut) and
although they haven't turned off the water yet,
I don't feel any safer here or any less stupid for
what I'm about to say to you.

Marga has offered me a job in Paris, where
she's going to open an art gallery. I would pay
off my fare in installments, out of my wages.
Poor Marga, she's so kind to me, and yet I almost hated her when she made me the offer.
She was forcing me to choose.

The chance of a lifetime! To go off in search
of a better fate than just scraping an existence
in this inhospitable, servile city. Paris, where an
artist is not considered a delinquent. Paris, where
life goes on far from this murky pond, far from
this dry husk of a world that closes in and chokes
you before you find your real voice. Here we
don't mature, we just grow old in darkness and
silence.

But I didn't accept. I doubt if you'll understand. I'm not sure if I understand myself. My
reasons are so trivial that they won't stand up
to intelligent analysis. What keeps me here?
Perhaps it's my imagination that makes a cow-

ard of me and shows me another possible side to Paris: being a nobody except within the safe walls of a colony of exiles; becoming a caricature of that tangle of virtues, defects, and habits that I have been and am without realizing it; losing the language it took me so long to acquire only to plunge into another; embracing a nostalgia for something I never much loved. What keeps me here? Perhaps just a kind of animal loyalty: the smell of these streets, familiar sounds, the area where I live now, the food I eat, a tree, a friendly face, my conversations with you, the café on the south side. I feel too an unhealthy curiosity about where the world I know is going, what will become of the theater, how we'll put on the new version (in English and in furs) of *Hamlet,* when the attractive painter and set designer, Claude, will ask me out, etc. As you see, a feeble plot.

I said no, and you should have seen the fuss Marga made. Wanting to be discreet, I didn't ask her her reasons for leaving. Intense as ever, she said, "Darling, this is not the time to think, now we must act. I'm going back to the fountainhead."

It's the flow of a river, not its origins, that interests me, so I'll never find the fountainhead. But I swear to you, Emilio, that when I said good-bye to Marga, when I started walking back toward my house and saw the lovely autumn light in the streets and heard the bruised, piquant Spanish of this city weaving together the unknown voices of the people I passed, tying them up in a strong knot, in a tacit, involuntary embrace, I knew I'd made the right decision.

Don't tell me off if you disagree. I'm longing for your return so that I can explain to you in person my sentimentality, my stupidity, and my cowardice.

Renata

· 26 ·

THE SIDEBOARD swayed for a moment on the windowsill and then began to fall.

It was falling so slowly that Bonday, his head back, his mouth open in a scream, could see the fantastic stillness of the glasses and the creamy relief on the Wedgwood pottery before the crash came and he felt the warmth of his own blood bubbling out from his crushed flesh. He was still dying, in midscream, when he woke up.

His wife was snoring gently, her stout body curled up, one hand beneath her pillow. He pushed back the sheet, slid noiselessly to the floor, and left the room. He went to the bathroom to look for a sedative. "I must sleep, I must get a night's sleep." He opened the bathroom cabinet, had his hand on a bottle of pills, and was turning the tap when he remembered that sleeping meant dreaming. And in his dreams lurked the sideboard. He put the top back on the bottle and replaced it on the shelf.

He dragged himself to the kitchen, took some ice from the fridge, threw it into a glass, and went into the library, where there was a small bar. Bonday drank little and unenthusiastically; the bottle of whiskey, which he chose at random (unlike wines, he couldn't tell one spirit from another), was for the benefit of visitors. He didn't want to get drunk, just to numb himself a little while he waited for the dawn. He didn't notice that he'd filled the glass to the brim.

Slumped on a sofa by the window, he stretched out his legs and rested them on a low table while he took a long drink of whiskey. He moved his feet lazily, and his slippers fell to the floor. Bonday regarded the irregular fan of white toes, the little blue veins at the top of his ankles. For some reason the sight of his bare feet saddened him. He took another sip of whiskey.

"My big toenail's getting very long," he heard himself say foolishly out loud while he refilled his glass, surprised to find the bottle by him, thinking he had left it on the bar.

It was raining now. An unexpected storm. The shutters that opened onto the garden had not been closed, and the rain pounded furiously on the windows. A clap of thunder shook the house. Bonday looked out at the garden lit by a sudden lunar clarity. The sight made him tremble: The tops of the trees, disheveled by the wind, were bent over like human heads beneath the invisible hand of an executioner. The sky was the guillotine; the lawn, a vast platform onto which the heads would roll. Horrified, Bonday shut his eyes. When he opened them, everything was liquid and black, and the garden had disappeared. He quickly filled his glass again and gulped down the whiskey, almost choking, but he could still see the faceless heads tumbling onto the library carpet, as real to him as they had been on the carpet of grass in his garden, *All those dead people, all those dead people out there.* And he poured himself another whiskey.

In a brief moment of lucidity he thought, Who'd have thought it, I'm getting drunk.

"It's an emotional wound," he told himself, "the psychological consequence of an accident with no physical consequences." He cursed Dr. Ranisky and gazed at the bottom of his glass. No ethics at all. Here he was on the brink of madness, and there they were, the doctors, fleeing the country. There was no whiskey or ice left in the glass. And what if he went too? Did the nightmare justify the expense?

A second, longer, more intense flash of lightning laid the garden bare. Bonday, though he did not want to look, looked.

Beneath a sky of molten silver he saw the whole garden revealed to him, the drowned lawn and the trees struggling to remain upright. The night was so clear that in spite of the rain he could easily make out the black roses on the rosebushes, the fence, the gate to the street. No decapitated heads or executioners, but what he did see was a human silhouette leaping the gate. "Thank heavens it's just a dream," he said to himself between sips of neat whiskey, and started to laugh.

The dream was so simple—a man leaping the gate—so entirely free of sideboards, so pleasant, that Bonday celebrated the fact by drinking directly from the bottle.

Two minutes later, he'd stopped celebrating and stopped laughing. He put his hand to his forehead. He felt an iron band there and another in the pit of his stomach. And that wasn't the worst of it. "Oh, God, now I'm going to get sad." Though he'd faked it often enough, nothing depressed him more than genuine sadness. "It's that sideboard," he moaned, "it's that blessed sideboard. Before that, I knew what it was to be happy." Of course, he had good reason to be sad. His novel, for example. He'd been stuck on Chapter 2 for months now. But it was quite a different matter to be seeing heads rolling in the garden and a man leaping the gate! Perhaps it was Don Matías, the gardener. Crazy old man, coming out in a storm like this to protect his rosebushes!

A third lightning flash lit up the garden. Astonished, Bonday blinked. There was another human figure jumping over the gate. He shook his head and tried to get up. He couldn't. In a thick voice he announced to the world, "It's the failure of all the great hopes I had. . . ." Yes, that was it. The novel was a failure, and ten or fifteen years had gone by since he published his last book. Was it really that long? It couldn't be. But it was. His generous impulse in joining the Cultural Campaign had failed too. Since his foolish flight from the Jardin des Plantes, Captain Beh hadn't phoned him. He tipped up the bottle to finish off what little remained of the whiskey. The alcohol burned the back of his throat. He started to cough. His ears were buzzing now. But he heard the noise in the room quite clearly. Still coughing, with watering eyes, he looked around. Nothing stirred. Only his own body rocking gently back and forth on the sofa and something shiny and yellow that was moving on the library door. The brass door handle.

"Oh God, it's my wife."

He didn't want to see her or want her to see him like this. He imagined his wife coming in, her stout body and flaccid skin, her thin hair dyed a modest chestnut, unruly from sleep, her voice first reproachful, then affectionate, that awful doglike loyalty. Genuinely moved, Bonday realized he was crying.

"A man without love, a failure and a man without love . . ."

The door half-opened. Bonday closed his eyes. Overcome by nausea and dizziness, he plunged headlong into a bottomless pit. He became tangled in and then fell through a cobwebbed mesh of images. The first three lines of that second chapter, chess tables set out in the middle of a jungle, a boy's laugh, a pair of blue eyes, and at the bottom of the well, a naked girl playing with a water pitcher. The nymph from the little square. Bonday held out his arms to her but never reached her. In her place stood a tall, elegant man with a melancholy smile. The man said, "If we're all a little paranoid, brother, it's because we have every reason to be." Bonday shook hands with Bonday and woke up.

Lucidly tipsy, he at last managed to get up from his seat. He'd fallen asleep in front of the big mirror, and he now caught sight of his own reflection. He took a few steps, stumbled, and had to lean against the wall. "The morning after," he groaned. The man in the mirror made him feel indignant, ashamed. "I drank a whole bottle, what an animal." Fixed by the frame of gilt garlands, he observed himself with horror and fascination. "A sick, slobbering wolf." He removed his hand from the frame. Something square and white fell to the floor. As best he could, he crouched to pick it up.

The following day, an ice pack on his head, the wreck of a writer who had once boasted that he never got drunk, Bonday lay on his bed of pain and read, for the hundredth time, the letter he'd found by the mirror.

Señor Santiago Bonday
Arroyo Manso

By hand

Esteemed Poet Laureate,
    We have pleasure in informing you that the Inauguration Ceremony for the post of director of the President Herrero National Theater will take place next Wednesday at 09:00 hours in

the reception room of the above-mentioned establishment.

We assume you will be present at this historic event and take this opportunity to inform you that, in accordance with Decree No. 7658, you have been appointed literary consultant to Category Z-k.

> Our most sincere congratulations,
> Your humble servant,
> Hugo Pantaenius

◦ 27 ◦

The power cuts are becoming more frequent. With the approach of autumn, the days grow shorter, and there is no lighting in the streets to help prolong life there for a few hours more. I hear the silence growing in the city: black, thick, and as toxic as a cloud of poison gas. It stops my neighbors' conversations in midflow, as they stand at the front door scolding their children and waiting for their husbands to come home. It silences the music on the portable radio being played by a group of young people on the corner, boys on the lookout for girls in a war in which love never shows its face. I hear the old people taking in their chairs from their front-row position on the pavement. I hear the last angry word of an argument about football. On the balconies I hear the dripping of water on plants and the clatter of shutters closing on the floor above. A whistle lights up the darkness of the street. I recognize the tune, as persistent as childhood memories. The man is coming home late and, troubled by this new silence in the city, he whistles to keep up his spirits. Trembling, I take comfort in that solitary sound. . . .

Dear Emilio,
　　Don't be surprised at the state of my hand-writing. I'm in bed, ill. Now I'm shut up here,

coughing and sneezing, this apartment seems bleaker and sadder than ever. When I get out of bed to make myself some soup or a cup of tea, I mourn Gertrudis's absence. To cap it all, I'm feverish. The fever makes me see strange shadows, shifting half-shadows in everything about me.

You once said that I had a fevered view of the world, and ever since then, because your remark wounded me, I've tried not to. I confront the world with a steady temperature of 98.6 degrees, I make my skin icy cold. And yet, sometimes, like now, when the thermometer registers a natural rise in my body temperature because of the flu, when, as the mercury rises, presentiments, threats, and ghosts are only to be expected, paradoxically I rebel against your judgment. Were you right? Couldn't it be that my fevered view of the world is the correct one? From my bed in this lonely room I look back on the full dress rehearsal and I see more than I saw then, more than I'm scribbling now in my notebook to distract myself, my temperature normal, with a coldness lent by distance.

"O! that this too too solid flesh . . ."

"He tries so hard to sound like Gielgud, but comes over instead like a cross between Marlene Dietrich and Laurence Olivier, don't you think?"

The Kid's laugh crosses the room and reaches the stage. Hamlet does not turn his head.

"Klappenbach," whispers Burgossi from the row in front, twisting his neck round to see the boy, "if you feel unable to respect the actor, at least have the generosity to respect the man."

The Kid colors. "Don't get huffy with me, Grandad, it was Ariadna who made the joke."

"To die: to sleep . . ."

I close my eyes. The sight of that thin body dragging itself painfully about the stage, encumbered by the weight of a heavy fur coat, makes me feel ill.

"And by a sleep . . ."

The voice is touchingly young. I don't want to look. I slide down in my seat until I feel the back of the chair against my neck. You see, Renata, you may be suffering, but you're also indirectly responsible for part of this ridiculous act.

A hand shakes my shoulder. "Don't close your eyes, dear," purrs Ariadna. "You'll miss the best scene: Hamlet and Ophelia, a lovely couple. There's a tiny age difference, but who's to notice?"

I open my eyes when Ophelia comes onstage. Wrapped in an otter-skin cloak, the youngest actress in the cast advances unsteadily, looking behind her.

"Nymph, in thy orisons . . ." Carrying imperturbably on, Juan's beautiful voice greets Ophelia.

Ophelia takes a few steps and hesitates. The bunch of plastic flowers she carries in her hands is as tremulous as her smile.

"Ophelia lowers her head and curtsies!" shouts Dr. Altamirano, Z-k, Social Services Division, and by chance the director of the English version of *Hamlet*. "Juan, give her the cue again."

"Nymph, in thy orisons . . ."

Ophelia lowers her head and curtsies, and her bouquet falls to the floor.

"No, no, no! You drop the bouquet *later!*" Furious, Dr. Altamirano rises from his seat in the front row. "Now Ophelia raises her right hand, covers her eyes with her left, and takes a step backward. For heaven's sake, Ophelia, do at least try!"

Ophelia, motionless center stage, looks at Juan with wide, terrified eyes.

"Nymph . . ." Juan takes out a handkerchief from the sleeve of his fur coat and mops the sweat from his face.

"Doctor," says the sweet, desperate voice of our Ophelia, "I can't quite remember . . ."

"Poor thing," murmurs Burgossi, "with no words, reduced to mime. A thankless task for such a young actress."

"So what?" snarls Ariadna from behind a cloud of cigarette smoke. "The rest of the cast copes all right. But not the little princess. The little princess needs coaxing."

Burgossi turns his melancholy face toward me, and says with a feeble, troubled smile, "You know, of course, Renata, that I never agreed to this ridiculous version. Of course, I set out my reservations in writing on the appropriate form. *Mutatis mutandis,* the version in English is an absurdity legalized by Decree 4025."

"Mutatis mu what?" The Kid collapses in a fit of giggles.

"To put it bluntly"—Ariadna is also laughing—"not one of the actors knows English. And as for that jumped-up neurotic, he got it off the John Gielgud record. He can manage 'To be or not to be' but he doesn't even know the English for 'good morning' or 'thank you.' "

Burgossi's bowed shoulders give a little shrug. "The public don't know much English either, but they're happy enough to go to seasons of German or Russian theater put on by touring companies, and they don't understand a word of them." He adjusts the silk scarf he wears round his neck. "Anyway I've registered my protest . . ."

Ariadna's face, heavy with makeup and ill will, comes close to my silent presence. "The head of Wardrobe protested *ever* such a lot too, didn't she. And yet there are all those lovely furs."

"A pity you didn't give the furs to us, Renata," says the Kid. "It's freezing down here."

I look at the still-unformed face of an eighteen-year-old struggling to acquire a manly firmness. He gives me a friendly smile, expressive of a kind of canine glee: the unpredictable and playful enthusiasm of a puppy. I nod and smile. My hands and feet are frozen. When we talk, our breath rises in clouds above our little group in the stalls.

"I don't know why they couldn't have waited a bit longer before taking away the theater's only boiler. I dread to think what it'll do to my throat," says Burgossi, tugging at his silk scarf.

"But, Burgossi, they did wait," says Ariadna. "No one paid the final installments. What's the point of paying debts, dear, if this theater doesn't exist?"

"No, no, no!" shouts Dr. Altamirano again. "Do it again, Ophelia, and do *try* this time!"

Ophelia turns toward the stalls and stretches out her arms in a gesture of weariness and entreaty.

"Stay there, *señorita*, don't move," shouts a voice. "I'm testing the lights on you." A yellow nimbus surrounds the figure of the leading lady.

"She's so pretty," sighs the Kid.

Yes, she is pretty. She has curly chestnut hair, and large blue liquid eyes. And there's a sweetness about the delicate oval of her face, tender dimples in her cheeks when she smiles. I remember a scene in the foyer. She and Claude in a corner, talking with easy intimacy. I had thought then, They share the same physical grace. The memory troubles me now.

"She's stupid," says Ariadna dismissively. "She's got a mental age of about five. Just right for our Van Gogh."

Indignant, I want to answer back that Ophelia is not stupid, that she's charming. I can't. My desire for justice drowns in a new feeling, intense and disagreeable.

I look at Ophelia and I see her as I did when I first came to the theater. I see my own image in her but deformed as in those distorting mirrors at carnivals. Dark eyes versus pale; peasant features versus that finely sculpted face; mousy blond versus that warm chestnut; woman versus woman. Astonished, disconsolate, I realize that the reason is Claude.

"And what's become of Claude?" asks Burgossi, innocently divining my thoughts.

I shake my head; the name hurts me. But the rehearsal is beginning again, the stage lights all go up at once, Juan confronts the ghost.

"Why, what should be the fear?"

An icy draft sweeps the stage. The Kid's furious voice rises out of the darkness. "Shut the door!"

"I do not set my life at a pin's fee . . ."

From the auditorium doors comes the noise of something being pushed toward the stage. The ghost comes out of his niche in the scenery.

"Silence in the auditorium!" orders Dr. Altamirano.

We turn round to look, but the lights blind us.

"Oh, no," groans Clara, "it's the order from the baker's!"

There's an enormous box in the center aisle. Two dark silhouettes are dragging it, two pushing it. There are murmurs of protest among the actors.

"Don't let them interrupt the rehearsal!"

"We'll never finish if we go on like this!"

"What's going on?" asks the ghost brightly.

Juan raises a hand. "Please, ladies and gentlemen. Let's continue."

Burgossi stands up. Ariadna puts a hand on his shoulder. "No, Burgossi. It's worse if you pay attention to them. You know how much the M-bs hate us. They'd do anything to keep us here all day."

"They're not M-bs," says the Kid.

"Yes, they are," insists Ariadna.

". . . *And for my soul, what can it do to that . . .*"

The enormous box is at the foot of the stage, the actors leave their places to look at it, the ghost gets down from his platform, Dr. Altamirano stands up, the Kid leaps into the aisle, Ariadna click-clacks after him, Clara starts to cry, and Burgossi sadly shakes his head. Only Hamlet stands his ground, his head held high, indifferent to the whirlwind of bodies and voices.

"Being a thing immortal as itself?"

"They'll sack me," sobs Clara, "instead of delivering the order to me in the foyer, they've brought it here and interrupted the rehearsal."

"What order, Clara?"

"The buffet for the ceremony."

"What ceremony?"

"I don't know, I don't know. There's some sort of ceremony. I don't know, but my head's pounding."

A ceremony? All I know is that I got a circular telling us to be at work at eight in the morning for, it said, a full dress rehearsal.

There are more people on the stage now. Technicians and clerks have joined the cast of *Hamlet*. Confusion grows, angry voices are raised.

"Where's Claude?" I ask Clara, but she has her face buried in her handkerchief. I stand up and move toward the stage, when suddenly the lights go out. An abrupt silence falls in the equally abrupt dark. Then comes Juan's clear voice.

"Electrician! Use the emergency equipment."

"Yes, sir."

A yellowish bell-shaped light descends to the stage, where Juan has carefully removed his fur coat. There's another burst of protests. Alarmed, I stand stock-still in the aisle. Then Candini arrives, pushing his way through the actors. He's wearing a blue suit, a white tie, and a white flower in his buttonhole. The only light on the stage falls on Juan and Candini.

"Brothers and sisters," says the deep voice. "Brothers and sisters. The hour of the Fleur-de-Lis has come." There's a stupefied silence, out of which comes a peal of laughter. Hamlet is laughing.

"Angels and ministers of grace defend us."

"The hour of the Fleur-de-Lis, brothers and sisters, has . . ."

"Say, why is this? wherefore? what should we do?"

"The moment of liberation has come!"

Dumb with amazement, actors, stagehands, employees, heads of departments, all of us watch the duel taking place, even more absurd than the play currently in rehearsal. We watch without intervening, without smiling or applauding. Every eye is fixed on the circle of pale yellow light. No one notices the men who have opened the box, no one sees them climb on to the stage, but moments later, two shadows with two pairs of hands snatch Juan Martínez Tormi from the spotlight. Laertes fleetingly crosses the yellow bell of light, in pursuit of Juan. I hear Ophelia's shout, then Candini's intense, solemn voice.

"Nothing stops the advance of history. No one can oppose the Revelation. The Fleur-de-Lis is with us and for us."

Still standing in the aisle, I'm unable to make a move. There is total darkness in the auditorium. Suddenly all the lights come up. I blink, dazzled, almost blinded. The enormous box is open; among the broken planks I see a flower. A gigantic white plaster fleur-de-lis. On the stage, among the other figures, some stumbling, others retreating or advancing, stands the quiet, erect, triumphant figure of our mystic, our astrologer, our preacher,

Fortunato Candini. And from behind the scenes a group
of strangers hesitantly emerges. A tall man with graying hair and mustache and gray eyes looks about him,
uncomfortable, perplexed; another man, stout, with a
thick mop of brilliantined hair, goes resolutely up to
Candini, holding out his hand; behind him, a diminutive priest enters, taking short steps, carrying a fat book
in his hand, the purple of his stole knotted, around his
neck like a scarf.

"The buffet!" Clara shouts from beside me, and rushes
toward the stage.

Four stagehands have come in now, behind the new
group, and are laying a long table with a cloth. Others
come in with chairs. "Let's get out of here. We've got a
minute and a half!" It's Claude, who has grabbed me
by the hand. I want to pull away from him and ask
why, but his hand tugs at mine, and we run down the
aisle to the doors of the auditorium.

"*Sacré Dieu!*" He stops. "It's too late. Our only hope
is the stage."

Confused and out of breath, still clasping Claude's
hand, I'm suddenly up there with the others.

Languidly, the thick, dark, unstoppable water advances from the auditorium doors like a huge crawling
creature that grows, rises, almost licking the edge of
that impoverished raft from where we, the ship-
wrecked, watch, with varying degrees of fear, curiosity,
and anger, the grubby sea out of which poke the bronze-
edged backs of the stalls seats and one pure white wing:
the flower of Candini's madness.

· 28 ·

A unique moment. A crossroads. This morning saw a
historic event, the assumption of his new post by the
director of the National Theater. This particular ob-
server did not miss a single detail of the scene.

Bonday put his pen down on the open diary and leaned
back in his seat. Tonight it wasn't the sideboard that
kept him from sleeping. What was it about the long,
fair hair, the dark eyes, the slim body, that reminded
him of the bronze nymph in the Jardin des Plantes?
She didn't have a Greek profile, nor was she carrying a
pitcher in her arms. It was something about the way
she inclined her head to one side. Something about that
half-smile, innocent and mocking. It wasn't that she was
beautiful either, at least not in the ideal way the statue
was. And yet there was a resemblance.

He got up and went over to the window. "The moon,"
he wrote mentally, "covered the silent garden with her
silver mantle." What if he went out for a walk? No, he
told himself firmly, bitterly. Stendhal and Maugham and
several others recommended that a novelist should always keep a diary. Obediently, hating them for the advice, Bonday kept his diary. But only now and then,
when he had nothing better to do, on sleepless nights,
like this one.

"I was present at the ceremony. A historic event." A fiasco, he thought. If it hadn't been for . . . In what way were they similar, the nymph in the Jardin des Plantes and the blond girl?

His appointment at the theater was at nine. At 9:20 on the dot Bonday entered the foyer, desperately tired but with a smile on his lips, more than ready for the inevitable introductions and eager admirers.

The foyer was empty.

Disconcerted, he looked around him. The only proof that he had the right day and right time for the ceremony was a poster.

OFFICIAL CEREMONY
TODAY AT 9:00 IN THIS ROOM

An employee in blue overalls was hammering in the last nail that held up the poster. Bonday went over to him.

"This official ceremony, is for . . . ?"

"You're early. Why don't you go for a little walk?" With his hammer he indicated the long table in one corner. "Look, they haven't even delivered the buffet yet."

"What buffet?"

"For the party."

As if *party* were the magic word, the foyer began to fill up with people. Bonday looked at his watch. Half past nine, he thought irritably. This thing's never going to get started.

"But the party," said the man in overalls as he closed his toolbox, "comes after the ceremony."

A very small, pale, chubby woman came up to them with a tablecloth in her arms. "Pedro, I have to put the tablecloth on."

"So?" said Pedro.

"I can't do it on my own, Pedro. Will you help me?"

"Me? I've got to go to the auditorium now. Why don't you ask this gentleman?"

The small, pale woman raised pleading eyes to Bonday, and gave him a tremulous smile. "Oh, you're an M-b, I didn't recognize you. You know, I've got this splitting headache."

"I'm a *what?*" Scandalized, Bonday rejected the table-cloth the woman held out to him.

"Clara! Clara!" A dark-haired, dark-skinned young man, extravagantly dressed, ran up to them. He was wearing a paint-splashed red painter's smock and a black beret. The smock, the beret, and his black hair were all dripping. "It's pouring with rain out there. Have you seen my notebook, Clara? I left it in the Salon de Thé, and I can't find it now. Ah, Santiago Bonday, the writer! Wonderful. I'm sure *you* must have a bit of paper on you. Come on, just a sheet will do, time's running out."

Bonday stiffened. "I don't always go around with a notebook on me, young man."

"Claude," sniveled the pale woman, "I have to put a cloth on the table, and I can't do it on my own. Pedro wouldn't help me, and the gentleman here says he isn't an M-b. . . ."

"Didn't I tell you it was going to rain? I must warn Renata," said the young man in the red smock, and ran off again.

"Renata, Renata," said the woman to Bonday. "Young people only think of themselves. And my head's splitting. Oh, sir, don't go. Look, it's easy, you take one end of the cloth and I take the other and . . ."

Bonday fled. In vain he searched for a friendly face among the people now thronging the foyer. Although he knew Marga Hedelstoff would not be there, her absence saddened him. Not a sign of the captain. He was almost missing Pantaenius's unctuous smile. Where on earth had everyone got to? He searched the room again in vain. There were more men and women there, and none of the women was pretty or even young. The doors to the auditorium were shut. It was ten o'clock. "Is this thing never going to begin?" he said to himself, moving nearer the doors. He could hear voices inside. Quite clearly, above the rest of the noise, a remarkable voice rose.

"To be or not to be: That is the question."

"Bonday, my friend!"

Ah, Pantaenius at last.

"Whether 'tis nobler in the mind . . ."

"We were afraid you weren't coming, Master."

"What the hell is all this about?"

"To die, to sleep . . ."

"Ssshh!" Pantaenius, a finger on his fat lips and indicating with his other hand that Bonday should follow him, tiptoed away from the auditorium doors. They went into a side room, and Pantaenius turned the key in the lock. "So that we won't be interrupted," he explained, smiling at Bonday.

They were in a vast, gray room that smelled damp and musty. They were not alone. Standing in a corner was a well-built man with a pale face in which burned two febrile eyes. He was dressed as if for a funeral or a wedding in a double-breasted suit and white tie, and he had a white flower in his buttonhole.

"Congratulate him, Master, congratulate him," whispered Pantaenius, pushing him toward the stranger.

The brilliant black eyes and the smile revealing long teeth emerged from the shadows. Rather apprehensively Bonday took the proffered hand. The man looks ill. Either that or mad, he thought.

In his honeyed tones Pantaenius whispered, "Santiago Bonday, our poet laureate. Fortunato Candini, the new driving force behind our campaign."

"Pleased to meet you. Why are you whispering, Pantaenius?"

Pantaenius raised a hand to his mouth. He was shaking, and Bonday realized that he was laughing. "Because of the priest. So as not to wake him up."

"What priest?"

"Ssshh!" He pointed to an armchair. An old man in a black soutane was asleep in it, his purple stole wound round his neck, a heavy book on his lap. He looked so small, his rumpled hair so white, he was sleeping so peacefully, curled in the large velvet upholstered armchair with its wooden carving, that he reminded Bonday of a white cat happily installed on its favorite cushion.

"What's he doing here?" he whispered.

Pantaenius took his arm and led him to the other end of the room. The large, pale man joined them.

"The priest came for the ceremony," explained Pantaenius. "As it's an official ceremony, we asked the Church to send a representative. You know, to bless the equipment and so on."

"Oh, I see. But where's Captain Beh? Hasn't he arrived yet?"

Pantaenius smiled at him affectionately. "Bonday, Bonday, the captain knows what he's doing. He won't be coming."

"What?"

"Sh! you'll wake the priest. The captain is foregoing the pleasure of sharing this historic moment with us. With his usual lucidity he thought that with you and Candini here in charge of the promotional side of the campaign, his presence was unnecessary." Pantaenius half-closed his eyes. "But the captain is with us in spirit.

I left him there alone in his office, dreaming of stage one of the process for change."

Bonday tried to imagine the captain alone and dreaming. He couldn't. Instead he imagined the captain and Pantaenius talking, arguing about something. He suspected that Pantaenius had triumphed in some way over the captain's true intentions. The idea of a submissive captain troubled him. No, he said to himself, everyone's afraid of the captain.

"Let's get on with it, then," whispered Pantaenius energetically.

"First, Candini."

"I know what I have to do. I'm ready, so are the boys," Candini said in a deep, resonant voice.

Surprised, Bonday asked politely, "Are you part of the Campaign then?"

The other two looked at each other. With a beatific smile Pantaenius said to the other, "He's an intellectual. A creature living in a world of his own." And to Bonday, "Master, Señor Fortunato Candini is the new director of this theater."

He closed the notebook. He was more drawn to the garden that night than to dutifully writing in his diary. He opened the window. It wasn't cold. The air smelled of damp grass and dried leaves. A great gulf separated the Bonday looking out into the garden and the Bonday trying to describe the trivial events of the morning, the utterly unimportant official ceremony. "In what way are they alike, the blond girl and the nymph in the Jardin des Plantes?" And suddenly he knew. It was an unexpected insight. He felt the blood rush to cheeks that had long ago forgotten how to blush. Deeply moved, he went back to his diary, picked up the pen, and wrote down the only true comment of the day.

Slender Renata, symbol of fleeting youth.

· 29 ·

My fever's subsided. I can get out of bed now without feeling dizzy. Slowly I'm getting better. I don't know why I feel so anxious. Alone here I've had more than enough time to scrutinize the memory of my last contact with the world, searching for the root of this invisible plant whose scent so troubles me.

I've been sad often enough before, and I've been alone and ill before too. But I've never felt this shadowy embrace before, this feeling of desperation that deprives me of air, ignites sparks behind my eyelids when I close them to try and sleep. Now and then I do sleep. I seem to be sinking down through the pillow, through the now rather grubby sheets and the mattress that supports my body in the void, and then there's a moment of calm victory when I hear myself say (to no one in particular, perhaps to the universe, which has somehow taken on human form), "I've vanquished him. Mission accomplished, I'm coming home." And then I feel the scream in my throat, a solitary, silent scream, because he has me by the throat again, pressing hard, and this time he's going to kill me for real.

I've often had nightmares before, but never one like this. In my own room, in the solitude of these last few days, I search for the key to a closed door. But I can't

even find the door. I can't come up with one reason
that can honestly justify my panic. Certainly not in the
area I explore with an obsessiveness verging on the id-
iotic. And yet, before I dream that I've vanquished the
monster, before I dream that I'm being strangled,
the memory of the flood drifts back to me, and I'm
on the raft again with the others.

Using the microphone an M-b has connected up for
him, the man with the brilliantined hair and the ingra-
tiating smile says, "Keep calm, ladies and gentlemen,
keep calm. This slight inconvenience of a purely technical nature will not prevent us continuing with our
ceremony with the public-spiritedness that distin-
guishes our people. . . ."

"Ceremony?"

"What ceremony?"

"You'd be better off calling the Fire Department."

"The phone lines are down because of the rain, idiot."

"A short ceremony, with no speeches"—the man smiles
smoothly and raises a hand—"and then we'll serve the
buffet."

"A buffet? *Now?*"

"Not a bad idea, really. We're going to have to hang
about here anyway."

Yes, we'll have to wait. The protests die down. Someone laughs. It's cold, people shuffle around looking for
somewhere to sit, take off wet shoes if they haven't been
careful enough about where they've stepped on the
stage, while I pretend that neither of us notices that my
hand is still in Claude's hand, discover with surprise
and joy a friendly face I thought was lost, and realize
that the tall, elegant man contemplating the flooded orchestra pit with alarm is the prizewinning author Santiago Bonday, the Master.

"Can I have your attention for just a moment," asks

the voice into the microphone, "for the reading of De-cree 4358 appointing Don Fortunato Candini director of the President Herrero National Theater . . ."

"Candini!"

"Candini!"

"Who's *Candini?*"

"Silence, please!"

Claude's hand squeezes mine. I stop listening to the man at the microphone. The beating in my blood deaf-ens me.

"Cold hands, warm heart," whispers Claude, and brings his face so close to mine that instinctively, out of modesty, I move away.

"I'm freezing," I say, my face burning.

Claude smiles. The white teeth against the dark skin, his dark eyes looking into mine. One second, two, three, an eternity of suspense in which I struggle frantically against my mouth's impulse to kiss that other half-opened mouth, to see if the pleasure my mouth antici-pates is anything like the dizzy pleasure of being skin to skin, hand in hand. There's no voice over the micro-phone. There's no decree appointing a new director. There's just the fear of letting myself be carried away in public toward those arms and that mouth. On our island on the raft Claude takes a pair of gloves out of his pocket, makes me put them on, and says something incomprehensible about my cold hands, and I, con-sumed by fire, filled with the consternation that accom-panies the discovery of love, that mysteriously precedes all happiness and all unhappiness, look away from him and politely murmur some clumsy words of thanks for the gloves.

"My child, would you be so kind as to hold this for me a moment?" The priest is talking to me and has already put a book in my hand when the voice over the microphone brings me back with a start to my senses.

"Over to you, Father."

Agitated, his cheeks red and his white hair disheveled, the little priest scuttles about the stage, wafts some incense around, and bestows a blessing in Latin on the onlookers, the flooded auditorium, the Fleur-de-Lis, and me with his book in my hands.

"Right, that's it. Thank you so much, my child."

"Gibbon's *Decline and Fall of the Roman Empire.*" I smile knowingly.

"Oh yes. You've no idea what a comfort the old heretic is in difficult times. I take it to all these official ceremonies. It clears my head of foolish thoughts, makes my cross easier to bear. I'd recommend it next time you have to get some document processed or line up at the baker's."

The white plumes of hair, the blue eyes, old-fashioned round glasses on the tiny nose.

"Don't you remember me, Father?"

He looks at me over the top of his glasses. "Of course. The Daughters of Mary."

"No."

"You're right. I know. The lecture on Byzantine art."

"Wrong again."

"Wait. I have a terrible memory for names, but I never forget a face." He waves his *Decline and Fall* at me. A student from the course on Sex and Morality!"

I start to laugh. "You give classes on sex and morality?"

The blue eyes look at me in horror. "Not so loud! How could you think I . . . it's that awful little priest at the Chapel of Casamanta!"

"I'll give you a hint . . . Gilgamesh . . . Tea . . . Rain . . ."

Father Collins's face lights up. "Of course, the Gilgamesh girl! We had such a pleasant talk. How are you?"

"I'm fine now. But if you remember, I was very sad that afternoon."

"That's right. Poor thing. Hold the book for me a moment. Thank you," and with an impatient gesture he straightens his stole. "Still lovesick?"

"Not anymore." I laugh and turn to Claude, but he isn't there.

"Just as I told you. Nothing lasts for ever, etc. Or did I tell you something quite different? Yes, yes, don't deny it, I gave you some advice." He makes a face. "What's to be done? It's an occupational hazard. And, of course, you ignored my advice. Quite right too. In short, since no one takes me seriously, when they come to me for advice, I just say the first thing that comes into my head."

"You didn't give me much advice, Father. You just said that God would provide, and that if He didn't, how could one even conceive of His goodness?"

He looks at me over his glasses again. He has freckles on his nose. "Did I say that?"

"Yes."

"And did He provide?"

"From that day on my problems were over."

"Ssh! Don't tempt fate! Just say that particular problem was resolved. Come on, let's go and eat something, I'm hungry. Let's hope there's something sweet to eat. I love sweet things. They're my secret vice."

I shake my head. I want to be near Claude, but I can't see him. Father Collins takes my arm.

"Oh, no, you're not going to leave me alone! According to the rules I have another half hour of public pastoral work. If you stay with me and people see us chatting, it's just possible the faithful will keep their distance. That way I save myself the embarrassment of having to explain the latest encyclical, that way I don't have to hear anyone's confession." He sighs deeply. "The faithful want to confess all the time, you know. None of this going to church on Sundays, oh no. You have to listen to them and forgive them all the time, it's a terrible cross to bear."

I let myself be dragged toward the table where the other shipwreck victims are already hurling themselves on the food. And alas, that's where I find Claude too. I see him pouring a glass of wine for the lovely Ophelia, smiling that incomparable smile of his. And I congratulate myself for letting my will win out over impulse. Common sense is always best. I would have kissed a mouth that wanted another mouth: the delicate lips of our beautiful Ophelia.

"Father," I say angrily, acidly, "why worry about an atheist and neglect the faithful believers?"

Father Collins, on tiptoe, is studying the food on the table. "I could try and save you."

"What do you mean 'save'?" I ask impertinently, to let off steam.

"There you are, calories, vitamins, proteins," he laughs mockingly, handing me a plate of sandwiches. "Eat up, you're dreadfully thin."

"Father Collins! How good to see you."

"Charmed, I'm sure," says Father Collins, his mouth full.

The tall, elegant man has come up to us, his pipe in his hand, his gray eyes smiling. Santiago Bonday, the Master, is looking at me; he waits to be introduced.

"Do you know this young lady?" asks the priest, waving his plate at me. "Don't you think she's too thin? It's the fashion. Women all starve themselves to death nowadays."

The writer smiles. "The young lady is very beautiful. But you haven't introduced us, Father."

"No? Is it really necessary? No one ever remembers anyone's name anyway. Introductions are a futile ceremony, really. Tell me what your name was again, child, then I can introduce you."

"Renata."

"Of course, Renata. Renata, now let's see, this gentleman is Ronday, a sculptor."

The man with the pipe laughs. "My name's *Bonday*, and I'm a *writer*. Don't you remember me? We met at the opening ceremony of the Flower Gardens. And you blessed the Society of Authors' new library."

"How could I forget! What a day! In the morning I'd had to bless a Japanese locomotive engine at a ceremony for the National Railways. Have another sandwich, child."

I couldn't read more than a page of *The Soul and Other Vagaries,* and I'd never much fancied reading his other books. But he can't take his eyes off me.

"I'm so glad," he says, talking to Father Collins but looking at me, "that you should be the Church's representative in this theater where we'll be performing."

Father Collins stops, a chocolate-coated fruit halfway to his mouth.

"Perform? Didn't you say you're a writer? And what role have they given you?" The small blue eyes look the tall, elegant man up and down. "Not Hamlet, of course. Polonius? No, you're not quite right for Polonius yet. Horatio! A bit too old, but with makeup on . . ."

Bonday laughs, quite unperturbed.

"It's his Irish temperament," Bonday says, trying to excuse him.

Father Collin's white hair ruffles. "Irish! Please. My family has been in the Americas for three generations, and people still think I'm related to those madmen, crazy people with no respect for anything, lunatics with not a sane thought in their heads, absolute devils."

The Master considers it prudent to change the subject. "What do you think of the new director, Fortunato Candini?"

Father Collins passes me a dish of canapés. "They're cheese and anchovy I think. Very good against the cold. Who's this Marini?"

"*Candini,* Father. Decree 4583. You listened to the speech. . . ."

"No, I didn't. Do you think at my time of life I still listen to speeches? I hear them, that's all. There's a semantic difference between the two verbs, thank God. Another canapé, child? They're delicious. Isn't he a friend of yours, this Marini?"

Bonday takes a sip of wine. "I wouldn't go so far as to call him a friend. But he'll do well in the post. He has conviction, drive. He's got *charisma.*"

Father Collins points to the white wing poking out of the water in the orchestra pit. "He's got a fleur-de-lis," he murmurs, frowning.

"A symbol," says Bonday, giving me an enigmatic look.

"Symbols!" exclaims Father Collins with unexpected fury. "Don't talk to me about symbols! They grow like mushrooms, take up the little empty space left on this planet, and absorb all the oxygen people need to breathe. If they planted gardens instead of symbols, think how healthy life would be in this vale of tears. I suppose now they'll put that thing in the foyer and, God forbid, call on me to bless it."

Bonday taps his pipe and smiles, amused. "Is the Church jealous, afraid people will abandon their faith and run after other gods?"

Father Collins roars with laughter. He laughs uncontrollably. He laughs like a naughty boy. His plumes of white hair grow wild, his blue eyes fill with tears.

"Water, please, give me some water!"

I hand him some, and he drinks it, laughing and spluttering. Bonday looks on, astonished.

"Other gods!" Father Collins is still laughing, but he's calmer now. "All through the centuries the Church has watched even the most faithful of its faithful flock running after other gods. Believe me, we never triumph over other gods. We just put up an artistic front to conceal our defeat."

Father Collins shakes his head and looks at Santiago Bonday with sad mockery. "Believe me, it isn't men's faith in the teaching of Christ that has allowed us to survive for nearly two thousand years. It's our wise, prudent alliance with men's weaknesses. I'm surprised you should be so ingenuous."

Bonday makes a wry face. "I never thought of you as a cynic."

"I'm not a cynic," says Father Collins with a sad smile. "A cynic has no beliefs. I have one: Love your fellow man." He hands me a piece of cake. "Apart from that," he adds with a sigh, "apart from that, nothing much else matters."

· 30 ·

It was three in the morning when Bonday, exhausted after a long battle with the falling sideboard, at last managed to get to sleep.

"Tacho, the phone."

"Don't answer it."

"Tacho!"

"I'm asleep."

"It's still ringing."

"They'll get fed up."

"What if it's your friend Captain Beh?"

Bonday covered his head with the pillow. His wife picked up the receiver. "Hello. Yes, just a moment. Tacho, it's the captain."

"Oh, God. Hello, yes?"

"No doubt you're surprised that I should call you at this time in the morning. Never forget, Bonday, that we're working to defend our national culture, and the man who works for culture does not sleep. Now wake up and listen."

"I'm listening, Captain."

"I've got some news that will have you leaping out of bed: The architect has finished the plans for remodeling the theater."

"How nice."

"Is that all you have to say?"

"You don't know how happy that makes me, Captain. Congratulate the architect for me, tell him that—"

"You can have the pleasure of telling him yourself. We're on our way there now."

"Where?"

"Why, your house, of course. A working meeting. I'm sure your wife won't mind making us some coffee."

"Captain—"

"Time is of the essence, Bonday. We'll be there in a few minutes. And don't go back to sleep."

Bonday heard the click cutting them off and stared dazedly at the phone.

"If it's not the sideboard, it's the captain. How long is it since I slept? They won't let me sleep, they won't leave me alone. I've had enough."

"Just tell them no, dear."

Bonday smiled bitterly. "Elsa, the man who works for the culture of his country does not sleep."

Half an hour later, a car drew up in front of the house. From the window Bonday saw the captain get out, followed by Pantaenius and three other men. One of the three was the big, pale man with eyes of fire. He didn't know the others, but there was something familiar about the heavy, cautious way they moved. Policemen? Bodyguards?

"Lovely house," said the captain.

"A palace," said Fortunato Candini, scornfully.

"It's very comfortable," said Bonday with an involuntary rush of pride, and showed them into the library.

Pantaenius was carrying a small black briefcase. He put it on the desk. "Don't try and hide it, Master. We know you're dying to see the plans for our theater."

Only then did Bonday notice that someone was missing. "Didn't the architect come with you?"

Captain Beh laughed.

"The architect is right in front of you."

The person in front of him was Hugo Pantaenius. Bonday looked at him, surprised. "You're an architect?"

Pantaenius bowed his head humbly. "By vocation, Master, only by vocation. But the captain, with characteristic generosity, has approved this little plan of mine, given it the go-ahead."

The captain smiled with a warmth that Bonday found even more surprising than the news that Pantaenius was an architect.

"Don't play the shrinking violet, Hugo. His plan is no better or worse than anything those deservedly unemployed architects swarming all over the city could offer me. Let me tell you why. Are you listening, Bonday?"

Bonday was listening.

"In moments of grave historical crisis," said the captain, patting Pantaenius's arm with his chubby, freckled hand, "loyalty counts for more than diplomas."

Everyone, apart from the heavies escorting them, went over to the plan Pantaenius was spreading out on the desk. Bonday had never understood plans. Mentally he clung on to Pantaenius's finger as it rested on a series of enigmatic right angles and curves.

". . . And we'll get rid of two doors here, eliminate a wall there, open up a corridor on the left, block up two rows of windows at the front . . ."

There'll be nothing left, thought Bonday.

"And is there enough money for such extensive work?" he asked cautiously.

The captain replied with his own question. "I bet you can't guess how much it will cost."

So as not to be caught out or left looking foolish, Bonday ventured an impossible sum of money.

Captain Beh, Pantaenius, and Candini burst out laughing.

"What a sense of humor, so like an intellectual," said Pantaenius. "Bonday, have you forgotten where we live? Double your figure, multiply it by eighty percent to cover inflation, and you'll have the approximate cost."

Bonday felt irritated by their mockery of his numerical abilities and the veiled accusation that he was ignorant of economic and financial matters. He could tolerate patiently enough some critic's jibes about the value of his literary work, but, as a man who had got rich because he'd known how to find his way through a jungle of royalties, publishers, booksellers, film and television producers, it annoyed him to have his common sense called into question.

"For that money," he said sharply, "you could build two new theaters."

The captain frowned. "Pantaenius has been up all night working out the accounts, Bonday. I'm not going to quibble over figures. What's a centavo here or there?"

"Believe me, Master," said Pantaenius, giving him a beseeching smile, "all I've done is follow the captain's instructions. 'Hugo,' he said to me, 'make it a theater that is functional, solid, majestic, that fulfills our needs and fits the image we want to project.'"

Candini, who until then had remained silent, confronted Bonday. His fiery eyes glinted menacingly.

"Are you against the Fleur-de-Lis?"

"The Fleur-de-Lis?" asked Bonday weakly, thinking, This madman takes himself very seriously.

"The theater will be a temple to a spiritual revolution. There we will light the torch of a new era."

Fixing Bonday with his gaze, Candini pulled out all the stops on his organlike voice.

"What is culture without a soul? What is a play without spirit? What is the essence of the nation without the Fleur-de-Lis that represents it?"

"Magnificent! Quite magnificent!" applauded Pantaenius. "Out of this world! Ah, Candini, we'll never reach the heights of your ideological passion. You see what a good choice we made, Captain?"

Candini kept his terrible gaze fixed on Bonday's face.

"Brother," he said, measuring his words carefully, "if you can offer nothing else, at least give your loyalty. The Fleur-de-Lis expects nothing more from people like you. Your loyalty, nothing more." He turned his head to look at the bodyguards, who, although still standing by the mirror in the library, appeared to be asleep. "Because if you're not with us, you're against us. Right, boys?"

Bonday leaned over the plan. "And what are those pretty little figures?" he asked Pantaenius.

But it was Candini who answered him. "Heaven weighing down on all the fates of Earth."

"Ah."

"Astrology, Bonday. The Fleur-de-Lis encompasses everything in its plans. Have a good look. The circle represents the celestial sphere. The twelve dividing points between the houses are the cusps . . ."

Bonday noticed that neither the captain nor Pantaenius interrupted the madman's bizarre speech. On the contrary, they listened respectfully, as if to a famous actor who has condescended to give a performance in private. Astrology! What secret path linked a National Theater, a campaign for the cultural reconstruction of the country, and a game fit only for ignorant, superstitious women? Confronted by this mystery, Bonday prudently said nothing.

". . . The symbols at the top identify the mental and physical characteristics and earthly destinies. The elements are indicated by symbolic colors. Positive elements in red, negative in black . . ."

"I see," said Bonday, not even attempting to disguise a yawn; a sleepless night, the sideboard, Pantaenius the architect, the astrologer/director of the theater, were all having their effect on him.

"We take into account the progressions of the Moon. . . ."

"Of course."

"If the Sun is the active principle, the Moon is the passive one. One gives out, the other receives. With Scorpio in the asc—"

Elsa came into the library, carrying a tray of coffee. With infinite relief Bonday rushed up to her and took the tray.

"A cup of coffee's just what we need." He smiled. "So, Captain, our vision is becoming reality, we'll have a great building for our great national theater. I confess I'm astonished at the speed with which we're moving toward our objective."

The captain knocked back his coffee in one. Like a caged tiger, he started to pace the room. Half-closing his eyes, he exclaimed, "The theater! The Campaign for Cultural Reconstruction! Yes, I can already see those strong walls built to defend the embattled roots of our culture. Enough of Shakespeare! Hugo, how will the headlines in the newspapers read?"

"Citizens: This is *your* theater," suggested Pantaenius.

"Put your back into Cultural Reconstruction!" shouted the captain.

Candini raised a hand. The captain and Pantaenius fell silent. With an ironic smile he said in his deep voice, "The Hour of the Fleur-de-Lis has come."

"Quite true, I'd forgotten," agreed the captain.

Pantaenius showed him a piece of paper.

"Perfect," said the captain, after glancing at it. "Now you can sign, Bonday."

Bonday's eyes were already heavy with sleep. His eyes almost closing, he asked, "Sign what?"

"Just bits of paper, Master, bits of paper," smiled Pantaenius ingratiatingly. "It's the budget. On the back we've already collected the signatures of many faithful friends, impresarios, professionals, politicians. We just need your signature to complete the formalities."

Bonday saw a list of names, but weariness prevented him from reading it. Yawning, he signed. He was giving Pantaenius back his pen when he noticed that one of the heavies was touching the frame of the mirror, as if assessing its weight and size.

"Hey!" Bonday was suddenly awake.

Candini's hand rested on his shoulder. "Let him be. My boys appreciate art as well, you know."

"Captain . . ."

But Captain Beh and Pantaenius were already on their way to the door.

"Go to sleep, Master," said Pantaenius.

"Good-bye then, Bonday, but don't rest on your laurels," said the captain.

Candini held out his hand. "Aries," he said in his intense voice. "They have a good character, altruistic, modest, passionate, sensitive. But if they don't keep their head at key moments, they may come to a nasty end. It's a great sign, yours. I congratulate you, Bonday."

Bonday dragged himself back to his bedroom. Feeling exhausted and battered, he undressed and got into bed.

"Elsa."

"Mmmm?"

"What sign am I?"

"You've never believed in . . ." Surprise roused her.

"I don't. I just wanted to know."

"Aries. Why?"

Bonday didn't reply.

The morning light and the noise of birdsong in the garden found him wide awake and full of dark fears.

· 31 ·

Dear Emilio,

I no longer expect to get any letters from you, and you needn't expect any from me.

When I opened the door today, the postman greeted me, removing his cap. *"Señorita,* I've been delivering mail to this district for thirty years." Congratulations, I said, and then sneezed in the sudden cold draft. "You congratulate me for having to live out a drama?" And he burst into tears, hugging his bag of letters to him. To prevent my flu turning into pneumonia, I asked him to come in, and made tea for us both. "Thanks, dear, you're an angel."

Suddenly he looked around. "Have you got a phone?" No, I said. "That's a relief, because I was just thinking how nice you were. Then for a moment I thought you might be one of those people who are helping to dig our grave." Your grave? "The telephone people." He noticed my incredulity, my surprise. "You're very young, *señorita,* you don't know the world, you probably even expect to receive the occasional letter." Of course I do, I said. Everyone who writes letters expects to receive letters in return. "Inno-

cent creature. I haven't brought you a single
letter." Why did you come then? To drink my
tea? "Don't blame me. As if I didn't have enough
on my plate. I've got a sick wife, two grown-up
sons with no jobs, and me with an empty post-
bag." He took out his handkerchief and blew
his nose. "Today I put it to the boss straight. I
said, Boss, in my thirty years here, have you ever
had any problems with me? Tell me the truth.
If there are no more letters, will you sack me?
Let me have it straight. He told me everything,
señorita. He told me what his boss told him. Brace
yourself, *señorita,* you're not going to believe it."
I'm bracing myself, I said. "There's a campaign
by the telephone people to ruin us postmen!"
That's incredible. "You don't believe me because you're very young. I can understand that,
I didn't believe it either. My boss had to repeat
it to me several times. The telephone people
want everybody to use nothing but the telephone." But it's not the same, I said, a letter
isn't the same as a telephone call. "Of course it
isn't the same. But they don't care. They just
want to destroy us. But they won't win. And do
you know why?" No, I said. *"Because the telephones aren't working!"*

A complete madman. I showed him the door.
He picked up his empty bag. "And do you know
why the telephones aren't working? Because we
postmen are getting ourselves organized. That's
what my boss told me, they're not going to get
away with it that easily. Well, he's not going to
lie to me, a gentleman in his position, who got
into management when he was only half my age,
and without ever walking the streets with a bag

over his shoulder." I almost shoved him out into the corridor. "You're too young to understand. But remember this: One of these days I'll bring you a letter. That letter, *señorita,* will be one small victory in the long struggle that lies ahead." He waved his cap to me from the stairs. "If one of your family works for the telephone company, tell me. I like you, and I'd hate to punch someone in the face then find out afterward that he was your brother or your boyfriend."

Emilio, the poor postman was completely mad. But this much is true: There are no letters. For some weeks now my neighbors have been complaining about the lack of mail. But they don't blame the telephone people. In this building the enemy is the porter who's begun a campaign to harass the tenants.

Love from a confused
Renata

Dear Emilio,

I'm writing to you by candlelight. Another power cut, another sleepless night, alone at home with no word from you.

I think of the countryside near my village. There night and silence are just an extension of life. Did you know, my friend, that you can feel the earth's heart beating when it sleeps? But this cement body has an artificial heart. Streetlights and noise are all the city provides us with, no sun, no green spaces. And the only blood here is the flow of conversations and gestures and attitudes that substitute for real action. Made in the image of this monstrous god, we never question, never doubt. Only when we flick the light switch and the light doesn't come on do we feel a slight tremor. Has the city died? Are we dead? But morning brings an explanation and relief. The newspaper tells us all about the electricity cuts and when they occurred in which districts. Fine. Now we can go quietly about our business, because the newspaper, the radio, or the television, our faithful Mercuries, have brought us a message from Olympus. Ah, teachers, judges, comrades! What would become of one in the big city without a printed reality, without a reality with sound and pictures!

In delegating our lives to miserable urban abstractions, we've also delegated the truth. The one thing that troubles this smug way of life is when we flick the light switch and nothing happens.

"Another one. See what I mean? It was an epidemic," Burgossi is saying when I enter the Salon de Thé. "We haven't had such a hard autumn since 1938. It's in today's paper. Five degrees centigrade, but it feels like minus two. A record for this time of year. My dear child, don't come too close—though there's nothing one can do to avoid catching it. I can feel it in my throat."

"It's not the cold that does the damage," says Clara, "it's the damp that kills you."

Ariadna sneezes.

"Bless you," said Burgossi, starting to cough.

"Anyone got any aspirin?" growls Ariadna.

"Bloody weather," says the Kid, and beats rhythmically on the window pane.

"My dear young Klappenbach," Burgossi says, giving him a worried look, "it is to be hoped, for all our sakes,

that the glass is strong enough to withstand your vigorous hand. As it is, the room is only moderately warm,
and the slightest hole or crack made in the window
would let in the increasingly heavy rain from outside."

"I can't help it. The rain depresses me."

"Ah, the lost generation," croons Ariadna before
sneezing violently.

"Perhaps," I said, looking around for Claude but not
finding him, "it was that soaking that made us ill."

"Soaking?" Burgossi arches his eyebrows.

"The flood."

"What flood?" The Kid turns around from his place
at the window. "When? Where?"

Disconcerted, I look at each of my colleagues in turn.
In every face I see, as well as various manifestations of
cold symptoms, the same perplexity.

"The day of the rehearsal," I say timidly, "the theater
was flooded, wasn't it?"

Everyone, without exception, laughs.

"Van Gogh's mania is contagious," says Ariadna.

"We were fine up there, and the buffet was just perfect," says Clara.

"I've never had such a good time," says the Kid.

Burgossi shakes his head. "No, Renata. The real cause
of our deplorable physical state does not lie in a phe-
nomenon which, though it might seem peculiar to a
stranger, has for a long time constituted part of everyday reality for the people working here. No, my child,
the culprit is this autumn we've having." Beneath the
silk scarf something crackles. Burgossi smiles at me sadly.
"Newspaper. The wool sweater, my dear, is no longer
enough. It was so different twenty years ago. People
almost never wore an overcoat, and one rarely had to
reach for a scarf. But the climate has changed. It's all
these atomic explosions, trips into outer space, and

aerosols. They destroy the atmosphere, change the climate. Soon there'll be coconut palms in Siberia and sleighs in the main street here."

"Sleighs!" sighs Clara. "I've always wanted to ride in one!"

An orderly comes in pushing a trolley.

"At last!" cries Ariadna. "I'm starving."

"The only thing that can prevent and cure a cold is a strict diet of broth and green vegetables," says Burgossi, selecting a sandwich and two sticky buns.

"I haven't got the patience to follow a diet," says Ariadna, biting voraciously into a sandwich. "I just go to the pharmacist and he gives me some antibiotics."

"I can't bear injections," says Clara. "And they destroy your body's immune system. The best thing is hot tea, lemon juice, aspirins, and if I have a really bad cough, cough medicine. Oh, you bad boy, you haven't brought any ham and tomato!"

"Is Claude ill?" I ask the Kid quietly.

He has his mouth full. He mumbles something that could be a yes or a no. I go over to Burgossi, who has a cup of tea in his hand.

"Any news about Candini? Has our director been away too?"

Burgossi wags a reproachful index finger. "Renata, don't drink too much coffee. It upsets the nervous system."

"Burgossi," I whisper, "you've been here for a long time now. Does no one care at all that we have a new director and that that director is Candini?"

He rests his pale, thin hand lightly on mine and replies in an equally low voice, "My dear child, how I envy your youth, how I delight in your innocence! It's true. No one cares about Candini's appointment. Not because it's Candini, my child. Poor man, he's a bit eccen-

tric, a bit 'touched' if you'll forgive the expression, but
then, who isn't? And, in the end, my dear, it's his post
that will cure him." He gives a deep, sad, weary sigh.
"I'm an old man, Renata. I've seen many directors come
and go. And some of them were well-intentioned, intelligent, energetic. But the same thing happened to all
of them, my dear. The very decree that raised them to
office obliterated them. Before getting that post, they
had convictions, ideas. The minute they took up the
post, they discovered that their duties consisted in
nothing but repaying favors to the people who'd given
them power and battling against those who'd opposed
them." He pats my hand. "However you do the sums,
Renata, the answer is always zero."

· 32 ·

"Telephone, Tacho."

"Oh, no!"

"Please, Tacho."

"It's four o'clock in the morning!"

"Tacho . . ."

"All right. Hello? Yes, Captain, of course I'm awake."

"Congratulations, Bonday! The Campaign is a success."

"Thank you, but—"

"We're proud of you. Have you read the newspapers?"

"They don't usually deliver our papers before dawn. It's still the middle of the night here."

"It's your loss. The smell of fresh ink makes success all the sweeter. I'll leave you to find out for yourself. But I didn't just phone to congratulate you. You must give me the name of that friend of yours, the director of the national news agency. Pantaenius asked me for it. Naturally he'll mention your name."

"Whose name?"

"Yours, Bonday, wake up. Didn't you say you were a close friend of the man? Pantaenius thinks the time has come to introduce the image of Candini to the national media, with a photo and everything. Now what did you say your friend's name was?"

171

Bonday yawned and gave him a name, promising that later he'd look up the telephone number in his address book.

"Later just won't do. As you know, the man who works for the culture of his country . . ."

". . . doesn't sleep," moaned Bonday, fumbling through his address book, his fingers still heavy with sleep. "Captain. One question. How's the rebuilding work on the theater going?"

"We're in the first stages of the process, Bonday. Rubble everywhere and Pantaenius battling with the workmen. Why do you want to know?"

"Because of my office, Captain. My house is besieged by journalists. When can I have an office at the theater? Anyway, it's time we gave some thought to which play should replace *Hamlet*. I've already come up with an excellent comedy by a national author—"

"Bonday, Bonday, don't be impatient. We've got our whole lives to worry about the play. If it's your consultancy fee you're concerned about, you'll get it anyway. It's only money. . . ."

"It's not the money!"

"Then just carry on talking to the specialist press and leave us to do the rest. Good day, Bonday."

"Captain, I—" *Click.*

Elsa was sleeping peacefully. Bonday looked at her enviously; he no longer felt in the least like sleeping. He got dressed, went to the kitchen, and resignedly made himself some coffee. By the second cup he was wide awake.

He cautiously poked his nose out of the door that opened onto the garden. It wasn't cold. The wet garden smelled sweet, reminding him of the scents of a summer's day. "It's going to be hot," he said, both grateful and irritated. "What a country! It's like summer in winter and like winter in summer." He left the garden. Blue-green shadows of night still lingered in some corners, but a golden haze was already rising from the leaves of the oak trees along the avenue. He started walking along the path to the road. Soon he'd hear the approach of the newspaper boy's creaking tricycle. Instead he was startled to hear the noise of someone hammering loudly. The noise was coming from the direction of the rosebushes.

"What's all this about, Don Matías?"

The old gardener raised a ruddy, wrinkled face to him. He held up the hammer and proudly showed him the poster nailed to a stake among the rosebeds.

FLEUR-DE-LIS—INTRESTED PARTIES
PLESE APPLY TO THE JARDINDESPLANS

"It's that flower you go on about, people keep coming into the garden and trampling all over the flower beds. If they want to study flowers, sir, they'll have to go to the Jardindesplans, which is chocabloc with them and all for free."

"Don Matías . . ." Bonday protested, though only mildly because the old man had a short fuse.

Don Matías removed his battered felt hat and dusted it off against his knees.

"I'm rather pleased with the lettering. At least I learned something at school. Not like this one, Don Bonday." He indicated a small boy who came trotting toward them from the garden gate with the newspaper in his hands. "My grandson," said the old man, dusting off his hat again.

The boy, who must have been about eight or nine, stopped in front of Bonday, said a polite, "Good morning, sir," and handed him the newspaper.

"I didn't know you had a grandson. He's a fine boy, Don Matías. I congratulate you."

"Don't congratulate me," grunted the old man. "It's a sad affair. Ramón doesn't go to school anymore. He's got to knuckle down to work now like his grandfather and his father."

Bonday said severely to the boy, "But you must study, boy. You must go to school and devote yourself to your books and do well. What's all this about leaving?"

The old man gave his hat a few more buffetings, this time on his arms. "You don't understand, Don Bonday. Ramón wants to go to school. It's his father who won't send him. . . ."

"That's very irresponsible of him!"

"Listen, sir," said the old man, his face wrinkling ominously, "my son isn't whatever you said he is. He wants to send him to school, but he hasn't got a job. Ramón has brothers and sisters, and they have to eat. And who's going to pay for his books and his uniform?"

"I see," said Bonday, feeling uncomfortable, looking at the boy and noticing for the first time what he was wearing: shoes with holes in them, trousers that were too short for him, and only a thin cotton shirt against the cold. "Yes, I see."

"Don Bonday," said the old man, frantically beating his hat. "I mean, I was wondering if you wouldn't mind, that is, if Ramón could come and live with me."

"Of course I don't mind. What made you think I . . ."

The old man looked at him with a humiliated, pleading face. "Ramón will help me in the garden, and he's already fixed himself up delivering newspapers. He's a good boy, and he doesn't eat much, really."

Horrified, Bonday interrupted him. "How can you set him to work at this age? The boy has to go to school." He tapped the child's head with the newspaper. "All right, young man, from today you go back to school. Buy whatever you need, and your grandfather will pass the bill to me."

The old man's eyes filled with tears, which he brushed away with the brim of his hat. "You're a real saint, Don Bonday."

Bonday smiled and made a dismissive gesture. But an awareness of his own generosity brought a lump to his throat. In a hoarse, falsely imperious voice, he said, "Well, that's enough of that nonsense. And you, young man, off to school with you!"

He'd turned to go, newspaper under his arm, when the boy called after him.

"Sir, sir!"

Bonday turned to him, smiling.

"Sir, tell me which school I should go to."

Bonday shrugged his shoulders. "Well, yours, of course."

The boy shook his dark head. "I can't go to my school, sir."

Bonday looked at him with sudden distrust. "They haven't thrown you out, have they?"

"No, sir," said the boy vehemently. "It's just that there isn't a school anymore. They closed it down, sir."

"What do you mean, 'closed it down'?"

"There weren't enough boys, sir. They all left like I did."

"Good heavens, what are we coming to? What a country, dear God, what a country!"

The boy waited respectfully. Bonday wanted to read the paper.

"All right, Ramón. Your grandfather will find you one somewhere or other. If he can't find one, well, then we'll talk about it again. Later, eh?"

Sitting at last at the table, the paper open and a cup

of freshly made coffee before him, he said to his wife,
"No doubt about it, Elsa, this country's going to the dogs.
When education, the very foundation of a free nation
. . . Aha! here's the bit of news the captain was telling
me about! He was right. It *is* a success."

And with a voice brimming with pride and pleasure,
Bonday read:

WRITER SANTIAGO BONDAY ACCLAIMED

ENTHUSIASTIC WELCOME IN THE NATIONAL CONGRESS.
DR. ELADIO MARTÍNEZ'S MOTION CARRIED.

The presentation of the blueprint for a monument to the Fleur-de-Lis to be erected in the
foyer of the President Herrero National Theater
was given an enthusiastic welcome in the latest
session of Congress. We give below an extract
from the speech made by that ever-popular figure Dr. Eladio Martínez. This extract clearly
shows that a strong wind of change *vis-à-vis* cultural matters is blowing through the corridors
of power.

Dr. Martínez stated:

"We have been inhibited, nay, paralyzed, by
centuries of imitating foreign cultural models.
We needed the invigorating, pioneering action
taken by our greatest writer, Santiago Bonday,
to wake us up, to make us aware of the traditional values of our own culture. We are not just
talking here of our native Fleur-de-Lis, from
which one ill-fated day we looked away to fix
our gaze obsessively on Europe. What is at stake,
gentlemen, is the fate of our culture, which to-

day is being reborn in the President Herrero
National Theater.

This side of the house, which I represent, de-
plores the fact that with our taxes we have been
subsidizing the promotion of a foreign artist.
Since 1920 British imperialism has imposed on
us one author and one play. This humiliating
foreign domination has undermined the foun-
dations of the traditional style of life in our
country. With shame we acknowledge our previous passivity. But today, at this grave juncture
in our history, let us join forces to win. For the
Fleur-de-Lis, for the President Herrero National Theater, for the culture so nobly represented by Santiago Bonday, let us all put our
shoulders to the wheel in the name of liberation."

Deputy Dr. Eladio Martínez's motion was carried by an overwhelming majority.

The letter Bonday sent that same morning thanking
Deputy Martínez was published in full on the front page
of all the newspapers.

° 33 °

Dear Emilio,

After several days off sick I went back to the theater. All or nearly all my colleagues have the flu or a cold, and are busy defending themselves against this winter, which they describe with enviable powers of recall and the passion of the hypochondriac as the worst in living memory. Don't ask me what last winter was like. I can't remember, and meteorology isn't my strong point. All I know is that it rains and rains and rains and is endlessly cold. It's not a fit subject for conversation. But the Creative Department could talk for hours about it. Not a word about Candini and his amazing rise to power. Just aspirins, antibiotics, lemon tea, and a lot of sighing and sniffing. Coming from people who were on tenterhooks to know the contents of that letter addressed to the Wardrobe Department, this indifference is, to say the least, surprising.

I ask myself if perhaps I'm wrong to be so curious. I've been here such a short time. Compared with me, they have a lifetime of experience at the theater. I'm inclined to think that just as the flooding, by virtue of having become routine, is nullified, doesn't exist, is simply a

mania of Claude's, so the reality of Candini's
appointment fades before the sufferings of their
beleaguered bodies and the fearful tortures
of flu.

Claude wasn't in the Salon de Thé. Not that
I had any great hopes of him, I just missed his
almost physical ability to take everything as a
joke. At least between jokes he'd have something to say about it. Off I went in search of
him, but I didn't find him immediately. I walked
a long way through the empty theater looking
for him, and for Juan Martínez Tormi too.
Claude and Ophelia say the old man has resigned. Poor Hamlet. I can understand why. The
way they dragged him off the stage on the
morning of the dress rehearsal! The humiliation of having to wear those furs, the interrup-
tion of the rehearsal by Candini: his last
appearance onstage. I would like to have said
good-bye to him. But he was right to leave without saying anything to anyone. Fewer witnesses
to the defeat.

I've nothing more to tell you. As time passes,
I lose confidence in the reality of these letters.
Far away in France, in the room where you work,
why should you be interested in these stories
about people you've never seen—just uncon-
nected pictures.

I await your return with some anxiety. It isn't
just the solitude that troubles me. I need some
friendly plot of earth to stand on. That plot of
earth is Emilio. But don't be alarmed. Next time
I see you in the café on the south side, the earth
will seem as wide again as it was in our talks
together, and I'll leave you in peace.

No, I put the blame for my unease on this

winter, the worst we've had in recent years, and
the flu, which has left me battered, weak, hy-
persensitive.

Love from your ever-more-stupid Renata

What lies. I wasn't looking for Juan, I was looking for
Claude, and only partly to talk about Candini's rise to
power. Because *my* body wants its share of life too. I
wanted to see him despite my disappointment, to catch
a glimpse of him from behind my mask of disillusion.
I wanted to prove, with the ridiculous tenacity of those
in love, that perhaps all was not lost, that perhaps he
didn't really like Ophelia that much, that perhaps . . .
So off I went. Not me, but the demon of love that pos-
sessed me, the same demon that can monstrously trans-
form the pain of rejection into the obscure pleasure of
the voyeur. To see him, to see him just once more, to
see him as often as possible. Off I went with the clumsy
excuse of returning the borrowed gloves, with my
opening speech down pat, hiding behind my veil of
gratitude, my words covering the true nature of my
need.

And that's where I'm going tonight as well. Down the
path I know by heart. Looking for Claude.

I walk and walk aimlessly. There's not a soul in the
icy corridors. The epidemic has decimated the theater
staff. As I cross another corridor, go up and down another staircase, open and close another door, a curious
feeling begins to grow inside me. *However fast I walk I
always seem to stay in the same place.* I notice details about
the theater and yet it all feels very far away. An old
velvet curtain, the finely carved frame of a window, a
broken chair leaning in a corner, make me sad and
anxious. I don't know what it is that moves me, changes
me. I walk quickly, without stopping, and yet I stay in

the same place. The four walls of a bare room with friezes of garlands and cupids, the yellow texture of light from a lamp, still or swaying in the wind, the noise of my shoes on the wooden floor, the crackle of rain on the windows, the bubbling of water gushing down a gutter outside. All these empty rooms, all these staircases leading nowhere, these shabby, useless objects, are, like me, as much a part of the theater as one's hand is of one's body, and the theater is part of the city, just as the city is part of the world.

Out loud I say, "Somewhere in this silence lies the truth."

My own voice frightens me. I start to run. Breathless, I reach the door of the Wardrobe Department. It fills me with relief, this joyless room, this leaden light. I'm out of breath from running, and I hear the sound of my labored breathing. I go over to the window and look out at the choppy water on the river, the sunless shore. I rest my forehead on the glass and feel the beating of my pulse, echoing the beating of my heart. I try to calm myself.

Why did I leave the protection of the Salon de Thé? I sit down at my desk and stare at the notebook with the blue covers. I've nothing to do. My job is a farce, my hard work a sham. I brood on the farcical nature of it all. And then something tugs at me. Like a coin at the bottom of a pool, it gleams in my memory for a second, then is gone again, buried in the mud. What is it? Exasperated, alarmed, I get up. I look around me. Yes, I'm alone. I open the door of the wardrobe room itself, in search of the company of costumes and masks. I switch on the light. The lovely, mysterious vision: the sky with spotlights for stars, the extravagant cast, mummified clothes vainly waiting to be someone. I take a red satin cloak edged with sequins off its hanger. I throw it over my shoulders. No, I'm no longer ashamed to play this game. It's the only pastime the theater allows us, not because it's innocent but because it's secret. I take a few turns about the room in my cloak. It's so long that to turn I have to kick it aside with my foot. I trip and fall to my knees, my hands resting on the bundle that made me trip. It's a bundle of black cloth. Sitting on the floor, I open it and find a shirt torn into shreds and a pair of black velvet trousers. Hamlet's costume.

I stand up. My hands tremble as I remove the cloak and return it to its hanger. I go toward the desk, and taking a key ring out of my bag, I open one of its enormous drawers. The black velvet cloak with the silver clasp is still there. I close the drawer. When I go to put away the key ring, I look at my hand. It's covered in dust. But there's something else in my sweat-damp palm. I hold it up to the light from the window. I see a faint red trace.

You were right, Emilio: I do have a feverish view of the world. There is a vein of madness in me, but I'm not proud of it; it terrifies me. When I hear someone boasting about being a little mad, when I hear applause and laughter greeting a show of madness, I feel envy and dread. They have both feet firmly in the real world. They can allow themselves the luxury of admiring the unreal. I can't. That's why I cling to their view of a solid universe. And I deserve the corrective slap in the face, the harsh lesson of common sense.

When I opened the door to Ophelia's dressing room, the mirror at her dressing table showed three people: Ophelia and Claude sitting down, their heads very close together, looking at a drawing of Claude's; the third, at the door, agitated and uncertain.

They both gave me a friendly, cordial smile.

"Renata, have you got over your cold? Claude told me you'd been off for a few days."

"You look very pale," said Claude.

"I'm sure you'd like . . ." began Ophelia, but Claude took the drawing from her hands, rolled it up, and put it on top of the dressing table.

"Let's go and get some coffee. It's freezing down here in these abandoned regions."

Ophelia laughed. "Abandoned by her companions, the leading actress without a leading role survives flooding, flu, and other such plagues. Hardly anyone's come today. At any rate, we actors all left earlier than usual." She said "we" as if she weren't there with Claude.

"Didn't Juan come either?"

They didn't know. They looked at each other questioningly. Is that what you wanted to see, Renata? A loving couple? I told them about finding the torn costume. A weird discovery. Like my jealousy.

"It can't be Hamlet's costume, Claude," said Ophelia, shaking her lovely chestnut hair. "He never leaves it at the theater."

"Aren't you forgetting the dress rehearsal? Poor old man, there was no way he could hang on to his role, not even by agreeing to wear those ridiculous furs. And we know what he's like, don't we, Ophelia? Why the hell would he take the costume with him?"

"Juan may have been temperamental, but he was also the soul of kindness."

"That ridiculous version of the play was sheer stupidity. They took everything away from him. *Merde,* he didn't want much. He just wanted to be Hamlet forever. To die repeating that stupid soliloquy dressed in that stupid costume."

"He's not stupid, Claude. He's a good actor."

"I know that. But he was old. Finished. He resigned, ripped up his costume, and left. *C'est tout.*"

"He didn't destroy his cloak or the silver clasp," I said dully.

They looked at each other again, surprised.

"He gave them to me to look after."

With affectionate, playful ease Claude gave me a quick peck on the cheek. I moved away, indignant. "Good girl," he smiled. "The old man was fond of you."

"When I touched the costume," I stammered, hating myself for it, "I got something on my hand." I held out the palm of my hand to them. "Blood," I said.

There was a second's silence. Ophelia's eyes were wide open like great blue flowers.

Claude took my hand. A moment later he burst out laughing, that light laugh of his that I love and hate. He showed Ophelia the golden pin caught in the sleeve of my dress, and the red scratch on my wrist.

"Those costumes from Wardrobe are a real menace," said Ophelia, shaking her adorable head. "I always have a good look at them before I put them on. I don't know why they fill them with pins. Maybe they'd fall to bits without them."

Brusquely, without a word, I left the dressing room. I heard the two of them calling after me. I didn't stop. When I knew I was far from them, safe, alone in a dark corner of the empty theater, I leaned against a wall and cried my heart out with rage.

· 34 ·

Decree 45498

In view of the fact that the play by the Swan of Avon, William Shakespeare, entitled *Hamlet, Prince of Denmark,* has now had 856,904 performances at the President Herrero National Theater; and in view of the fact that the above-mentioned play fails to fulfill the cultural needs of the country which the National Theater was founded to meet

WE HEREBY AUTHORIZE:

Article 1. The elimination of the above-mentioned tragedy by the said Shakespeare from the national stage.

Article 2. The replacement of the above-mentioned tragedy by another whose subject, treatment, and language will tend to the exaltation of our traditional way of life, which will, without falling into gross errors, draw its inspiration from the very deepest roots of our national psyche.

Bonday stood at the door of the TV station while he waited for a taxi to appear, thinking, No, it's too early to go home.

What about going around to a few bookshops? He was sure that the broadcast would improve the sales of *The Soul and Other Vagaries*, but not yet. Anyway, it was pouring with rain. What about Marga? Marga Hedelstoff lived in Paris now, another source of distraction lost. The Writers' Association? Never! There'd be a crowd of old women writers there, a melancholy sight. No, he only went to the association at times of extreme depression. And Bonday was feeling the special excitement that flattery creates, the stimulation of the nerve ends that comes from wallowing in praise.

The reporter had asked some quite good questions, and Bonday had been clear and decisive in his replies. He applauded himself for having deflated the emergency decree with a few sharply critical words. "Being an upright citizen, I will of course adhere to the government's latest drastic resolution, but as an artist I cannot deny that there is in William Shakespeare a smidgen of poetic inspiration, the odd effective scene, and the occasional memorable character."

The taxi came.

"Where do you want to go?" the cabdriver was asking for the second time.

Without thinking, Bonday gave him the address of the theater.

"So this is what Captain Beh means by 'the process,' " he said to himself, annoyed, standing on the pavement outside the theater while he opened his umbrella against the torrential rain. A mound of debris with a deep ditch behind it prevented him from approaching the door. On the threshold a stagehand sat chewing a toothpick.

"Looking for someone, mister?"

"No. I want to get to my office."

The orderly took the toothpick out of his mouth. "M-b, Z-k, R-x, or D-m?"

"I'm sorry?"

"The management reserves the right of admission. What section do you belong to?"

"My name's Santiago Bonday," said Bonday firmly, because the water was pouring off the edges of his umbrella and soaking his shoes. "How the hell do I get in?"

"You don't, mister, if you're not on the list."

"Look, who are you and what right—"

"Listen, mister, rules are rules, and it wasn't me who made them. We can't let just anyone in, not when it's in this state. Are you blind or what?"

Furious, Bonday said, "No, I am not blind. Let me talk to the director."

"Brother Candini?" the orderly stood up. "Have you got an emblem?"

"Have I got a *what?*"

Standing on tiptoes on the steps, the clerk looked him up and down. Then he pointed to the lapel of Bonday's raincoat.

"You should have said, mister. You'd need a telescope to see that from here."

Surprised, Bonday looked at his lapel. There was a little white ribbon pinned to it. Then he remembered that a woman in the makeup room at the TV station had pinned something to his raincoat. He hadn't taken any notice, thinking that it was a ribbon for some charitable organization. Now he could make out, drawn in fine black lines on the white ribbon, a fleur-de-lis. That lunatic, he thought. And immediately corrected himself. The crafty devil, he's commercializing the idea already. Mumbling excuses, the orderly picked up a broad plank and dragged it over to the ditch. Bonday was just regaining his composure, and already preparing his complaint to Candini, when the door opened and a girl peered out. The girl from the Wardrobe Department! Bonday felt his pulse begin to race. He forgot about the orderly. He forgot about Candini. He forgot everything. All he wanted was to cross the ditch.

"Renata! How nice."

The girl, who was looking anxiously at the ditch, raised her eyes.

"It's Santiago Bonday, don't you remember me?" asked Bonday from the other side.

She smiled the half-smile of the fountain nymph.

Adorable, so shy. Overwhelmed at being in the presence of a famous writer, thought Bonday, overcome with happiness.

"Wait, *señorita*," said the stagehand, out of breath after adjusting the plank, placing it between the step and the pavement. "Okay, give me your hand."

There she was, the nymph from the Jardin des Plantes, prettier than ever. Bonday ran to shelter her under his umbrella. "What a pleasant surprise!"

She half-smiled, without looking him in the face. Terrible weather, said Bonday. And you've no umbrella. Oh, you lost it. He was always losing umbrellas too. But what did it matter? He had one with him now and she didn't, and he'd be quite happy to walk her home. Nothing like walking in the rain. She declined. She's shy, thought Bonday, so shy that she feels intimidated by a man of the world like me. And what about a coffee, to celebrate their bumping into each other? No, she was in a terrible hurry. Shy but stubborn. In fact he wanted to talk to her about the play. What play? she asked, looking toward the street. Shy, stubborn, and not very bright. The play they're going to put on, that he himself . . . The girl said, You're mistaken, there is no play. Yes there is, said Bonday, it's just a question of getting down to work on it. There's no play, she repeated. But I . . .

"Master!"

The shout made him turn his head and then raise it a little, because the woman who had shouted was extremely tall.

"What are *you* doing here? The great genius!"

Bonday hadn't the slightest idea who this shrill-voiced Valkyrie was. He mumbled a resigned "How are you," and when he turned around, his right hand still grasped by that of his admirer, it was too late. The girl was waving good-bye to him with that same half-smile, running toward a waiting taxi. She got in, and the taxi disappeared into a sea of cars. Defeated and depressed, Bonday saw his dream vanish into the city and the rain, and found himself alone with the enormous woman with copper-colored hair.

He never understood why he allowed himself to be dragged to a café, why he put up with her awful conversation, why he downed several glasses of brandy and answered her ardent looks with his own feigned emotion. He never knew when the hotel was mentioned or which one of them mentioned it, nor how they got there (except that it was in a taxi and that the copper-colored head rested like a limp reading lamp on his shoulder), nor how they reached the rented room (except that it was in an elevator, together with a bundle of dirty sheets) nor how, since he was never able to get to sleep, at some point he woke up.

The woman took his face between her hands, told him to call her "tu," said that her name was Ariadna, and that love had brought them together so that they might drink deep of its passion and fire.

She wasn't ugly, just very big and much taller than he was. Gentle freeing himself from the caressing fingers with their long nails, Bonday turned over and buried his face in the pillow.

· 35 ·

Dear Emilio,

My friend the warmongering postman has not returned with the letter he promised me. Is this a victory for the telephone people? Or haven't you had time to write to me yet? Without my conversations with you, my life is like a desert island.

But I shouldn't exaggerate. On this desert island today I have Father Collins. I like to go to the church when I feel lonely. I like this tiny, eccentric priest who doesn't demand my religious credentials before plying me with tea and mounds of sticky cakes. I like the generosity with which he lends me books and the gusto with which he demolishes them. I like the way he's interested in my novel and yet never misses a chance to point out to me that the novel is a vicious and corrupting genre, a child of Lucifer condemned for pride. I think he likes my primitive ingenuousness, and finds my ignorance, my youth, and my candor a breath of fresh air in the hothouse world of confessional and ceremony.

When I'm not at home writing, Father Collins's church is the only place where I feel more or less comfortable. There was a time when the theater was like a second home to me; since the appointment of Candini, although little has altered there, a lot has changed for me, and it just isn't the same.

Perhaps man's true homeland is a handful of friends, a handful of affections, loves, and old habits. You sense the existence of that secret homeland when someone disappears from your personal geography: The landscape doesn't change, neither does the climate nor the architecture, but the soul that gave it a sense of humanity and belonging has died. We're less patriotic and less lucid than we think.

Juan Martínez Tormi has not returned to the theater; they say he resigned. Claude, to whom I was so attracted, prefers another girl. Quite right too; I've given up trying to conquer him. Candini, whom we never see now, encourages the previously tolerable defects of the Creative Section; I've given up trying to get on with my colleagues. And Emilio Rauch doesn't write to me; I've almost given up hope of receiving a letter.

Nothing has changed much, although the theater buzzes with bulldozers and building workers. They've closed some rooms off, opened others, bricked up two or three windows, knocked down a few doors. That's all. The only thing that's new is the play. We have a play. The play that will replace *Hamlet, Prince of Denmark* by the banned dramatist, William Shakespeare.

*   *   *

"We've got to stick together if we're going to stop that wretch getting his own way," said Ariadna, perched on my desk in the Salon de Thé.

I ask her if I can sit down.

"You're just in time," she says, remaining where she is. "We're deciding what to do. We're going to confront Candini."

Burgossi has his head in his hands and looks so dejected that I ask him, "Are you ill?"

"Not physically, Renata. But spiritual pain is worse than physical pain." He raises his hand to his chest, making the newspaper underneath crackle. "Only two more years and I can retire. Now I can neither resign nor consent to the assassination of culture, not without besmirching all the precepts that have guided my humble passage through this world. I'm caught between Scylla and Charybdis—"

"Is Scylla and Charybdis what you call the pension a Z-k gets?" says the Kid scornfully. "The assassination of culture! Come off it, Grandad, you'd assassinate your own mother if it meant you'd get your pension."

"*Ça va, petite?*" Claude's dark head looks out from behind his easel.

I open my bag and take out a pair of gloves.

"Thank you."

"Oh, great, I thought I'd lost them."

"You lent them to me," I say quietly, resignedly.

"Really?"

Ariadna and the Kid are arguing loudly.

"Mind your own business, brat!"

"Oh, I see, someone else drooling over culture!"

"No, you idiot. What do I care about culture? What I care about is not letting some worm, some creature with absolutely no class, come and give orders to people like oneself."

" 'People like oneself'! Who are 'people like oneself'? And where's *your* family tree, *señora?* I'll tell you where: standing in a cemetery for complete nobodies, the same as Fortunato Candini."

"Don't come on all working class, Klappenbach. We all know about your daddy, the nice bourgeois factory owner who sends you a check every month to make up the salary that his little baby plays at earning in this miserable theater, because he's the failure of the family and the only thing he could do was 'art.' "

The Kid's eyes fill with angry tears. "I haven't got a family!"

"Oh, come on, Klappenbach," snarls Ariadna sarcastically. "Your memory's failing you, dear, but don't worry, you'll get it back at the end of the month when your check arrives."

"Oh dear." Clara hides behind her knitting while the Kid advances, his childish cheeks flushed, one hand raised, and Ariadna leaps from the desk, her nails at the ready.

"That's enough!" Claude comes between them. "Are you mad? That's enough, Klappenbach! And you should learn to hold that tongue of yours, Ariadna."

"Hold her tongue?" The Kid struggles in Claude's arms. "Someone should put a bomb under her!"

"Oh yes?" Ariadna laughs, sitting down on my desk again and primly crossing her legs. "So it's up to the boy to decide who should live and who should die, is it? Congratulations, Klappenbach, I certainly couldn't do that—"

"Cheap bitch! Of course you couldn't! You'd get someone else to do it."

"That's enough, both of you! Stop it, Klappenbach! Don't be such an idiot. Have you already forgotten what

it was that was so important to you? Wasn't it the play?
The fate of the theater? Culture?"

A silence falls. The Kid stands motionless, sulking.
Ariadna lights a cigarette.

"Okay, van Gogh. Okay. Very good. Bravo. We knew
you didn't care two hoots about it. The only thing that
matters to the artist is his own work, isn't that right, van
Gogh?"

"That's right," says the Kid, pulling away from
Claude's restraining arms. "He's the egotist around here.
The only thing he cares about are himself and those
daubs he calls paintings."

"Art for art's sake," laughs Ariadna. "And did you
hear the superior tone he took, Kid?"

Claude looks at them openmouthed, stunned. He
looks at Clara and Burgossi. Everyone is looking at him
with varying degrees of reproachfulness.

"*Touché!*" exclaims Claude at last, smiling and shrugging his shoulders. A moment later he's cheerfully
whistling.

"Ah yes, violence," mumbles Burgossi, and mops his
brow. "Violence was the nightmare of Marcus Aurelius.
You know, Renata, scenes like this make me sympa-
thize with that philosopher and his feelings when he
walked the wall that separated Rome from the barbar-
ians."

Because there is little of Marcus Aurelius's sto-
icism in me, my hands are shaking when I put down
my cup of tea on the desk. I want to turn to Claude
and beg him for a crumb of that sense of humor
that allows him to whistle gaily as if nothing had happened. But I daren't do it. He'd just make fun of me
again.

In a shaky voice I say to Burgossi, "I'd like to see the
play."

*   *   *

Communiqué to the Creative Section

In line with Emergency Decree 45498 the management of the President Herrero National Theater suggests the production of a play to be staged next season.

Deadline for script completion: 30 (thirty) days from today's date.

Basic plot: A young brother of the Fleur-de-Lis has a vision of our Marvelous Guide, which, after many doubts, makes him determined to confront his enemies. The triumph of the young man will be represented by a sculpture of the Fleur-de-Lis placed in the center of the stage and surrounded by the corpses of the defeated.

I look up from reading Candini's communiqué. Everyone is looking at me, awaiting my reaction, to see which side I take.

"Barbarism, my child, barbarism," prompts Burgossi.

"They *suggest.* Did you get that, they *suggest,*" hisses Ariadna.

"Basically I'm not against the idea, Renata," declares the Kid. "At least it'll be a change—the Prince of Denmark was getting pretty moth-eaten. But Candini has overstepped the mark. We can't let him think he can just order us around as if we were slaves."

"A month isn't long," sighs Clara tremblingly. "Not long at all."

"So what do you think of the new play?" The question comes from Ariadna, but it's what they all want to know.

"It's Hamlet all over again," I say honestly and firmly. "Murder as the solution to a dilemma. It's just good old Shakespeare again."

The silence wraps around me. Disappointed, suspicious, alienated, they observe me. What have I said to provoke this hostile silence? I look at Claude. His black eyes gleam with repressed laughter. He finds the silent but eloquent indignation of my colleagues funny. I see in his eyes the experience I lack. I see that they weren't asking for my opinion; they just wanted another soldier for the war, support for their interests. Claude is amused.

"I'm not going to say *touché* like Claude." My voice trembles with loathing. "I won't!"

Now they all stare at me in amazement, then look at one another.

"Oh dear, oh dear," says Ariadna at last with feigned horror, "aren't we temperamental! Don't get upset, dear. After all, who was asking for *your* literary opinion?"

They don't know what it is to be really alone. I found out today, and I still hurt from the pain of that revelation.

· 36 ·

EXHAUSTED FROM YET another sleep plagued by nightmares, Bonday went out into the garden to clear his
head and found a surprisingly springlike morning.

He stood on the step, his eyes stung by the intense
sunlight, and blinked in astonishment. Not a cloud in
the sky. During endless weeks of rain he'd prayed for
a change in the weather; now he'd do anything for a
passing storm. Instead an impeccably blue sky over-
flowed onto the shining grass. There would be no post-
ponement of the picnic. Any excuse he proffered to get
out of it would only offend the captain and arouse the
anger of the overly touchy mystic. He was committed
to going. Even worse, his name was on the program of
events and in the morning papers.

He went into the house and sought refuge in the library. Sunk in an armchair, his head resting on the
chairback, he closed his eyes.

"That sideboard will be the death of me."

In investigating the possible causes of his nightmare,
he now had enough material to write a book. But he
didn't want to write a book. He wanted to sleep.

He opened his eyes and saw himself reflected in the
big mirror. "Good God!" He was all too conscious of
the terrors of the night, but he hadn't imagined their

ravaging effect on his face. It was the face of a tormented, bitter old man. He felt shaken by this vision of a repellent double. He thought of Renata, the nymph-girl. Would he let her see him like this? The picnic was an official event; she was bound to be there. But then so was the other one. How awful, the Valkyrie with her kittenish voice, purring: *Love brought us together to drink deep of its fire and passion.* No. Definitely not. He'd be very polite, very gallant, but beneath the kid gloves he would conceal an iron fist. He wouldn't let himself be trapped again.

A good hot shower, the prospect of seeing the girl with blond hair and dark eyes waiting for him (like the nymph in the fountain) in some corner of the Jardin des Plantes, did wonders for his body and smoothed away the hard lines on his face.

"Are you sure you don't want me to come with you?" asked his wife while Bonday kissed her loyal, plump, faded cheek.

"No, you'd only get bored, and the damp garden would play havoc with your rheumatism. For your own good I forbid you to come."

When Bonday left the house, he found Don Matías and his grandson working in the rose beds. "Beautiful day, Don Matías," he said gaily. "Makes one feel ready to face the world."

"It's all right for you to say that," grumbled the old man. "You don't have to break your back working or looking for anthills."

The old man, his hat on, his grandson at his side, was in his usual ill humor. Bonday smiled. "Everything's as it should be, the old man's his usual happy self."

Cheered by the lovely morning, his head cleared by the fresh air, filled with curiosity and desire to see the girl from the theater, Bonday was humming to himself as he started the car.

Not for one moment did the thought of the sideboard cross his mind.

CULTURAL CAMPAIGN PRESIDENT HERRERO
THEATER FUND-RAISING PICNIC
IN AID OF THE FLEUR-DE-LIS

The huge canvas banner hung above the iron gates of
the Jardin des Plantes.

Very nice, thought Bonday generously, and walked
past the long line of guests snaking up the path.

"I'm Santiago Bonday," he said to the two guards in
black trousers and shirts, one sleeve of which bore the
Fleur-de-Lis design.

"And I'm Brigitte Bardot," said the one holding a
book of tickets.

"Don't be impertinent. I am Santiago Bonday, literary consultant to the theater. Now where's the picnic
being held?"

The one with the tickets shook his head. "Don't get
smart with me. Get in the line like everyone else."

"One, two, three, four, five, six . . ." The other guard
was counting a group of small children gathered around
a man in a blue windbreaker but, out of the corner of
his eye, he was looking fiercely at Bonday.

"Listen, my name is Bonday, and I'm due to speak at
the ceremony—"

"Get in line and you can talk until the cows come
home," said the man with the tickets.

"One, two, three, four, five, six . . . You made me
lose count, you stupid bastard!"

Bonday took a step back, bewildered. The man in
the blue windbreaker and the children laughed. Exclamations and protests were beginning to emanate from
the line, which was growing ever longer and rowdier.

"All right," said the one with the tickets wearily, "show me your emblem, sir, and let's be done with it."

"What emblem?"

The men in black looked at each other. "Not another special guest," said the one counting the children.

"Another smart-ass who's forgotten his invitation and hasn't got an emblem."

Bonday was white with rage. He said in a low voice, enunciating each syllable, "We'll sort out who's who with Brother Candini."

"Now don't be like that, sir," the guard said in conciliatory fashion. "We'll let you in, okay?"

Bonday, with never a backward glance, flounced through the iron gates. Nevertheless, he was in a nervous sweat by the time he got to the little graveled square and the fountain with the nymph. A crowd in their Sunday best were disappearing down the hill. And now what? he wondered disconsolately. Because not only was the garden an endless labyrinth of little paths and identical small squares, there were a lot of people there simply sunbathing or reading, with no intention of taking part in the picnic.

The man in the blue windbreaker and the cluster of children passed near by him. The children looked at Bonday and laughed. Bonday felt tempted to follow them. No, their father wouldn't be taking them to a festival of culture. He walked once around the fountain. There were no signs showing the way and no familiar faces. The nymph was smiling, lost in her pathetic, waterless dream.

"Sweet girl," Bonday said to her tenderly, "my only friend, what's to become of us?"

Well, he sighed, either I walk back through those gates and later have to explain myself to the captain, to Pantaenius, and to Candini, or I plunge into this garden, get lost, and spend the night camping out in the jungle. The idea of having to explain himself to Candini decided him; he started walking. Fifteen minutes later, hot and out of breath, he stopped. He'd reached a small stone bridge. It seemed familiar. But two paths led away from the bridge, one to the left, one to the right. Bonday spread a handkerchief on the grass and sat down. He closed his eyes.

"Hello."

Bonday jumped. Had he dropped off?

A boy with fair hair and intensely blue eyes was looking at him, very seriously.

"You're lost," said the boy.

The young freckled face shone as if freshly scrubbed and wore the grave expression characteristic of boys his age. Bonday thought of the gardener's grandson. This boy was blond, but nevertheless there was a resemblance.

"No . . ." he began and stopped; after all, this was only a child. "Yes, I am lost."

The boy nodded understandingly, like an adult.

"When my dad first brought me here, he'd never let me wander around on my own. But now I can find my way around blindfolded."

"How nice," said Bonday distractedly.

"Are you leaving the party, or just arriving?"

"Which party?" Bonday asked, suddenly interested.

"The picnic."

"Arriving, but I can't find the way."

"Well, that's the way." The boy pointed to the small bridge.

Bonday looked at the two paths.

"I can only see two paths."

"No, there's another one in the middle. What happened was that it got overgrown with grass after all that rain. Do you want me to come with you?"

They set off. Bonday felt grateful. "Do you go to
school?" he asked amiably. "What year are you in?"

"You asked me that the other day. I'll tell you if you
like, but you've already asked me."

"When?" Bonday couldn't remember ever having seen
him before. He simply thought the boy looked familiar
because of the similarity with the gardener's grandson.
In fact all children looked the same to him: He could
only distinguish them by their sex.

"At the last tournament, don't you remember? You
were lost that day as well."

Now he remembered. For some reason he felt suddenly cold. He'd only been to the garden twice, and on
both occasions he'd met the boy. The little chess
champion!

"There weren't any more tournaments after that,
you know. My dad's furious. He says surely the garden's big enough for everyone. And why do they have
to take over the terrace and why put up barbed wire
round it?"

"Who?" Bonday ducked to avoid a low branch.

"The gentlemen who came with you. And the gentleman my grandmother likes. My grandmother, my aunt,
and an older cousin, they all say they belong to the Fleur-
de-Lis, and they've got emblems and everything. My dad
gets angry. My mom says she's got enough to do with
the house and all that."

Bonday could see the arbor now. The entrance was
almost hidden by clamorous red bougainvilleas.

"I used to like playing chess. But I like the Fleur-de-
Lis as well. My grandmother brings me, and they give
us sweets."

"That's nice," said Bonday while he looked at the
bougainvilleas in flower and wondered if it was the right
season, or if the plants, like people, were letting themselves be fooled by the weather.

"They drive me mad, you know. They say the Fleur-de-Lis isn't for children, that chess isn't for children. In fact, the only thing I really like is this garden."

"Is this a path?" Bonday peered inside the arbor, and saw the green-black mouth of some sort of tunnel.

"A secret one," said the boy, his blue eyes shining. "There's another one, but this is the prettiest. You see all kinds of things here."

He took Bonday's hand. They went in. Bonday almost had to grope his way along, clasping the small, rough hand. When the boy stopped suddenly, Bonday almost knocked him over.

"What's wrong?"

"I'm going to show you my secret place. Look, look."

In the wall of interwoven branches and leaves was a circle of light, an opening.

"You don't want to look," said the small voice, disappointed.

Afraid the boy might abandon him there, halfway along the tunnel, Bonday meekly bent down and looked. Framed in the circle of light was a small wooden hut. The boy's secret was a gardener's hut, abandoned and almost overgrown by weeds.

"Wonderful!" he said as enthusiastically as he could.

"You won't believe me, but things go on in there."

"I believe you, sonny, I believe you, but I'm going to be late."

The boy tugged at his hand, forcing him to crouch down again.

"I tell you, things go on in there. The other day I stayed in the garden until it got dark, and I saw them bring a man and put him inside there."

Bonday thought, Children and their imagination . . . God preserve me from all that fantasy. The captain and Candini waiting, and me stuck in the tunnel talking to a child.

"Oh, you saw a man," he said.

"No, not a man. An old man. He had strange clothes on, and he was acting oddly. He was crying. Men don't cry."

Bonday decided that things had gone far enough. "Of course men don't cry. But that wasn't a man."

He sensed that the boy was holding his breath.

"It wasn't a man," repeated Bonday, deepening his voice. *"It was a vampire."*

"A vampire!" The blue eyes shone in the half-light.

"There are vampires in the Jardin des Plantes," continued Bonday, half-irritated and half-amused by the delay and by the story. "But no one has ever seen them until now. I congratulate you. You've discovered a great secret."

"Vampires," the boy repeated.

"Now let's go," said Bonday, pulling at the boy's hand.

Silently, almost glued to Bonday's side now, the boy obeyed, and soon they emerged from the tunnel.

"Right, young man." Bonday smiled. "Many thanks for your company."

The boy looked at him with his blue eyes very wide. "Are you sure they're vampires."

Bonday nodded, impatient now. He could hear the sound of voices on the terrace. The picnic had started. "They're really good fun, vampires. Now, off you go and play. People are waiting for me."

He turned around to give a last wave to the fair-haired boy, who was still standing by the entrance to the tunnel. "Ah, childhood, childhood! Me, Santiago Bonday, using my creative imagination to entertain a child! We're all so susceptible to the faith children have in adults."

He'd gone a few steps when something made him turn his head. Did he call me? he wondered. But his young guide to the garden, the precocious chess player, wasn't looking at him. He was looking thoughtfully at the tunnel entrance.

I just hope, thought Bonday, with inexplicable unease, that I don't meet him a third time.

· 37 ·

Dear Emilio,

I'm writing to you here alone at home in the small hours of the morning with all the lights on. Night sends me sliding back into childhood. *I'm afraid of the dark, and I can't find words to express myself.*

I don't know how to tell you today's incomprehensible little story without slipping into childish fantasies. At times like this, when some trivial event keeps me awake, I really miss Gertrudis's scoldings, and her lime-flower tea. The thing is, the Wardrobe Department was burgled. This afternoon Ophelia showed her perfect face in the Salon de Thé. The men gave her a unanimously warm welcome. Miss Heartbreaker's arrived, I said to myself bitterly. Claude put down his brushes, the Kid hid his chewing gum, and Burgossi stopped reading. But Ophelia was looking for me. Surprised and curious, I followed her into the corridor. Her white face was whiter than usual. She told me that a man had come into her dressing room without knocking. He asked her where they kept the costumes for *Hamlet*. Since the abortive dress

rehearsal, all the costumes are filed away in the
Wardrobe Department, and as Ophelia thought
the man was an M-b, that's what she told him.
The stranger asked her for a key. There isn't a
key, said Ophelia. There is, said the man.
Ophelia got annoyed. There's no key, and anyway, who are you? You'll pay for this, said the
stranger, if I find out you've lied to me, you'll
pay for it. And with that he went.

Ophelia seemed frightened. "He wasn't an
M-b. I've never seen him in the theater." I said
maybe he was an inspector looking for me. "He
wasn't an inspector." She shuddered. "He had
yellow eyes, and red hair." Ophelia had waited
nearly an hour after the man went before coming to look for me. "Is there a key, Renata?" she
asked me before I could find out why she'd
waited so long. The door doesn't lock, I said,
but let's go and have a look. Then she took me
by the arm as if to stop me. "What's wrong?" I
said. She shook her head. "You didn't see his
eyes," she said with repugnance, "you didn't see
his eyes."

I thought Ophelia was exaggerating a bit.
There was nothing of value in the Wardrobe
Department, even if anyone did want to burgle
it. So there was no need for a key, and the open
door didn't surprise me. Then I saw the desk
drawer. There was a hole in the lock, and then,
furious, I remembered that there *was* a key. I
had it in my bag in the Salon de Thé. There
were splinters of wood on the floor, and the
drawer was empty. They had stolen the cloak
and clasp that Juan had asked me to take care
of for him. I pushed open the other door, the

door of the wardrobe room itself, and for the
first time my fantastic friends frightened me.
Impassive, the court of Denmark hung from
their metal hangers. Everything was in order.
The only thing missing was the bundle contain-
ing the ruined costume. It was as if someone
had erased the last traces of Hamlet from the
theater. Deeply saddened, I said to myself, "Juan
sent someone to get his things."

Juan, the old fool, would be quite capable of
stealing, as long as he didn't have to humble
himself before anyone. I turned to say as much
to Ophelia. She was very still, looking at something she'd picked up from the floor. It was the
coronet of flowers from her own costume. The
wire was twisted, the flowers crushed. We didn't
say a word. Ophelia threw the coronet into a
corner. I laughed nervously. "It's stupid," I said,
"it's all just stupid. But we'll have to report it."

For the first time, from behind Ophelia's lovely
mask I saw another person surface. Her blue
eyes held a strange authority. "No," she said,
"we won't report it. You must promise not to
let anyone else find out about this. For now at
least, Renata. Later we'll see."

Don't ask me why I accepted that pact of silence. I think it was out of amazement at seeing
this unknown face slide over the face of the
Ophelia I knew, a fleeting face, as if someone
had leaned out of the window of a house, just
for an instant, only to disappear the moment I
spotted them. For the first time I felt friendly
toward her. Although inexplicable, the burglary
of the Wardrobe Department brought us together.

We walked for a while before going back, she to her deserted dressing room, which now served no practical purpose, and I to my people in the Salon de Thé. We had a long, frank talk about Juan, about Hamlet, about the theater. Ophelia habors no false hopes, and I never had many. I'd almost forgotten what had brought us together when Ophelia, as we parted, said with a sweet smile, "I'm glad I had at least a little courage. Enough not to have given him your name."

Now, before going to sleep, I remember those words. They mingle muddily with a new friendship that consoles me in your absence.

Love from your fanciful,
sentimental,
bewildered,
Renata

· 38 ·

THE TERRACE that Bonday remembered as being a lake of mist on which floated chess players seated at marble tables was now an amphitheater packed with a noisy crowd of people eating and drinking, sitting among their opened packages and picnic baskets, sheltered from the sun by the shade of gigantic trees and canvas banners.

WELCOME TO THE AGE OF THE
FLEUR-DE-LIS!
DOWN WITH SHAKESPEARE!
WE NEED YOUR SUPPORT!
IF YOU'RE NOT WITH US, YOU'RE
AGAINST US!
HAMLET NO, FLEUR-DE-LIS YES!

Pure McLuhan, thought Bonday, amazed. The tribe and the message. The Campaign has certainly caught the tone of the times.

In the middle of the amphitheater, on a wooden platform, there was a long table with a cloth, and vases of white flowers. He saw Pantaenius, Candini, and Captain Beh eating and drinking among some other people he didn't know.

"At last, Master," Pantaenius held out a hand to help

him onto the platform. "We were beginning to think we'd have to finish the ceremony without you. The captain was getting worried."

There was an empty seat next to the captain. Bonday sat down.

"Who'd have thought, Captain, that the first major display of mass support for the Campaign would be such a success." Bonday smiled, covering the glass that Pantaenius was trying to fill. "No, no wine for me, thank you. If we get this much popular support now, the day the play opens, there won't be an empty seat in the house."

The captain nodded without looking up from his plate.

"And talking of plays, Captain, I've been looking at some interesting little works for our repertoire—"

"Please, Bonday, don't bother the captain with the repertoire, he's got enough to think about with the infrastructure."

The captain still didn't speak. Bonday looked at him, intrigued.

Pantaenius smiled. "You must understand, Master, the captain's position is a very difficult one, one of immense responsibility. Although he knows, of course, that we won't abandon him at this historic juncture."

"Is something wrong?" Bonday asked Captain Beh. The chubby, freckled hand pointed at the floor. There lay his three-cornered hat with its red plume. The captain made a gesture. Of fury? Of impotence? Bonday didn't understand. But he had no time to inquire further because a small hand, its skin as transparent as glass, was laid on his shoulder.

"Poet laureate," said a tenuous, unemphatic voice.

"Your Excellency!" exclaimed Pantaenius, standing up.

The man was very short. He rested his free hand on

a stick with a mother-of-pearl handle and politely inclined his round head, which, like his hand, also seemed
made of glass. His short, fair hair, growing close to
the skull, had the lightness of some gilded, translucent
fiber.

"No titles, my dear," said His Excellency with a crys-
talline laugh. "And no names. What value do they have
here?" And he wagged one of the pale, heavily beringed fingers that rested on Bonday's shoulder. "What
a pity we're so far away!"

Far from where? wondered Bonday, tortured because although the man seemed very familiar to him,
he couldn't remember who he was. A flurry of exclamations, of chairs being pushed back, ruffled the table.
People rushed forward.

"I hadn't expected your support," exclaimed Captain
Beh, picking up his red-plumed hat and pressing it to
his breast.

"How could His Excellency let us down?" said Pantaenius, smiling and informal.

"Under the new Constitution of the Fleur-de-Lis,
there's room for everyone," said Candini in his ringing
tones, holding out to His Excellency his open palm, on
which shone a small metal object.

"Charming, delightful," said His Excellency, picking
up the emblem of the Fleur-de-Lis with the tips of his
fingers.

Pantaenius offered him a seat. His Excellency waved
a beringed hand.

"Impossible, gentlemen, I have to go. I just wanted
to see this extraordinary spectacle with my own eyes.
You were right, dear Hugo, it was worth it. It's all so
primitive, so spontaneous. . . ." He fluttered his fair
eyelashes. "Oh, if only we weren't so far away!"

A languid smile, like a trail of bubbles in a fishbowl,

accompanied the movement of a hand that blew a kiss in Bonday's direction. Bonday started with shame and fury.

"Oh no, dear, don't get up to say good-bye. I'll just slip off. I'm going back to my retreat, to my cell, to a life of contemplation surrounded by only the purest of young men and a few works of art. . . ." His Excellency's voice moved off down one of the paths of the Jardin des Plantes until it was lost in the lustrous green mesh of the garden.

"Good," said Pantaenius with satisfaction. "Another supporter."

"Who was he?" Bonday asked quietly.

Pantaenius murmured a name.

"Surely not!"

"It most certainly was," laughed Pantaenius.

"I didn't recognize him. The only time I ever saw him, he was wearing a suit of armor."

"From his own valuable collection, Bonday. Very rare and very pricey."

"Support from *him*!" repeated Bonday in astonishment.

Pantaenius shrugged. "He has to come to terms with inflation and the rising cost of living just like everyone else, Bonday. And his tastes aren't exactly cheap."

"But how did the Campaign . . . ?"

A roar came from the loudspeakers.

"They're testing the microphones," said Pantaenius. "We have to get on with the speeches."

It must be the sun, the wine, the food, either that or the people who say we're a sad race are quite mistaken, thought Bonday, overwhelmed by the applause and the shouting. Candini stood up. He approached the center of the platform and opened wide his arms, as if he wanted to press the whole world to his blue-black suit and the white flower in his button-hole.

"Brothers and sisters!" He received a seemingly endless ovation. "The hour of the Fleur-de-Lis has come!"

Suddenly Bonday saw the girl, sitting in a corner. She was silent, still, like the nymph in the fountain, lost in a dream of secret games, her absorbed face beautiful and childlike, her eyes blank among all those eyes fixed on Candini, graceful and abandoned amid the left-overs, the trampled grass, the oppressive afternoon heat. Bonday held his breath, unable to follow Candini's harangue, or to hear the promises made by the cult, or the enumeration of the stars that were marking out another path for the Cultural Campaign. All he saw was the girl sitting among the greenness. And then, dear God, he saw the other one, the Valkyrie, waving to him. *Call me Ariadna, now that love has brought us together to drink deep of its fire and passion.* Bonday shuddered.

Never again, he swore, never again would he have anything more to do with that woman, with that particular mistake, or with any of those other women, those other mistakes.

· 39 ·

They came running in. They were wearing black uniforms and carrying guns. They burst into the Salon de
Thé during one of the many meetings called to oppose
Candini's play, ripping through the threads of our discussions like a stone thrown at a spider's web.

As I remember it, one minute we were immersed in
the Kid's insults, Clarita's crying, Ariadna's sarcastic remarks, Claude's jokes, Burgossi's Latin tags, my refusal
to join in with them (the vicious circle in which we spun,
waving our ragged banners), the next minute we were
gripped by astonishment and panic.

They ordered us to lie down on the floor, and we
obeyed without thinking, cowed by the metallic click of
those weapons, which we were seeing for the first time
in our lives. They ran to the window and pointed their
guns down the street. We lay there, flat on our stom-
achs, faces to the floor. It seemed an airless eternity.

"Brothers and sisters."

The deep, ringing voice was at the door, but sounded
far off and somehow different.

"It's all over, brothers and sisters. We're well-pro-
tected, safe from any attack."

Slowly, one by one, numb, confused, and humiliated,
we got up from the floor, brushing down our clothes,

caught in the bewilderment that follows fear. No one asked a single question. Why ask questions of a dream? I can still hear the affectionate tone of Candini's voice as he explained what had happened, while the men in black moved away from the window and leaned indifferently against the wall, the picture of lassitude and tedium.

". . . enemies who are trying to invade the theater," Candini says again tonight in my notebook, by the light of my reading lamp. "Enemies who wish to destroy the play, prevent the law being carried out. I, Fortunato Candini," that changed voice repeats now from far off, "appointed director of the National Theater by Decree No. 4358, repository of the spiritual orders of the Fleur-de-Lis, which, beloved brothers and sisters, our enemies would harm, will not allow that to happen."

It's only in my memory that I hear his words, because at the time I didn't. I was only half-listening. "I will not allow that to happen, not now that a process intended to promote the well-being of all has been set in motion. . . ." Because at the time I was looking at the other man. ". . . There are steps to be taken to bring that process to a happy conclusion." He also announced promotions for the Creative Department. I stared at the man. And increased salaries and bonuses. "Chief of our Provisional Security Forces, brothers and sisters." And he gave us emblems with a fleur-de-lis on a black background. "Thanks to our heroic Security Forces, no one need fear another attack like the one we suffered today." And we had to hand over our keys to the chief of the Security Forces, to the man I was staring and staring at. "All the theater keys."

"He doesn't need keys." I was startled to hear my own voice.

All my colleagues turned to look at me. In the silence I looked at the man and the man looked at me.

With strange deliberation, weighing his words, Candini said almost gently, "Nothing is born without violence, Renata. You must understand, as must your brothers and sisters, that it's all just part of the process."

The chief of the Security Forces has red hair and repellent yellow eyes.

· 40 ·

THE FOUNTAIN NYMPH appeared to be retreating, she was moving imperceptibly toward the backdrop of branches and leaves. She's going! Bonday trembled. No, she wasn't going. A red-haired man stopped her. Bonday could have kissed his involuntary ally. The other woman, the Valkyrie, was throwing him impassioned glances. Fascinated by the girl who seemed on the point of disappearing, frightened by the gestures of the other woman, he didn't hear the clamorous applause that greeted the end of Candini's speech, and found himself suddenly in an island of silence.

Hugo Pantaenius went over to the microphone.

"With his usual modesty, the pillar of this campaign for Cultural Reconstruction, Saturnino Beh, captain of cavalry, retired, has declined to make a public speech. Instead your humble servant will read the report on our Campaign's progress."

"Take notes, Bonday," ordered the captain in a low voice. "It's for the press."

Bonday looked over at the girl to assure himself that she wasn't going anywhere, then he took out his notebook and pencil and blindly wrote: *Communiqué no. 1 . . .*

The girl was arguing with the red-haired man. Good

God, thought Bonday, she'll go and I'll be stuck here
unable to do anything.

". . . three hundred forty-two square meters of work
carried out on the building . . . fifty-three contracts
signed . . . minutes of advertising time on television . . ."

A dark-haired young man wearing eccentric clothes
was talking to the girl. She lowered her head. The dark-
haired young man was putting his arm around her
shoulders. Bonday felt his jealousy mingle with relief;
the girl wasn't leaving.

". . . the purchase of a plane is in hand . . ."

The applause startled Bonday, who was noting down
in his book the word *plane*.

". . . And now I want to introduce the man who has
touched the very roots of our culture, our award-winning author, Santiago Bonday."

Without taking his eyes off the girl, Bonday stood
up. I shaved twice this morning, he thought, not a
shadow of a beard. He smiled. The smile seemed di-
rected at the rowdy, anonymous crowd, but it was intended for the nymph still contained miraculously in a
square of green.

"It's much too beautiful a day to bore you with a long
speech," he began, determined to speak as long as was
necessary because at least standing up there on the
platform, he would attract the girl's attention.

"Bravo!" shouted a thick voice.

"Other, more authoritative voices have spoken elo-
quently of the dangers threatening our national culture. I will, therefore, deal only with the reasons that
have obliged us to eliminate William Shakespeare from
our theater."

"William who?" shouted the voice, and the people
laughed.

"William who. Exactly." Bonday smiled. "Why should we know this man's name? His dramas—"

"No more Shakespeare!" howled the drunk.

Bonday nodded. "Yes, sir, exactly, no more Shakespeare. But let us look clearly at the reasons. Perhaps it's the baroque language that has tortured generations of Spanish translators? No. Is it those long speeches that require constant recourse to the scissors? No."

"We're wasting time here," shouted the voice in slurred tones.

"Neither of these reasons lies behind our farewell to William Shakespeare. What we reject is his ideology. An ideology of ambiguity, a dangerous ideology. Can we allow criminals like Macbeth or Richard the Third to awaken the sympathies of the spectator? Or a cynic like Falstaff to amuse audiences? Or permit, in *King Lear,* that the fool and not the king should be the embodiment of wisdom? Or—"

"Down with Hamlet! Long live the Fleur-de-Lis!"

This time, other voices joined the voice of the drunk. Bonday couldn't go on. It was Candini who managed to impose some order on the public, by simply raising a hand. A glance over to where the girl was still standing decided Bonday. He should finish his speech before it was too late.

"Wholeheartedly committed to the here and now," he mumbled, "we will not be like the Prince of Denmark. We will be ourselves. There need be no dilemma over this course of action."

"Death to Shakespeare!"

"Long live the Fleur-de-Lis!"

Bonday sat down again. "How much longer before the ceremony is over?" he asked Pantaenius.

"There's just the children's choir."

Good God, Bonday sighed, not a children's choir. A

little group of children dressed in black uniforms mounted the platform. At the top of their voices (to the tune of "Mambrú Is Off to War Again"), they started singing.

"The Fleur-de-Lis is off to war
To fight our foes and beat them raw."

Bonday noticed desperately that people had begun to leave. He half got up from his seat to look, because every now and then the people leaving blocked his view of the fair-haired girl.

"For every brother cruelly killed
For every drop of brave blood spilled
A thousand foes will die."

Pantaenius, Captain Beh, and Candini were clapping along to the rhythm of the song. They wouldn't notice his absence, thought Bonday. And, indeed, they didn't see him when he slipped away from the table and began to make his way toward the girl from the Wardrobe Department, the fountain nymph.

"For your voluntary donation," a man in black said, pointing to a box full of notes.

Bonday took out a few pesos and tossed them into the box, furious because the man, stopped right in front of him, momentarily came between him and the girl. When the man in black stepped aside, the girl was gone.

"My love, you shouldn't have run off like that, I was waiting for you. I would have waited until death itself."

Horrified, Bonday moved away from her. He'd fallen into the trap. "The sideboard was warning me of this encounter," he said to himself, weak with sadness.

"I'm terribly busy, Ariadna. It's my novel, a particularly difficult chapter, I . . ."

Ariadna was clinging to his arm, and Bonday closed his eyes with dizziness and fatigue. "At least don't let me be seen with her."

"Let's go," he said.

"Where to, darling?"

"To the exit, but we'll take a secret route."

He stopped at the entrance to the arbor. He raised his hand to his forehead. He was bathed in sweat. For some reason he was trembling. Thoughts of the sideboard? Now? He felt cold.

"You naughty boy. Trust you to choose a nice dark place."

Behind Bonday, anonymous feet crunched over the gravel. He pushed the woman into the arbor. They felt their way along, with her caressing him and him swearing vengeance. He would not be a gentleman, no kid gloves. A brutal good-bye and then he'd speed off in his car.

They reached the exit: a circle of light in the distance, framed by the green penumbra. The woman at his side screamed, but to Bonday the scream seemed to come from another world. He couldn't utter a sound. Like a sleepwalker, he crouched down over the small body, the fair head twisted horribly to one side, the wide but lifeless blue eyes, the freckles on the cold cheeks. Like a sleepwalker, he stood up and, once over the shock of recognizing the young chess player, he thought to himself how little the boy weighed; that the black fancy dress cloak and the silver clasp seemed heavier; that his own body seemed to weigh him down as did the nightmare, the green penumbra.

The darkness was filling with people, but Bonday did not release the body.

"It's the father."

"They don't know how to look after their children, they deserve to be lynched. . . ."

"He fell from that tree. . . ."

"It isn't the father, he just found the body. . . ."

Bonday, with the boy in his arms, looked so fiercely possessive that no one approached him. Not until a red-haired man came shoving his way through the onlookers, pushed aside the weeping woman next to Bonday, and shouted, "Everyone back! You, put the body down on the ground, an ambulance is on its way."

Bonday did not put down his load.

"Please, Master . . ."

Very slowly, he began to come to. The boy was dead. Very slowly, Pantaenius's mellifluous voice reached his ears. "Master, please, keep calm." Very slowly he let himself be persuaded, and they took the boy from his arms. "A regrettable accident . . ." "These trees . . ." "These things happen . . ." Blindly he let himself be taken to the car. Someone (Pantaenius perhaps) offered to go with him, begged him to take a taxi. Bonday shook his head, closed the door, and started the engine.

With no memory of how he had got there, he stopped the car in front of the house, climbed out, crossed the garden, walked past his wife without looking at her or speaking to her, went into the bedroom, undressed, lay down, and pulled the sheet up over his head.

This time it was a daytime nightmare, and there was nothing enigmatic about it. In the nightmare, Bonday was saying to a boy whose eyes were wide with astonishment, "There are vampires in the Jardin des Plantes. I congratulate you on having found them. Now off you go and play, my little friend." And the boy went off and disguised himself in a black velvet cape, climbed up to the highest branches of a tree to hunt the vampires Bonday had invented, and he fell. It wasn't the sideboard now but a freckled boy, the boy chess player, who fell again and again to the hard, trampled earth of a path in the Jardin des Plantes.

His wife opened the door and saw him smothering his tears in the pillow, biting back his cries. Gently she closed the door and tiptoed away.

· 41 ·

Dear Emilio,

The postman came back, but he didn't bring me any letters.

"Not yet, *señorita*. We're only in the first stage of the process." You seem happy, I said. "I'm very happy. I don't mind about having an empty bag now. Neither do my children. I showed them the form, and it's all so easy they couldn't believe it. The boss has a heart of gold. They pay us well. We've got enough to eat." If you haven't got any letters for me, why did you come? "I just took a liking to you. Do you think I've forgotten about the tea? All these years working in the area, and no one has ever given me more than a good morning. That's why your word's good enough for me." What word? "Your word that you haven't got any books." Books? "Books by what's-his-name, William Shakespeare." Ah! "Have you? You haven't, good, I'll cross you off the list and go." No, wait, I have got some. I've got loads of books. I've got the complete works. "Don't be like that, *señorita*. I'm on your side. Look at the list. See? I've crossed you out. And look." The uniform he wears is now black. He lifted his lapel to show me something. "See the emblem?" Get out of my house! "You're very young, you don't understand. That's why I'm going, see, I won't say anything, I won't put anything down. But be careful. And if you get a telephone worker coming around . . . They're something else again, they're dangerous, you know." Go! "Okay, okay, keep calm, I'm going. I hope they don't make me come back. And I thought you were so nice. Don't get angry with me. It's not my fault, you know."

It's not his fault. Whose is it then? I heard the explosion. I was hurriedly getting dressed because I was late for the theater. A gas leak, I thought. But when I went down the stairs, they were already bringing up a stretcher for him and putting him in an ambulance. The porter was looking at the pool of blood with greedy eyes, rehearsing a statement for the journalists: "A crime of passion. I never trusted that postman. He was always gossiping with the neighbors, always flirting with the women. I've been here thirty years and I always said . . ."

It was eight o'clock in the morning. A beautiful clear day. I went into a bar and asked for something strong. They gave me some colorless liquid that burned my throat, I drank it in one. I reached the theater in a kind of daze, more from the horror of that blood than from the alcohol I'd drunk. . . .

I find it hard to finish these useless letters to Emilio. It would be better to put it all down in the notebook or wait for him to get back to tell him everything. The letters are like a wistful dialogue for one. And yet they make me feel closer to him.

It's spring here now. I find it offensive, the smell of newness, the fresh earth in the patches of green in the city. It comes to me mingled with the smell of death that surrounded a body lying facedown next to an empty mailbag. It's spring, not summer, yet Claude insists on calling it tropical fever. And, smiling and smiling, he adds: It will pass. "Paint, write, sing, shy, vagabond soul, and leave your life to take care of itself."

But that was in the afternoon. The morning and the spring contained the death of the postman, the confused smell of greenness and corruption that floated in the street. I went into the Wardrobe Department and closed the door.

There, safe from fire and destruction simply because no one cared about them locked in this prisonhouse of masks, were the familiar stars on the plaster ceiling, the smell of old, damp cloth, the calm integrity of the fantastical costumes. And there too I found the seed, like the tiny seed in some ancient offering to a celebrated Egyptian mummy. The mummy had been long dead by the time it was brought to the museum, but not the seed. Centuries later, with just a little sun and water, it germinates, sprouts, can even give us nourishment, while no amount of sun and water will bring back to life the illustrious dead.

My anxiety subsided in the silent company of my imaginary friends. Growing inside me was the illogical but natural pleasure of being alive after a brush with death: Your skin gets back its feeling, your breathing returns to the intimate rhythm of your blood, you notice details and color again. I touched my lips. They were no longer tight or dry.

I wasn't surprised that Claude should be the one to invade my refuge, nor did I feel ashamed to be found wrapped in a red satin cloak, with a tiara of fake stones on my head, sitting among my friends in the wardrobe room, dreaming of another time, another play, another life.

He closed the door and lit a cigarette. For a long while he looked at me with those dark eyes, silent and serious.

"Solitary games make this world both beautiful and terrifying," he said at last, his voice hoarse.

"There's no terror when you know what you're playing at."

The light from the spotlights glinted in his dark eyes that seemed somehow closer to me than the figure leaning against the wall. I had all the time in the world to observe him, his body, the languid pose he affected, the cigarette burning itself out, the faintest hint of a smile on his lips, the steady gaze of his grave eyes that also had all the time in the world to observe me, my body, the languid pose I affected, the faintest hint of a smile on my lips, and my grave eyes gazing steadily back.

That was my world, my game. That's why I said, "I'm going to leave the theater, Claude."

He threw his cigarette to the floor, stubbing it out carefully with his foot. "No, you're not."

"I'm going to leave the theater."

"You're not."

Slowly he approached, bent over me, then knelt down in front of me. I had to raise my head to keep my eyes on his, to repeat gently, languidly, "Why? Why?" while his hands took the tiara from my hair, undid the clasp of the cloak, and he silenced my question with his mouth. There was no other answer but the slide into a nest of satin, the warmth and splendor of the two of us without disguises now, the silk of cool, burning skin, the two of us clasped together in the pathetic phantasmagoria of the wardrobe room.

∘ 42 ∘

"YOUR GARDEN'S really fabulous, but do you know what I think it needs? A statue. Something very simple, you know, a swan or a little gnome with a lantern, because, I don't know, there's something a bit sort of cold and sad about all this grass and trees."

Bonday smiled weakly at the woman in the blond curly wig and the plunging neckline against which gleamed a gold medallion. He picked up a cup to pour himself some tea, and the cup clattered ominously in the saucer. "I'm still not feeling very strong," he said to excuse himself.

They'd arrived unannounced around midafternoon: Pantaenius, Candini, this woman (who had rather taken Elsa aback and whom Bonday had scarcely looked at, having instinctively, like a reflex action, labeled her middle-aged, common, loose, good in bed, nice, easy-going, and fun), and Candini's bodyguards, now bearing the lofty title of Provisional Security Forces. Bonday, on his first day out of bed, had allowed himself to be dragged out to the street to be shown a couple of cars. "You really shouldn't deny yourself this pleasure, Master," Pantaenius had insisted. "They're just two examples of our whole fleet of cars." Leaning on Pantaenius's arm, Bonday looked at the cars.

They were Auburn 125s. For a moment he seemed to be thrown back into the past, and he was once again that poor, envious boy staring at the Auburn parked in the village square, with that same snout, like a metallic rodent, and in it a group of boys laughing, wounding Bonday with their laughter and the inaccessible party to which they would all be going.

"Wasn't there anything newer?" he asked, flustered.

"When you know a product works, it's a sin to look for something newer," said Candini severely.

The two black, shining Auburns troubled Bonday. "I suppose, Captain," he murmured to the man in the white uniform who was standing a little apart, "that my approval is of little importance. After all, I'm not going to use them. . . ."

He heard Pantaenius laugh. "You really are very weak still. You've mistaken him for Captain Beh!"

Bonday blinked. The man in the white uniform was tall and thin, with a long pointed nose. It certainly wasn't Captain Beh.

"Lieutenant Colonel of Cavalry Agustino Zé," the man said, holding out his hand. It was a hard, dry, firm hand. Perversely Bonday felt nostalgic for the feared but familiar hand of Captain Beh.

"Why didn't the captain come?" he asked, with no interest whatsoever.

"Ask no questions and you'll hear no lies," said Candini sententiously.

"Come now, Candini, the Master's an affectionate soul, interested in his friends." Pantaenius gave an unctuous smile. "My dear Bonday, Captain Beh has gone on a spiritual retreat."

"A spiritual retreat?"

"Yes, a retreat. Ah, if you could only see him in that calm environment, among all the greenery and the flowers. . . ."

"So he's gone to the country?" He didn't know why he was asking, out of inertia perhaps.

Candini's hand rested on his shoulder. "With the Fleur-de-Lis everything is possible. The Fleur-de-Lis has brought the country to the city."

"You should see how pretty it is now," said the blonde from the window of the Auburn, as she played with the steering wheel. "Fortu had some work done there. Do you remember what a dump it was? Now there's not a scrap of litter, and the fountains even have water in them. That one with the girl, you know the one I mean, the one holding up a jar like this, looks just divine now. Though the truth is I'm not that keen on the statue, it's a bit shameless if you ask me, when you think that families and children go to the Jardin des Plantes. . . ."

"The Jardin des Plantes!"

Pantaenius held him up. "Forgive us, Master, we've reopened old wounds. How thoughtless of us!"

Controlling his nausea with difficulty, Bonday allowed himself to be led across the garden to a wicker chair where they helped him to sit down. Someone raised a cup to his lips. It was the blonde.

"Take a little sip. It's tea, it'll do you good."

He looked up and regarded the course, heavily made-up face with spontaneous sympathy.

"Shall I call your wife? Wouldn't you like to lie down for a moment?"

He shook his head. "No, I'm fine now. It was just a moment's dizziness."

Bonday feared that allowing his disposition to cut short this unpleasant visit would only bring about a second invasion of his house and garden by Candini, Pantaenius, the men in black, the man in the white uniform, and the Auburn 125s. The thought terrified him. Heroically he said, "I suppose you came to talk to me about the Campaign."

"Perhaps this isn't the right moment, Master."

"I'd prefer us to talk now, Pantaenius."

In the late evening light the figures sitting around the table had a dark edge to them, and the garden fell silent. Bonday struggled against the torpor that was beginning to overtake him.

". . . and not only have we got your office ready, we've had a new play written. . . ."

"A letter, Don Bonday." It was Ramón, Don Matías's grandson.

"What's that uniform? Have you found a school?" Bonday took the letter and concealed a yawn behind it.

"No, sir."

There was so little light that he had to hold the paper close to his eyes in order to read it. Despite his weariness and the presence of the others, he exclaimed, "The Golden Fork!"

The blood flowed into his cheeks, strength returned to his limbs. There's still some pleasure left in this world, he thought.

"Good news, Master?"

"The Society of Gourmets has awarded me their highest honor, the Golden Fork," he replied, almost to himself.

"Allow me to offer you my heartfelt congratulations," Pantaenius said, shaking his hand.

"What are 'goormays,' Fortu?"

"People who eat too much," said Candini scornfully.

"Not at all." For the first time Bonday felt annoyed. "They're people who know how to eat, madam."

"If they give prizes for that, they should give me the biggest one then," she said, laughing gaily.

The simplicity of the woman won Bonday over. As if to a child, he gently explained, "It's not quite like that. It's a very exclusive club where the members cook highly original and refined dishes. Very few people can belong to this club, and fewer still win their highest honor, the Golden Fork."

"Gold-plated or solid gold?"

"Solid gold." Bonday smiled.

"We didn't come here to talk about forks," thundered Candini.

"That's true, Master, we came here not only to inquire about your health, but because we need help in the next stage of the Campaign. It's the Grand Membership Rally."

"Go on." But Bonday was already mentally composing his letter of reply to the Society of Gourmets.

"I took it upon myself to suggest a demonstration of public support. Candini approves this in view of the conflicts threatening the progress of the campaign."

"Conflicts?"

"Ah, Master," sighed Pantaenius, "it's human nature to rebel against everything that's good for us. Just at a time when the large financial corporations, the political parties, the sociologists, the psychologists, and even our inefficient but well-meaning civilian government are waking up to the fact that a passion held by the majority has more force than the cold arguments of reason, there's always some misfit who starts protesting about the rights of the individual."

"Of course," said Bonday, deeply bored.

"Let them protest," said Candini. "The Fleur-de-Lis can even make misfits fit."

"It's nearly dark," said the woman, "and I wanted to see the inside of the house. I'm mad about interior decorating, you know."

"The problem is," continued Pantaenius, "that the Campaign for Reconstruction is based on the principle of total collaboration. And just look what happens. Blind to our grand destiny, blind to how powerful we could be if we worked with the people, blind to our natural roots, the cult of the Fleur-de-Lis, up pop the Shakespearians and start protesting."

"The Shakespearians?" asked Bonday weakly, on the point of falling asleep.

Pantaenius sighed. "Would you believe me if I told you we've discovered a secret press and no less than a thousand annotated editions of *Hamlet*?"

"The work of a thousand pedants, if you ask me," murmured Bonday. "It doesn't seem so very serious."

"You don't understand, Master. Remember the man who's in charge of financing our play: The cultural can never be entirely separated from the economic. A reader of Shakespeare is no longer just a reader of Shakespeare, he's an opponent, someone who will not put all their efforts into the Campaign."

I must get some sleep, thought Bonday, I absolutely must get some sleep.

"It's odd," he managed to say. "People used to find Shakespeare so boring . . ."

"Let's get to the point, Bonday," said Candini, standing up. "The Grand Membership Rally, the first of other similar and equally vital ceremonies, will take place in the theater, before the television cameras and the press. You'll be better by then, and you'll be there."

"I want to see the house, Fortu."

"When is the ceremony?" yawned Bonday.

"We'll let you know, Master."

The darkness of the garden was suddenly rent by a shrill cry. "Santiago!"

Bonday woke up. In the lit doorway his wife was brandishing a broom.

"Santiago, this man was rummaging around in the library!"

A man in black staggered out of the house, protecting his head with his arms.

"What's going on?" Bonday found himself in the midst of a whirl of overturned chairs, figures moving in the darkness, voices, shouts.

"Master, you must forgive . . ."

"The Fleur-de-Lis allows no exceptions. . . ."

"He had a book, Brother Candini, a book by . . ."

"Fortu, now we've annoyed the lady, and she won't show me the house!"

"What book? What is this?"

"Madam, please accept my . . ."

"Get out of my house!"

"Just give me the order, and I'll take her to the car. . . ."

"I must be dreaming," Bonday was saying to himself as they helped him to the door, Pantaenius oozing apologies, Candini dispersing his men, the blonde sniveling because she wouldn't get to see the house, the man in the white uniform now just a white stain on the blackness of the garden, and the Auburn 125s in the street.

Lying in bed, while his wife dabbed at his burning brow with a moist cloth, Bonday stroked the covers of the banned book.

"What's going on, Tacho?" his wife asked tremulously.

Bonday shook his head and sighed. "Perhaps," he said, "it's all just part of the process."

· 43 ·

Something inexplicable has happened. Someone made
an anonymous phone call to the police reporting the
presence of armed men in the National Theater. We
don't know who the brave person was. They sent a pa-
trol from the Police Department. They didn't get beyond the foyer. They were received by Candini, the red-
haired man, and his Security Forces. Everyone in the
Creative Department watched the scene from the bal-
ustrade, I with a mixture of wonder and irritation. Who
had got in before I did? Why had I hesitated to break
my pact with Ophelia? We saw how Candini handed
the officer in charge of the investigation a piece of paper, how the latter read it and returned it, touching his
cap. Candini and the officer smiled, and they all went
out into the street together. Burgossi said, "We must
let the law take its course." No, it couldn't have been
Burgossi who informed them. "They're all in it together, the pigs," said Ariadna. Was it her? "They
weren't doing us any harm. But now they'll take against
us." It wasn't Clara. I looked questioningly at Claude.
He shook his head. The Kid was missing, and I thought,
Of course, it must have been that violent, rebellious child,
the Kid. I went down the stairs.

They were all outside on the pavement. The police,

the Security Forces, Candini, and the red-haired man. They were chatting as they examined an old car. The red-haired man was talking to the officer. Perhaps he was explaining to him how that grotesque mechanical relic worked. There was a boy sitting at the wheel, his hand on the gearshift. I heard him from the door. His face flushed with excitement, he was saying again and again, "An Auburn 125! An Auburn 125!"

Only then did I recognize him. He had a black uniform on. It was the Kid.

"Imagination is the evil fruit of the tree of knowledge," Father Collins said to me today in the courtyard of Santa Angela de la Piedad. "The Church isn't against knowledge. It just plucks the flowers of fiction that bloom too early, that poison the branch from which they spring. Prune your imagination, my child, before it's too late."

I doled out another ladleful of soup into a plate and put it down in front of one of the dirty, ragged children crowded around the improvised table of planks in the garden.

"But I'm not imagining the weapons, or the threats, or the fact that they burgled the Wardrobe Department. Just because they haven't shot anyone yet, just because their threats are mere words so far, just because I've no proof of the thief's identity, does that mean neither threats, nor weapons, nor crime exist?"

He turned a weary face to me. "Yesterday I had a meeting with my superiors. It was a long afternoon. We talked of the loss of faith in this century, which makes the salvation of souls so difficult. We talked of morality, the family, the pernicious inclination toward sex, money, drink. We condemned the cinema, literature, the playthings of our day." His blue eyes flashed. "I barely had enough time to find food to feed these poor unfortunates who don't come to hear mass or confess their awful sins. And you come along with your men in black, your ridiculous theater, your childish nightmares, and still expect clear answers from me, when what I need is bread and clothes."

"Father . . ."

"Don't Father me! This isn't the moment for discussions on truth and life. Leave all that leisurely nonsense to the institutions. Go to my office, read the bishops' statement, and leave me in peace."

As I write, I feel the same heat in my face as I felt then, the same burning of tears in my eyes. Father Collins saw it too.

"Dear God," he exclaimed, wearily, with terrible bitterness, "how little space and time we humans have for pity!"

Dear Emilio,

These last few weeks I just haven't felt able to write to you. My lack of enthusiasm isn't just because this monologue of a correspondence seems so futile. I've started to believe that each person is an island and that the long silence between the two of us is much wider and deeper than the ocean that separates us. The image of the island haunts me, and it's not at all pleasant.

Now I recall bitterly when, what seems like thousands of years ago, in our café on the south side we aspired to that mythical island. Who hasn't at some time longed to retreat to a small plot of land, ringed by water, far from the clamor of the world, to think and dream in freedom? But, my friend, there was a basic flaw in our idea of how that paradise would be. We imagined it as having constant fine weather and

sun. The island we drew for ourselves was set
in an immense field of blue sea, joined to the
coast by the invisible cord of a small boat. And
the island I find myself on these days lan-
guishes under a bank of mist, and nothing is
what it seems to be in this foggy web.

The Fleur-de-Lis took over a theater and is
now taking over the whole city. That white
mushroom of a plaster flower is growing and
growing in the mist. The deep ringing tones of
Fortunato Candini's voice, which used to preach
in an obscure corner of the Jardin des Plantes,
which amid the scornful laughter of the Salon
de Thé spoke so prophetically of its victory, now
boom forth from the radio, from the television,
at every public ceremony, and the fevered eyes,
the wide, slow smile, are endlessly reproduced
in a kind of general delirium in the press, in
streets, in squares.

It spreads island by island, no one knows why
or how. The mist is full of haranguing voices
exchanging shouted opinions, it's swept by a
turbid wave of celebration. But we don't receive
one single trustworthy piece of news. There are
no letters, no telephones, no electricity. The city
celebrates in darkness, people embrace in silence. Were we so alone that now we need to
huddle beneath the same ghostly eaves? Doesn't
anyone care about the proliferating Security
Forces? Is no one troubled by the strange cars,
the metallic threat that haunts the theater and
watches over the city?

No. In the Court of Denmark life follows its
usual course. We adapt easily. Beneath the Fleur-
de-Lis Ariadna continues to make her sarcastic

remarks, Clara is kept frantically busy with celebrations and ceremonies, Burgossi does not resign, the Kid is a trainee with the Security Forces, Candini raises our salaries. And me? Yes, I do the same. I take refuge in Claude's advice. "Paint, write, sing, and let life take care of itself." When I have nightmares, I remember Father Collins. "Imagination is the evil fruit of the tree of knowledge." If I feel ashamed about continuing in my job at the theater, I seek out Ophelia and Claude, and the three of us form the basis for an island of friendship and love. Ophelia is like a sister to me. She's like a sister to Claude. She's my friend. She's so sweet and simple. "Because I love you both so much, I always tell you everything," says my sister Ophelia. "Except for one thing, and that's a secret." She laughs and keeps that secret for the day when this tropical fever, this madness of the Fleur-de-Lis, is over. Our motto is: All things must pass. Our heads lowered in fear, hope, and confusion, the three of us move forward hand in hand through this bank of mist.

All things must pass. When you get back, Emilio, you'll find me laughing about this whole episode, exaggerating the details a bit to amuse you, to prove to you what a marvelous storyteller I am.

God, I miss you.

Renata

· 44 ·

Dear Dr. Sanz,

It is with great pleasure that I take up my pen to respond to your pleasant news. To be awarded the Golden Fork by the Society of Gourmets! Never in my wildest dreams could I have hoped to receive such a noble title, to join a group of people who . . .

"Whatever you do, don't buy onions from Pancho. He always sells you them when they're already sprouted."

"All right, all right."

"I'm warning you, Tacho. I don't mind closeting myself in the kitchen all day. I don't mind the pretense at the table, but I won't put up with Pancho's onions."

. . . Your praise for my stuffed onions, a modest speciality of mine, is, of course, exaggerated. They are not in the same league as the chicken in whiskey of Don Ceferino Estévez, our ranching friend and fellow member, nor the venison cooked in tarragon of General Heme, president of the Hunting Club . . .

Bonday had imagined that writing this letter would be one of the few pleasant moments he would enjoy at this time, but now he was having real difficulty finishing it. It was Friday. On Sunday he would receive the club authorities in his house at Arroyo Manso. He tried to return to a time, not so long ago, when his daily life was an agreeable round of flattering conversations.

"You've done so much for the Cultural Campaign, Master," he recalled the saccharine voice of Pantaenius saying on that dark afternoon during his convalescence, "that we're terrified you'll be laid low by the same kind of stress as Captain Beh. Rest, take the sun, get your strength back. I'll tell you the date and time of the Grand Membership Rally so that you can wear your victor's laurels once again in public."

Reluctantly he picked up his pen.

> . . . and I take this opportunity to point out the injustice of those frequent jibes from abroad implying we are savages . . .

The letter demonstrably failed to cheer him up. Since the death of the boy in the Jardin des Plantes, a shadow lay over everything that Bonday did. It was no use repeating with anguished tenacity: *It was an accident.* The shadow came from the lifeless blue eyes, spread out from the endless penumbra of the Jardin des Plantes, stretched over the greenery of his own garden, the refuge he had believed his house to be, and invaded the library where he was sitting. The letter he was writing seemed grotesque, and he himself, Santiago Bonday, just a vain and ridiculous old man.

He shuddered. If I've been ridiculous, if I am ridiculous, he thought with a bitter lucidity, it's not entirely my responsibility. It's other people's fault for taking me seriously. And in a blind impulse to hold on to the only way of life that he knew, he wrote almost angrily:

How can they possibly fail to recognize, Dr. Sanz, the great sophistication of a city that contains such institutions as the one over which you yourself preside, established to sustain, despite the encircling barbarity, the sensibility of the man of the world? Without the actions of people like yourself, we would be reduced to merely stuffing ourselves with food and gulping down drink like animals, refusing to savor as one should the bouquet of wine and champagne.

Yours in gratitude,
Santiago Bonday

He raised his head and looked at himself in the mirror. It reflected the image of a man in shirtsleeves who had not yet shaved that morning and who had slept badly. Confronted by that other man, he felt the irritation of the well-groomed toward the rumpled; confronted by that sad, alien face, he felt the pity a happy man feels for the less fortunate.

With desperate arrogance he sat up straight and tried to smile. "There must be some pleasure left in this world. Daily life, Saturdays, the market, Pancho, and yes, why not? this meal for the members of the Society of Gourmets."

· 45 ·

The doorbell rang. A letter, I said to myself. A letter from Emilio!

"I've come to repair your phone." I haven't got a phone, I said. "It doesn't matter," he laughed, "none of the phones work anyway." So? "Can I come in?" What for, if I haven't a phone? "No one wants to talk to anyone nowadays. Don't you want to talk either?" He was young, friendly, polite; I let him in. "Thanks." Well? He smiled. "I know you've got some books by Shakespeare." I took a step back. "No, don't be alarmed. Listen: 'Whether 'tis nobler in the mind to suffer the slings and arrows of outrageous fortune.'" Ah, I said. I was frightened. To be perfectly honest, I still am. You never know with this Campaign, and on top of everything else, I work at the National Theater. "I know, I know. I see you're aware of what's going on." It's not difficult to be aware of this lunacy, I said. "Of course. Becoming aware is the first step. You'll be ready to join us now." Us? "You'll be free to read Shakespeare." Shakespeare? "Yes, Shakespeare. Just listen to this stirring call to arms that you'll repeat along with us: 'Out, out, brief candle.' I don't understand, I said. "It's quite clear. That brief candle is man's brief life. It must be snuffed out if it interferes with one's dignity." Is that what you believe? "Me? It's not just me. There are a lot of us. More than you might imagine." You and all the others are mad. He looked at me in silence. He sighed. "Poor thing, you're caught in the trap of contradictions." There's no contradiction in my love of life! Of my life and the lives of others. "Depends who you mean. For example, what about a certain man with yellow eyes." If that man commits a crime, the law will deal with him. He laughed. "Remember what *Hamlet* teaches us: In the hands of the weak, the law is a dead letter." Look, I haven't got a phone, your Shakespeare makes me sick, and I don't want to snuff out any candles, so just go away and leave me in peace. "Okay. I like you, so I won't add your name to the list. But you'll have to decide. To be or not to be."

The explosion made the cups shake. "Don't be frightened, it isn't here." He looked at his watch. "Perfect. Right on time." He smiled at me coldly from the door. "You owe us something, and it's only right that you should know that. You remember the postman who threatened you? Well, he won't be threatening anyone anymore. It doesn't matter whether you've got a telephone or not. Believe in us. We're still on the same side. At least for now."

Dear Emilio,

It's forbidden to send letters via the airlines, but I've been told that some sailors will agree to take letters if you pay them well. I'll go to the port today to send you these few lines if I can.

I've decided to leave the city, to escape from the theater. I'm going back to my village to hide

until all this is over. I'll make my poor aunt
happy, and I'll clear my head a bit, get some
fresh air. I hate to think of being far from
Claude, of not having a friend there like Ophelia. I haven't said anything to them yet. I'm
ashamed to be fleeing from shadows, from my
imagination, my madness.

This is the address where you should write to
tell me the date of your return. . . .

My aunt's letter and my appointment as teacher in the
school arrived at Father Collins's church through the
good offices of the priest in my village. I was coming
back from the port with my letter to Emilio, having failed
to get through the barrier of men in black uniforms all
sporting their emblems.

Father Collins let me read the letters several times,
respecting my icy silence.

"Good," I said at last. I looked at the bookshelves.
Father Collins's eyes were observing me, worried, intent. "You're my friend, Father."

"Yes," he said simply.

I opened my handbag and smiled. "You must be patient with me. Remember, I'm one of your agnostics,
always susceptible, out of pure politeness, to the de-
signs of Our Lord." I gave him a bunch of keys. "They're
the keys to my flat. I have another set. It's just in
case . . ." He looked at the keys, then at me. "Don't
worry, Father, don't worry. Be patient, try to understand me. I can't prune my fictional flowers. I'm the
kind of tree that doesn't bear fruit."

Father Collins's small hand rested on my head. He
stroked my hair clumsily. Only then did I realize I was
crying.

My aunt's letter spoke of her love for me, of how

she'd done up my room, and of the little welcome-home party. The letter from the school announced my appointment, my salary, and the hours of work. There was a seal stamped on top of the provincial coat of arms: It was a Fleur-de-Lis.

· 46 ·

THE MARKET in Arroyo Manso was about ten blocks from Bonday's house, built on the edge of the residential area. Here the roofs of the big villas and the new houses like white cubes (born of the recent craze for Mediterranean architecture) were beginning to grow sparse. Maintaining only a precarious hold on their true roots, they teetered above an abyss of rubbish dumps and small tin shacks.

Bonday did the shopping at the market every Saturday, and although this Saturday was no exception, the events leading up to it made it stick fast, like a thorn, in his memory. What he enjoyed most about Saturdays was the market and the little village, a wall of poor but dignified houses, built between the rustic opulence of the residential area and a murky backdrop of poverty. He would set off early so that he could stroll the ten blocks and pause by civilized privet hedges and cascades of red hawthorn berries to chat with neighbors, conscious of his fame as a writer and proud of the humble simplicity of the walk he was taking.

He could have transcribed from memory his Saturday morning chats with those amateur men of toil—in fact prosperous citizens, tired of the prison of their carpeted offices, the phony atmosphere of the air-conditioning, the smoke and the tedium of the bar where at the end of each day they would have a few drinks before returning home along roads jam-packed with cars. At weekends they rebelled against their executive fate, threw off their suits and ties, put on old shirts and trousers and, ragged and unshaven, replaced a panel in the fence, pruned a tree, painted part of a wall, shouting orders to wives and children, who cooperated, comforting themselves with the knowledge that forty-eight hours later Monday and freedom would arrive.

Until halfway along the route nothing troubled the smooth calm of his Saturday, this country interlude wrested from the city by the liberal application of large amounts of money. The women, already dedicatedly toasting themselves in the sun, their skins shiny with suntan lotion, smiled at him with the usual touch of flirtatiousness; the men talked of politics. Politics bored Bonday, but he enjoyed being part of this world-weary masculine murmuring that was part of his Saturday mornings.

"The women talk about their children and husbands while the men talk about politics," he used to remark to his wife when he returned from the market.

One day, Elsa, unexpectedly sarcastic, had retorted, "The way you men talk about politics is no different from the way we talk about our children and husbands."

This Saturday Bonday wondered if she wasn't right. For the first time in a long time, for the first time in all those chats, the complaints about the government's ineptitude, the imbecility of the ministers of finance, the corruptness of civil servants, did seem to him curiously like the mingled resentment and vanity with which his women friends spoke of their husbands, and something in the phrase "this country" reminded him of the furious and obsessive note in the voices of mothers when they talked to him about their disobedient children. He'd reached the sixth block along the route when a thought stopped him in his tracks. *No one had made a single comment to him about the Cultural Campaign.* He looked about him. The carefully tended gardens were flourishing. A rain of petals fell delicately from a cherry tree. The air smelled deliciously of spring mornings. *Not one word about the Fleur-de-Lis.* But that strange and disagreeable well of silence, bereft of perfume, contained a phrase that his neighbors in passing, apropos of nothing, repeated to him again and again along the six blocks, "What this country needs is a firm hand."

Bonday smiled, amused. "That's where the sexes are in agreement: What women most admire is the strength of authority; what they find most repugnant is disorder. It seems that in all things we are the sons of women."

There was one person to whom he could tell this amusing crumb of knowledge, and that was Dr. Pita, the local doctor, who had a fine sense of humor and found the subject of politics as boring as he did. Dr. Pita was cutting the grass in his garden. Bonday gaily greeted the fat, bald man pushing the lawn mower.

"What a splendid day, Doctor."

"Fascist!"

Astonished, Bonday stood looking at him open-mouthed.

"Fascist!" the doctor said again.

"What's wrong, Doctor?"

The other man moved away toward the house, dragging the lawn mower behind him. He turned his head only once to shout again, "Fascist!"

It must be the sun, thought Bonday, horrified, the sun beating down on that bald head. A fascist? Santiago

Bonday, a fascist? Why would Dr. Pita . . . ? No, it couldn't be that. The Cultural Campaign? Impossible. But what else could it be? They'd known each other for years, they respected each other. There'd never been . . . Suddenly he understood.

"The Golden Fork!"

The doctor had also tried to get into the Society of Gourmets. Without success. He'd always been rejected, because he was too poor, or too outspoken, no one knew why. Someone must have told him about the Fork, and the meal on Sunday with the club lunching at Bonday's house, and the doctor not invited. "The power of envy. They don't award him the Golden Fork, so he accuses me of being a fascist. Well, I'm not going to let that old fool ruin my morning!"

Only a short way from the market he said bitterly to himself, "The one unforgivable sin in this country is success."

· 47 ·

I love Claude, I'm writing my novel, the jasmine on my balcony has flowered, and today we were summoned by Candini to deliver the new play. I get up early. The sky promises a hot day, the street smells of trees, water shines on the pavements, I feel glad to be young, to be alive. I don't take the bus to the theater. I saunter along the pavements; between the cracked paving stones the grass spreads and the flowering weeds bloom. A very old car passes by me like a dream. In it are some men in black uniforms, a human excrescence of that ridiculous car, and between them sits a man wearing a white shirt, who turns a very white face to the blind, deaf, and dumb spectators on the pavement and shouts, "Long live Shakespeare!" He's silenced with a blow. I hear the sound of the blow on his face. I love Claude, it's spring, I'm writing my novel, I'm young, I'm alive. It will pass, all things must pass.

Today there's the appointment in Candini's office to deliver the play that Burgossi may or may not have written, no one can remember and no one asks. Claude paints, I write, the Kid is in training with the Security Forces, Ariadna is busy organizing the brand-new Media Department of which she is now head, and Clara fusses over preparations for the next ceremony.

My steps, so sprightly as I walked along the street, become clumsy and slow as I start to go up the staircase. I know that when I open the door, I'll see, among others, a pair of dark eyes, a desirable mouth, a knowing wink, and that they will be enough to reassure me. But instead the first thing I see are a pair of amber-colored eyes and a black shirt. And I know that this very day, this very morning, I'm going to resign from the theater.

It's late. My colleagues look around at me when I go in. Candini is standing behind the desk, wearing his black suit, a pure white flower in his buttonhole. Burgossi, also standing, is holding a manuscript in one hand while with the other he nervously adjusts his silk cravat.

"I see that you don't understand, brother. . . ." Candini is saying while I sit down in a chair next to Claude.

"In my capacity as head of the Script Department," said Burgossi, "backed up by long experience in the theater, I merely suggested that an extension of the deadline might be convenient and would allow us . . ."

There's something about Candini's office that is familiar to me, and much that seems incongruous. A Manila shawl over a rocking chair; flowery chintz curtains at the window; a plastic fern in a porcelain pot, and, in one corner, a tiny altar.

"Brothers"—Candini strokes the flower in his buttonhole, and slowly shakes his head—"some of you have understood the situation. You're aware of the battle we're waging against the enemy. Others . . ."

I look at Claude. But it wasn't his smile I sought, and when he does smile, it hurts me. He finds the scene amusing. The Manila shawl, the plastic fern, the chintz curtains, the altar and Virgin: a disturbing, grotesque manifestation of humanity in power. The homely patina takes the edge off the black uniforms, off the ten-sion in the Creative Department, who, as one, bow their heads, lower their eyes, and, trembling, await orders. I look away from Claude's comradely smile. I feel abandoned by Claude. "There's a simple solution," says Ariadna's feline voice. "Burgossi should resign and someone else write the play."

Burgossi turns his head toward her. His astonishment at the unexpected betrayal makes his face, which has turned gray, seem even longer than usual. Ariadna shrugs her shoulders, crosses her legs, and lights a cigarette.

Hunched, mute, faded, Burgossi looks at us all in turn, in silent entreaty.

"We won't take his pension away from him, will we, Candini?" asks the Kid with an adult confidence.

"I'll arrange the farewell party," pipes up Clara, tremulous and happy.

"Burgossi hasn't said he's resigning yet," Claude puts in, his face serious, adding a scornful, "*colleagues.*"

"I resign though," I say, standing up.

"Enough!" Candini raises a patriarchal hand. He tells us gently with an ironic, almost amused smile, the deep organ notes in his voice lighter, in the tone of the preacher about to describe paradise to us, "You haven't understood, brothers and sisters. Let me explain again."

The red-haired man moves over to the door.

"No one's going to resign, brothers and sisters."

Burgossi drops down into a seat and dabs at his damp forehead with one corner of his cravat.

"I only said that Molière . . ."

"Molière!" The Kid gets up, his face red. "You stupid old fool! We haven't finished with Shakespeare yet and—"

"Enough!" Candini rests his hands on the desk, emphasizing each word, his voice hitting those deep, grave notes again. "No one is going to resign. United, we will triumph. Divided, we will be defeated. There will be no resignations in this theater. There will be no dissidents, no malcontents. There are only brothers and sisters of the Fleur-de-Lis. Where do you think you're going, Señorita Renata?"

My voice is trembling, and I hate that trembling. "I have no brothers and sisters, Candini . . ."

"Señorita Renata—"

". . . and if I wanted any, I certainly wouldn't choose them from among your uniformed hirelings."

Claude grabs my arm. He wants to hold me back, and I pull away furiously because just one second more and I know the impulse will be gone. I'm afraid. The red-haired man blocks the door with his body. It isn't rage or courage or an awareness of the importance of my stand that makes me confront him. It's the closed door, not being allowed to leave.

"Señorita Renata," I hear Candini calling me, patiently, with a mixture of weariness and condescension.

The red-haired man looks at me with his amber eyes, and there's the shadow of a smile on his somber lips.

"Let me pass!"

And then the door half-opens.

"Renata!" It's her. The blond wig, the chubby, rouged cheeks, the wide mouth in full cry. Then she's kissing me, hugging me, choking back tears. "Renata! My darling girl! Fortu, this is my Renata. I knew the Virgin of Casamanta wouldn't let me down. You see, darling, you see how she's kept her word? I made her a promise, if she'd help me find you. And I have, Renata, I've found you!"

Breathless, I murmur, "Hello, Gertrudis."

The others watch the scene in amusement. I can't free myself from Gertrudis's caresses. She's already ordering Candini to suspend the meeting so that we can celebrate this family reunion; she overwhelms us all in a whirl of introductions; she talks about the boardinghouse and loudly tells humiliating anecdotes. Clara and an assistant arrive with glasses and bottles. We must drink to the miracle, and above all, Fortu, we must raise her salary, my girl's a real jewel, so bright, so well-read, so good.

And the office of the director of the National Theater, Burgossi's humiliation, the Kid's arrogance, the threatening man with yellow eyes, all take on the absurdity and vulgarity of life. They take their place beside the plastic fern, the rocking chair and the Manila shawl, my friend Gertrudis, the Stella Maris boardinghouse, the nights of tears and lime-flower tea, Emilio in the café on the south side, and me rolling down from the heights of my dignity, me on the floor of this human comedy in which Gertrudis returns as the floozy of a poor mystic with ambitions to be a dictator, to reclaim her lost daughter. I look at Claude. His black eyes are shining. He's laughing. Knowingly. He's right.

· 48 ·

THE SECOND DEPARTURE from his Saturday routine
awaited Bonday at the entrance to the market. Clus-
tered round the gateway like an exotic kind of ivy were
the spice-sellers, the Indian women and their children,
who never failed to delight Bonday. The women were
so Indian, with their thin plaits, their almond-shaped
eyes, full lips, and dark skin. Each time Bonday en-
countered them, he was filled with admiration and
amazement to see these leaves sprung from the deepest
of national roots, plucked from primitive territories that
he promised himself he would visit one day, when he
had some spare time and was ready to risk life and limb
and his car on those unsurfaced roads.

As on every Saturday, he sought out the spice-sellers
to receive a small packet of something colorful and fragrant. He couldn't get near them; a wall of people
blocked his path.

"What's wrong?" he asked the fishmonger, who was
straining to see.

"Looks like one of them died."

"Good God!" He stepped back, wanting to get far
away from there. But the wall of people was opening
now. Two of the stall-holders were carrying the body
of one of their friends; her plaits dangled pathetically

257

from her head. Moved, Bonday whispered to the fishmonger, "What was wrong with the poor woman?"
"The Indian disease."
"Smallpox!"
"No," said the other man, "hunger."
"What a country. In the midst of plenty someone dies
of hunger." He was opposite the cheese stall now, looking at the pyramids of round cheeses, the triangle of
Gruyère, the bright blue-green veins running through
the Roquefort. The existence of the cheeses confirmed
that they were indeed living in the midst of plenty, as
did the behavior of the fishmonger, who was once more
cheerfully proclaiming the virtues of his merchandise
and joking with a long line of customers. Bonday regarded him with distrust. "Do we just tend to exaggerate? I'm accused of being a fascist because I'm awarded
a Golden Fork. And an Indian woman dies, and they
say it's of hunger."

The vegetable stalls were lined up to form a narrow
corridor. To the left was Pancho's stall. To the right
some new, round, perfect onions. Pancho had a long
line of buyers. He won't notice my betrayal, said Bonday to himself, as, without looking at Pancho, he sidled
up to buy the onions from the stall opposite.

"How are you, sir?" shouted Pancho just as Bonday
was about to join the opposition's line.

"It's useless," he sighed, "no one can go against the
ethics of the market." And, resigned, he crossed over,
in obedience to Pancho's call. Pancho was the king of
this particular kingdom. He was a plump, stocky figure,
extravagantly unkempt, his hair hanging in fringes about
his ears, a blackened cigarette glued to his lower lip.
He was always lively, sarcastic, and jolly. From his throne
atop a stairway lined with vegetables, beneath canopies
of tubers, parsley, and basil, he presided over a court

of irresolute women, forgetful old ladies, children clutching scraps of paper, and intellectuals like Bonday.

"What can I get you, sir?"

Bonday awoke from his impossible dream of sneaking away from the line and buying from the stall opposite.

"A kilo of tomatoes." As usual, the onions were sprouted.

Pancho took some tomatoes from the box, threw them onto the scales, and, not even looking at the weight, took the bag Bonday held out to him, all the while joking with a bony woman who leaned there, resting her cheek on one hand.

"The marrows you sold me yesterday were a disaster, Pancho."

Oh, no, thought Bonday, not with the club coming to the house. I'll have to buy the onions from the other ` stall.

"I wanted them for stuffing, but they were much too small," sighed the woman.

"The smallest marrows are the tastiest," laughed Pancho, his cigarette quivering on his lips. "Ask my wife if you don't believe me."

The woman reddened.

What a sad sight. She can only be about fifty, and she's nothing but a bag of bones, thought Bonday.

"All right, sir. What else did the missus tell you to get?"

"I trusted you, Pancho, and look what happens, the marrows were too small for the stuffing I'd made. . . ."

"Lettuce," said Bonday.

"They complain," said Pancho, shaking the water off the lettuce, "because they're women. Look at the gentleman here, he bought marrows off me yesterday, just the same they were, and he's not complaining. Weren't they good, sir?"

Everyone turned to look at a poorly dressed man with a sad, flaccid face and the shadow of a beard.

"They were fine," murmured the man.

"You are awful, Pancho," sighed the woman.

"I don't know about the marrows," said Bonday to the sad man, hoping to find an ally, "but the onions aren't any good."

The man didn't reply.

"Come on, sir, wake up!" Pancho was saying to him, because Bonday was still looking at the man. "Can I help you, sir? Let's see, no potatoes, but I've given you tomatoes. I've given you lettuce. . . ."

It was then, when the man reached out to take a bunch of chard, that Bonday noticed his hand. It was plump, freckled, and hairy: the unforgettable hand of Captain Beh!

Without thinking, stunned, he said, "Onions, I need some onions."

Captain Beh! Impossible. He would never have recognized him in that state, so scrawny and without his uniform. He paid Pancho and picked up his bag. Undecided, embarrassed, he confronted the man. "It's a small world, Captain."

The man dropped his bunch of chard. "I think you must be mistaken."

"Captain . . ."

The man was moving smartly away. The step was unmistakably that of Captain Beh. Curiosity forced Bonday to follow him. He had to run to catch up to him.

"Captain, there's no reason for you . . ."

The man stopped. "Come with me," he said, leading Bonday to a corner where there were no people, but where there was a bin in which some pieces of wood and rubbish were burning.

"Almost summer and it's still so cold," said the captain, shivering, holding his hands to the fire.

"I never imagined," said Bonday, shocked at the physical deterioration evident in that once-imposing man, "that a spiritual retreat—"

"Spiritual retreat? Is that what they told you?"

"In the Jardin des Plantes. Pantaenius was very worried about the stress you were under, and I . . ."

Captain Beh looked at Bonday. A remnant of his old fury smoldered in his narrow eyes. "Those two think they're so clever. . . ."

"Well, all of us who began the Campaign . . ."

"There is no Campaign," said the captain, looking thoughtfully at his fingers tinged red by the flames.

"The Fleur-de-Lis . . ."

"There is no Fleur-de-Lis."

Bonday no longer felt curiosity about Captain Beh's strange attitude. He wanted to get away from him, but his sense of politeness wouldn't let him.

"The National Theater . . ."

"There is no National Theater. . . ."

"He's mad, absolutely barking mad," Bonday said to himself, retreating just a step.

"Master—" The look in those narrow eyes was no longer authoritarian or angry, it was astute and cruel. "Master, I'm going to give you some advice. Leave."

Bonday didn't respond.

"Leave. Until the day comes."

"What day?" Bonday heard himself ask feebly.

"The first day of the Reconstruction." The captain was raving now, staring at his red palms. "We have the best of everything here. We must tear our obsessed eyes away from Europe, everything is here. Everything is possible. And when the day comes . . ."

"Good-bye, Captain."

"Wait!" The freckled, hairy hand gripped Bonday's

wrist. The hand was burning hot. "Look around you,
Bonday, and tell me what you see."

Alarmed, Bonday looked. The overflowing stalls, men,
women, children, the vendors' cries, laughter, the bus-
tle of the market, Pancho whistling. "What I see every
Saturday," he mumbled.

The captain let go of his wrist. "You're a fool, Bonday. Go, before it's too late."

He turned his back on him and started to leave. In a
belatedly rebellious impulse Bonday shouted, "But why?
Tell me why!"

The captain turned his head, his smile lopsided. Like
his look, it was a cruel smile.

"Because there are no more Saturdays."

Bonday remained standing by the fire as it died down.
For the first time in many years he would not go for
his final stroll, a final turn about the noisy, agreeable
world of the market. He picked up his bag and walked
slowly toward the exit.

Awaiting him in the street was the final departure
from his Saturday routine.

He saw the Auburn 125 before he saw the man being
dragged along and forced into the car. The man was
plump and stocky and was wearing an apron and a white
stall-holder's cap. He was struggling between two men
in black uniforms. The Auburn pulled away, and some
women, among them the woman who'd bought the
marrows, ran after it shouting.

"Pancho! Pancho! They're taking Pancho away!"

Pancho stuck his head out of the Auburn.

"Long live Shakespeare!" he shouted before being hit
with a blackjack, before being swallowed up in the brilliant black of the Auburn.

Bewildered and shaken, Bonday asked himself how
it was possible that Pancho, Pancho of all people, should
turn out to be a reader of Shakespeare.

· 49 ·

Dear Emilio,

It's three o'clock in the morning, and it's raining. I've tried reading because I couldn't sleep,
but I don't even know what book I had in my
hands. I've tried writing. I've watched the rain.
I've looked at the photograph we had taken in
the Jardin des Plantes. I'm waiting for you to
come back. I'm waiting for it to stop raining.
I'm waiting for something to shake me out of
this unbearable waiting.

I don't know what's wrong with me. I slowly
drift further and further away from myself. It's
useless scratching around, hour after hour these
days, for some good reason to justify my lethargy. Given the circumstances, I've no excuse,
since I fare better than the others. Gertrudis
protects me. To complain about her, about her
motherly concern, would not only be unjust, it
would be imprudent, and dangerous for other
people. Thanks to Gertrudis, I can get the odd
accusation withdrawn, can have the Security
Forces keep a distance from my friends, have
them ignore Claude's insolence, stop them following Ophelia in an Auburn 125. The only

charge one can level against the Security Forces is intimidation. But it's a highly efficient form of intimidation. Yet for many people they're heroes. To be on the safe side, I still always go to Gertrudis.

Love is the only human feeling that is truly anarchic. Candini loves Gertrudis; Gertrudis loves me. There are no other interests involved in those two loves, which each feed on themselves. Some might say that Candini has found in Gertrudis his ideal mate, his vulgar better half. But I see genuine tenderness in the wild, cruel eyes of this apostle of the Fleur-de-Lis, I see how he looks at her, how he listens to her, I see how Candini's love peeps out from behind his authoritarian mask, and I wonder if there isn't something monstrous in love's independence, in its ability to inhabit another world, obey other laws, within the same human body.

That's how Gertrudis's love for me is. In my cowardly way I respect it. There's something familiar about that barbarous language and an obsessiveness that I feel not so much incapable of as just too immature for. One Monday I went into my office in the Wardrobe Department and found Gertrudis, tense with emotion and pleasure, telling me, "I did it all to make you happy." I could neither reproach her nor protest. The gray room was now a red room. There were curtains at the window that gives on to the river. There was a Formica-topped table and a green armchair.

"The gray was so sad," Gertrudis said. She took my hand and led me over to a new door. She covered my eyes. "Surprise," she said.

It was a bathroom. A bathroom with blue tiles. Gertrudis's arm circled my shoulders.

"Like a little house," she said, her voice trembling with tenderness. "A little house for my little girl."

I calculated what that grotesque product of Gertrudis's language of love must have meant: workmen, materials, a race against time, an argument with Candini. A woman without a home, a woman without children, my poor friend from the boardinghouse, Gertrudis. I raised my head and looked into her eyes. I erased all consciousness of myself, of hatred for Candini, of my solitary, foreigner's soul, and said, "It's lovely, Gertrudis, really lovely."

It's still raining. Why are you still not back?

· 50 ·

"Is THAT WHAT they told you?" His wife raised her eyes from her plate and looked at him from the other end of the table. "That's all?"

Bonday put down his knife and fork on his almost untouched plate.

"Can I go now, sir?" asked the maid.

Distractedly toying with his wineglass, he nodded.

"Did you talk to Dr. Pita?"

"He refused to see me."

"Ah, that's a pity, he's got connections."

"For heaven's sake, Elsa, so have I, and a fat lot of good they do me!"

"It's just not possible." His wife shook her head stubbornly. "The ground can't just have swallowed him up."

"Well, he hasn't been arrested. I checked at the police station."

She raised her napkin to her face. "His wife came to see me, Tacho. She's desperate and I . . . I . . . I . . ."

"For God's sake don't cry, please, don't cry."

"Of course, of course, silly of me. And on your birthday too! It's over now, dear, I'm fine."

Bonday tried to smile. His birthday! Somehow they had engineered things so as to avoid a celebration like those they had held in previous years, parties that filled

266

the house at Arroyo Manso with friends, neighbors, students, and journalists. Bonday's last social gathering (the meal for the Society of Gourmets) had extinguished the dying embers of his enthusiasm for the social whirl. Even the committee members had noticed Bonday's amazing lack of interest. He'd watched them eat his much-applauded, award-winning stuffed onions feeling irrepressible disgust at the sight of those round, glutinous objects. He saw in the onions the head of the dead Indian woman, Captain Beh's hands, Pancho's open mouth shouting from the Auburn.

"Disappeared!" repeated his wife. "Is that what they told you?"

"Elsa . . ."

"Master, don't be taken in by appearances," Pantaenius had told him on the phone. "I understand your concern. Ah, you intellectuals! What enviable sensitivity! But you must confine your imagination to your work. An Auburn? Impossible! Are you sure? Well, since it's you, we'll look into it. I don't deny that with all the hullaballoo surrounding the Campaign and with the process in full swing, one of the cars may have escaped our notice and fallen into the hands of some delinquents pure and simple. What did you say your friend's name was? Pancho? Listen, Master, with all due respect, it's not going to be easy finding him among all these Shakespeareans. Try and get more details. Yes, of course, leave the matter in my hands. But I'd advise you, Master, for the good of the Campaign, not to tarnish your image for the sake of a market stall-holder. If he disappeared, he'll reappear. Who knows what this Pancho of yours was up to? For the moment you should just concentrate on the Grand Membership Rally. What's that, Master, don't you read the newspapers, don't you watch television? There's been masses of publicity.

Thanks to men like yourself, naturally. No, I can assure you, no, it wasn't the captain. Periods of transition like this, the tumult of an ongoing process, throw up all kinds of impostors. Believe me, Master, Captain Beh has not yet emerged from his retreat in the Jardin des Plantes."

"Elsa, would you like to go on a trip?"

His wife looked at him, surprised. "A trip? Now? But where?"

"To Europe." Bonday smiled, trying hard to sound casual.

He saw her face suddenly light up, a tremulous smile appear on her withered lips, her hand raised to her breasts, shapeless beneath the severely cut dress, and he felt ashamed. It was ages since he'd suggested any entertainment to her other than lingering on the edge of some dull gathering at a friend's house.

"Would you like that?" he insisted.

The light in her went out. She shook her head. She clung to her world of resignation: It was, when all was said and done, a world in which she felt protected and comfortable.

"Later," she said gently, "later, Tacho. I can't leave the house just like that, just dismiss the servants. . . ." And suddenly she looked at him distrustfully. "Anyway, why now?"

"Well, I could visit the psychoanalyst who was going to treat me for that business with the sideboard . . ."

"Tacho," she said reproachfully, "you don't dream about the sideboard anymore."

"That's true," sighed Bonday, "that's true." He folded his napkin and got up from the table. "I'm going for a walk around the garden," he said, excusing himself, feeling profoundly downcast.

· 51 ·

I just don't understand why.

I want to write about her, and I'm horrified to find that now she's become two people. One of them, yesterday afternoon, gave me a drawing by Claude. It was a portrait of me. "You were terribly jealous, Renata, and I just found it very funny because he was always complaining to me about your cutting remarks, telling me that he liked you '*beaucoup*' and how you were '*une très jolie fille*,' in that French he affects to hide his shyness. Claude is like a brother to me. I could never take him seriously. Now I'm happy. I like people to love each other, and especially when it's you two whom I love so much. I'm right, aren't I, Renata, you do love each other a lot, don't you? You'll get married, of course. Don't laugh, you wicked thing. Don't I always tell you everything? Well, almost everything. Now let's think about the wedding. The church, Handel, and your friend Gertrudis in some hideous dress, bawling her eyes out. Don't laugh like that. You'll start me off, and then I won't be able to stop. In times like these it would be better if I could laugh, at least until it's all over . . . and it will pass, I promise you, it will. Now, let's talk about the wedding, the church, Handel, and your friend Gertrudis. . . ."

That Ophelia belongs to yesterday. They found the other Ophelia today. In the hall of the theater. At the foot of the staircase. She'd tripped, fallen, and broken her neck . . . it doesn't seem possible.

Dear Emilio,

Ophelia, my friend, the sister I never had, is dead. She fell down the big staircase in the theater. Pedro, the electrician, found her. We heard the shouts, but when we got there, Pedro wasn't shouting anymore. He'd gone white and rigid, staring at the body, staring at the tangle of shining chestnut hair, loose and horribly alive, that spilled over the last of the marble steps.

As if in a dream, I remember being at my dead friend's side, surrounded by faces and voices. I didn't touch her. My impulse was to leave, to run away. It was as if I didn't see what I was seeing, as if I were dreaming it all.

Claude bent down, picked up Ophelia's hair ribbon, and crushed it in his fist. The Kid, in his black uniform, fell to his knees and cried, shamelessly, inconsolably, a lovesick little boy again. The chief of the Security Forces went over to Pedro, and the electrician backed off, unable to look away from the other's amber eyes. As in a dream, I saw Candini's double-breasted suit and the white flower in his lapel and a look of infinite amazement on his face, a tremor of disgust. Gertrudis dragged him away from the scene, pulled him over to a corner. Tears, sighs, exclamations, surrounded my dead friend. I couldn't cry. My last memory of the dream is the wailing siren of an ambulance, the doctors and nurses coming in, the stretcher, the figure of Candini bent double, vomiting in a corner, Gertrudis's hand on his forehead.

We all loved Ophelia, but not one of us could save her from that stupid death, from her fate on the staircase.

An irreparable loss, said Candini to Ophelia's mother at the wake. On the lilac ribbon decorating the lavish wreath of flowers were the words, in gold letters, *From her brothers and sisters of the Fleur-de-Lis.* Her mother had kept asking us, Where's Marta? Where's my daughter? No one had dared tell her that her Marta and our Ophelia were there in the bronze-handled coffin.

Only one newspaper mentioned the death of the National Theater's leading lady, and it published a photograph. Ophelia doesn't appear in the photo, Candini does, erect and serious. And the caption reads, *Despite the tragedy we will pull through. Our leading lady, snatched untimely from this life, would have joined us in saying, "The show must go on."*

And it goes on, it goes on.

It's four o'clock in the morning. It's impossible to sleep. The summer has arrived with a vengeance. Until a few minutes ago Claude shared with me the unbearable heat and the airlessness. And the silence. We thought we'd keep each other company, but neither of us had ever felt so alone. Claude kept playing with Ophelia's hair ribbon.

"I'm leaving," I said.

Yes, I'm leaving. I'm going back to the village, to my aunt's, to the school and the Fleur-de-Lis. At least there'll be open countryside, stars, the smell of grass, dogs barking. Anything to escape from this island hit by sudden summer, to leap this wall of endless ceremonies, to go off into pure silence, genuine night, until it's all over. He didn't say, "Don't go." He didn't say, "Let's go together." He just kept playing with Ophelia's ribbon, serious, distracted, not looking at me.

In the context of a recent death every action seems obscene, repugnant.

"Do you really want to hurt your second mother like that?"

There's no trace in him now of that revulsion that made him vomit near Ophelia's body on the staircase. On his pale face I see the joy of triumph. I'd gone into his office just as the journalists were leaving; his eyes are still full of the fire sparked by the flattery of cameras and tape recorders. He's a man of the theater, Candini.

"No, Señorita Renata, not before the Grand Membership Rally."

I'm on the point of begging him. I keep insisting, desperately. What does it matter if I'm not present at the wretched rally? There's a whole crowd, a whole city, to give their support, to carry his banners, and to cheer him.

"You have a duty to perform. You're the head of a department."

"I resign. Appoint someone else to the post."

He smiles. "You're very young, Señorita Renata. Don't you realize that measures are being taken to maintain our image?"

"What do I care?"

He slowly shakes his head. He's very sorry, but he can't allow it.

"To be or not to be: That is the question, *señorita*," he says mockingly, smiling, sure of himself.

"I'm leaving, Candini."

158   "Ah, you're too young to understand. These are very
159   difficult times. At this early stage of the process, out-
160   side the theater, beyond the protection your brothers
161   and sisters afford you, I wouldn't be able to answer for
162   your life."
163   My *life?*

⚬ 52 ⚬

BONDAY PAUSED for a moment on the threshold.

"The lion's mouth."

The mouth of that lion night was uniformly black, its breath smelling unpleasantly of damp, the tips of trees like the points of sharp teeth. There wasn't a single star in the sky, and the only lights down below were a distant lamp in the garden, and another on the extreme right.

He'd fled the oppressive dialogue with his wife, the strain of that miserable birthday celebration, by pretending he was going for a stroll in the garden. Now he couldn't go back. He lit his pipe and walked toward the one lighted corner, where there was a group of young birch trees.

The slender trunks, the silver bark, of the birches, shone yellowish in the lamplight. Until the old gardener had taught him otherwise, Bonday had confused birches with ashes and, in the belief that they were ashes, had bought them from the local nursery, attracted by the delicate femininity of the young trees that evoked for him girls from another time, bloodless and pale, reclining eternally on plump pillows. "Ashes! These are birch trees, and they're not worth the money you paid for them. In this climate a puny thing like that isn't going to survive one summer. Now an ash, that's what

I call a tree, Don Bonday." Purely to defy the old man,
to assert his authority, he'd ordered him to plant the
birch trees anyway and, without any real interest, reluctantly helped by Don Matías, he had watched them grow.
After endlessly explaining to visitors (who couldn't tell
a birch from an ash either), and endlessly looking at
them, his pretended affection had turned into love, and
he no longer needed the admiration of others in order
to like them. He was genuinely convinced that they were
the most beautiful trees in his garden, and when he
compared them with the ash or the oak, the latter
seemed to him coarse, vulgar, graceless.

In the thick darkness of the night, in the gloom that
was beginning to take hold of him, Bonday felt the consolation of those friendly trees. He reached out a hand
and passed it gently over a young branch: the gesture
of a man absentmindedly stroking his dog.

He heard a moan. Standing amid the tangle of birch
trees he looked about him. The garden, made larger
by a single shadow that obliterated the boundary fences,
seemed immense and impenetrable to him. In the long,
deep silence that followed, even his own agitated
breathing frightened him. Then, another moan. Instinctively he tightened the hand still gripping the
branch. From his impoverished refuge he suddenly
recognized the voice calling to him.

"Good God, now what's that old fool been up to?"

It was Don Matías, whose custom it was to go out at
night to defend his rosebushes from the ants. Concerned, but also furious at the old man's mania, Bonday strode blindly across the garden.

"Good God!"

The old gardener tried to get up. Bonday saw the
blood on his wrinkled face: He must have tripped and
fallen in the dark.

"Lean on me, Don Matías. That's it. It's nothing much, don't be frightened. I'm going to get Dr. Pita."

Bonday and his wife laid the old man on a sofa in the living room. Elsa brought a towel and wiped away the blood flowing from his nose.

"It's best if Dr. Pita sees him," said Bonday, "even though it doesn't seem very serious."

"Don Bonday . . ."

"Don't get up. I'm going to get the doctor."

"Don Bonday, Ramón has gone . . ."

Bonday and his wife looked at each other.

"He's gone." The old man's face crumpled. "His father left him in my charge, and I couldn't even look after him . . ."

Bonday's wife bent over and stroked his wrinkled forehead.

"Don't worry, Don Matías. The doctor will be here soon."

"Where's my hat? Where's my hat?"

At last they managed to make him lie down. He kept asking first for his hat, then for the boy. Bonday brought cognac and got him to take a few sips.

"It must be the effect of the fall," he said to his wife.

"He went off with those people, Don Bonday." The old man was crying now. "He won't come back to me."

"Calm down, Don Matías. You know what boys are like, he'll be out there somewhere. . . ."

The old man raised wild eyes to him. "Yes, you're right, sir. Ramón is out there, and later he'll come back. He's probably just helping them carry the great unwieldy thing, and then he'll be back. . . ."

Bonday held his breath. "What great unwieldy thing?"

"They covered my mouth so that I wouldn't shout, Don Bonday. They took it out through the big window, they hit me, and Ramón went off with them. They carried it through the garden, half-dragging it, they hit me and I didn't see anything else, I couldn't find my hat, and Ramón had gone. . . ."

"What great unwieldy thing?"

"The big mirror, Don Bonday, the mirror . . ."

Where the big mirror had hung, there was now a large rectangle of bare wall with a note pinned in the middle.

REQUISITIONED BY THE FLEUR-DE-LIS

Behind him, in a low, shaky voice, his wife said, "The boy's not in the house."

Without turning around, with the note still in his hand, Bonday said, "Tomorrow, whether you like it or not, we're going to renew our passports."

· 53 ·

I've gone down to my office to collect my things. I'm not even going to say good-bye to Gertrudis, I'm just looking for my handbag, the portrait Claude drew of me, and a couple of books.

"Renata." He's at the door, unsmiling.

"I'm leaving, I'm leaving."

"No," he says gravely, "not before the rally."

I look at his dark eyes, his lovely mouth, the sad brown face, the languid outline of his now-tense body.

"Did Candini send you?" I ask without believing it, but out of desperation and rage.

"Ophelia sent me." In his hand he's holding the ribbon Ophelia used to use to tie back her hair. I look at the ribbon. I don't understand. Claude says quietly, "It's best if we attend the rally."

Claude's hands untie the knotted ribbon. It seems an unnecessarily long ribbon to tie back someone's hair, even if it was the thick, shining hair of our friend as she fell down the stairs.

"Routine inspection."

Claude and I turn around. Neither the black uniform, nor the white badge, nor the weapon he's holding, lend maturity to the red, childish, furiously authoritarian face.

"Come in, little soldier." Claude bows.

The Kid doesn't reply. There are beads of sweat on his forehead. He looks at the door to the wardrobe room with worried eyes.

"It's just a routine inspection. If you tell me everything's in order here . . . that you're alone here . . ."

I don't know why, but I open the door of the room and put on the light.

"That's what I'm hiding, slave! Nothing that your Fleur-de-Lis can use. Nothing that will get you promoted. Nothing, absolutely nothing!" The spotlights are like dazzling stars whose light falls on the frayed, unused costumes. All the masks, jewels, and weapons shimmer. The Kid in his black uniform stands motionless. So does Claude. So do I, my hand still on the light switch. The three of us are looking at the man crouching in a corner, his face turned to the wall.

"Come with me," the Kid said, trembling.

Pedro didn't move.

"I'll have to take you by force."

"Klappenbach," Claude's voice dropped to a whisper, "take him *where?*"

The Kid just shook his head.

"I'm carrying out orders."

"Why him?"

"Don't ask me. I don't know. I'm just carrying out orders. I don't know why."

Claude put a hand on his shoulder.

"Kid," he said very gently. "Come on, Kid. We're alone here, no one knows you found him. We're friends, Klappenbach, surely you haven't forgotten that."

"This is ridiculous," I said, trying to laugh.

The Kid tightened his lips. "I can't." His voice was sharp now. "I can't. Come on, come with me."

Pedro looked around now and opened his eyes. "They're taking me to the Jardin des Plantes," he said.

The Kid raised his gun.

"Please, Klappenbach," pleaded Claude.

"Please," I begged.

"No one comes back from the garden," Pedro said.

"No one's going to take you away from here." Claude threw himself on the Kid to try to take his gun off him. I screamed. The two fought their last fight together, on the floor now, with a real gun between them; it wasn't just for a joke in the Salon de Thé, and it was Pedro, not Ariadna, standing on the sidelines of the scene. The shot made them freeze.

"Get up, you idiot, and you too, Mr. Hero. And you over there in the corner sniveling."

The yellow eyes looked scornfully down at the two on the ground. He held the gun from which the shot had been fired pointing up at the ceiling. Behind, there were other men in black, all wearing the emblem.

"Right, let's go, all three of you."

"Where are you taking them?"

The amber eyes turned to me. He didn't answer. Claude took a step forward. The red-haired man leveled his gun at him. "I just want to say good-bye to the young lady," Claude said with a heartrending smile. His dry lips brushed my cheek. "Don't be frightened, Renata. It'll all work out."

"I'm going to find Gertrudis, she has to . . ."

There was real terror in his dark eyes, and yet he was smiling. "Of course, *chérie*. But don't miss the rally, I want you to go, I want you to tie back your hair, don't forget the ribbon."

They pushed me back against the window and dragged Claude toward the door.

"Don't miss the rally!"

The door closed. I ran over to it, pushed against it, tried to force the lock, and beat on it until my fists hurt.

A long time afterward, kneeling by the door, exhausted with crying and shouting, I heard a voice from the other side.

"It's for your own good, my dear, it's for your own good."

It was Gertrudis, consoling me.

° 54 °

In the departure lounge at the International Airport, ten minutes after getting through the last check, Bonday was still examining a handful of documents. Tickets, passports, luggage-claim tags, embarkation forms. All the paperwork was in order, but he kept going through it again and again to make sure it was right.

From the other side of the vast windows a leaden sky threatened rain. Bonday took a deep breath of the artificial air in the departure lounge, dry and cool, but hostile too after the first moment of relief, when he felt himself torn from the damp, suffocating heat of the city, his feet about to cross the threshold into winter in Paris.

Sunk in her chair, hugging her handbag to her, his wife seemed to be asleep. Bonday walked over to the window. There was no city beyond. There was no street, square, district, that he could say good-bye to. He let his eyes wander over the cold terrace of a world between two worlds, a bridge of runways and machines.

Without quite knowing why, he shivered.

Dear Emilio,

For months I wrote you letter after letter. I never got a reply. I can tell you now that your silence wounded me, but that was unjust of me, as Father Collins has proved. He brought me

some books (to pass the time) and a packet of
letters. They weren't letters from other people.
They weren't letters from you. They were in my
own handwriting, my own words. The shock took
my breath away. That's the hellish thing about
mirrors, they only reflect your own face!

To protect me—though I don't know from
what—they've shut me up here until the day of
the Membership Rally. Don't worry, I'm getting
used to it. Gertrudis makes sure I lack for nothing, and Father Collins visits me. I've asked for
paper and a typewriter. Through the good offices of Gertrudis.

Father Collins brought me the draft of the
novel I was writing. I laughed out loud. Was he
hoping to console me with literature? Enclosed
by four red walls and a window onto the river?
All I have left now is my memory. The diary
and the letters never sent, intact, fresh, dead. I
work up some notes in the notebook, elaborate
a scene around some remark. How far away that
life seems now. In the memories that keep me
poised on the edge of the abyss, until they open
the door, I seem such a stranger.

For the hundredth time Bonday looked at the elec-
tronic timetable. The red dots indicating departures
blinked rhythmically, announcing other flights.

"Why did they put us in here if we're never going to
leave?" he sighed, bored, his elbows on the smooth wood
of the bar, a glass in his hand. The glass was empty. "I
shouldn't drink. It isn't wise." He ordered a second
brandy.

Beyond the horizon of hangars lay the city, and in
the city the theater, and in the Theater Candini, the
Fleur-de-Lis, and the final, obligatory ceremony. He'd

fulfilled his commitments. No one could accuse him of shutting himself up in an ivory tower. He'd given his best efforts to the Cultural Campaign and part of his heritage (the mirror) to the theater, and he'd accepted Pantaenius's aggrieved excuses without getting too indignant at Candini's voracity, his excesses. Now, in Paris, he would return to his real world, to his island. Books, lectures, articles, friendly faces, and a writer's nostalgia for the country he was leaving behind.

During the Membership Rally Pantaenius had embraced him affectionately. "Master, you don't know how much we'll miss you. But you're doing the right thing, you deserve a rest. The process has proved exhausting for us all."

The brandy, warmed in the palm of his hand, reminded him of how suffocatingly hot the theater auditorium had been despite the fans. The implacable summer heat had brought a rosy glow to the cheeks of Father Collins, who had been sitting next to him in one of the seats laid out in rows on the stage. Behind them Candini's men had stood in immaculate lines while Candini spoke into the microphone. There had been applause from the stalls as one by one the heads of departments from category Z-k came up, the cameras capturing the moment, the photographers' flashlights popping, amid the shouts and cheers of the audience. "Another brandy, please," Bonday said to the bartender.

I look back now and I see myself facedown on the floor, not crying anymore, listening to Gertrudis on the other side of the door. Terror claims me. No more shouting. That's enough tears for now. I stand up. It's not easy to move in this blanket of ice. I go to the bathroom, and I wash my face. I should cut my bangs. I cup my hand and drink tepid water from it. What's my role in this play? I tie back my hair with Ophelia's ribbon. I look immaculate, my face clean. The irony of that little red house. Soap and towel. Sky-blue toilet paper. I open the cabinet. It's empty. Why is there no cream, no talcum powder, no cologne? Really, Gertrudis, this isn't good enough! I turn on the shower. Only cold water. But it's hot in the room, God, it's hot.

The thunder of motorcycle exhausts, the wailing sirens, made Bonday turn toward the door of the departure lounge. Policemen in helmets and visors were escorting an Auburn 125 that braked sharply by the door.

"Let the ambassador through!"

The crowd of people who had gathered by the windows parted to make way for a short, heavily built man with gray hair slicked down with a thin layer of brilliantine. The man had got out of the Auburn, carrying his own heavy suitcases.

Bonday looked at him openmouthed, with his third glass of brandy in his hand.

I have to believe in Gertrudis. I have to accept her story that all these measures are purely to intimidate. Gertrudis is the sane side of the events that keep me prisoner. And in her mad way, she loves me. Why would she deceive me? To distrust that warm, sensible, generous woman is to deliver myself over to my imagination, my hell. With words, caresses, and scoldings she disperses the shadows that burn in my red office, she makes the screams of the devil seem the crude shouts of a rowdy mob.

It was Pedro, she says, who got us into this mess. Thank heavens Fortu is so good-hearted and won't let the Security Forces get out of hand. If that boy (meaning Claude) had done nothing, then nothing will happen to him. It was a bit foolish of him to try and defend

that good-for-nothing Pedro, who instead of talking to
Fortu talked to a journalist. Yes, the report was published, it wasn't very long, but it was published in one
of those sensationalist rags. No one took it seriously, of
course. How could anyone take such a vile attack on
the Fleur-de-Lis seriously, when everyone knows the
work that's being done on the National Theater? The
journalist? Just like all the rest. They throw their stone
and then run away. Not a trace of him. Poor Fortu, as
if he weren't already half-dead with exhaustion from
the Campaign! A martyr. It's only natural he should
rely on the boys in the Security Forces. After all, they
are loyal. There are some excesses that Fortu doesn't
approve of, but we live in a violent age, and what's one
more beating here or there? He had to congratulate
them for the job they did on the magazine. No one was
hurt, of course they weren't. Fortu would never have
allowed it. He's got a heart of gold. They just smashed
the furniture and one of those printing presses. And
all for what? For some idiot who thinks he sees things.
She can understand it. Poor Pedro. He was very shocked.
He really loved the girl, that actress. He said he saw
something or other, that it wasn't an accident. It's only
natural. It's difficult to accept that someone should just
die like that, because, well, it's fate, and, may the Virgin
of Casamanta keep us safe, Renata, but, like it or not,
there *is* such a thing as fate.

Claude and Pedro are well, Renata, she says. Under
arrest until the rally is over. In fact they're much better
off than you are, Renata, because they're among all that
greenery, in the open air, listening to the birds singing.
But she prefers to keep me here. Nothing can replace
a mother's love. Especially in times like these. So I
shouldn't complain. I should listen to Father Collins.

Gertrudis takes care of my physical needs, Father
Collins of my soul. Until the day of the Membership

"Good-bye, Master, see you again some time. In some
European city perhaps, who knows? Or, why not," Pantaenius's saccharine, voice was moving away now, "in
the National Theater itself, on the same stage. It's a
small world, Master, for people like you and me." While
they called him to board his plane, his flight, Bonday
saw the girl advancing toward him from the bottom of
his glass, from a tangle of yellowish birch trees, from a
fountain in a small gravel square, from a tunnel of green
shadows, from his own tortured memory.

She was coming slowly up the steps, leaning on Candini's mistress. Bonday looked at her in horror.

There was no half-smile, no trace of that secret,
childish playfulness that had made him fall in love with
her. She was wearing her long blond hair tied back with
a ribbon, and her girlish bangs had been savagely lopped
off to reveal a high, smooth, grave forehead. There was
nothing graceful now about that slender body Bonday
had pursued in his dreams. There was no beauty at all.
No fountain nymph.

"What's happened to that girl?" he heard himself ask
Father Collins hoarsely.

Father Collins had not deigned to reply.

Dear Emilio,

This is my last night here. Tomorrow I'll be
out.

I've had my last talk with Father Collins, my
last talk with Gertrudis. I've calmed them both
down. I don't know why they were so upset. In
the end it's just a puppet show, And we've seen
enough of those at the theater. Gertrudis swore
to me that I won't have to do anything. My job
and my category will be announced over the
microphone. Then I go up the steps, receive a

diploma from Candini, shake his hand, and smile for the television cameras and the press photographers. There are so many of us joining the Campaign (both in and out of the theater) that I'll slip through easily enough, back to the stalls, and then out into the street, with Claude and Pedro, as Gertrudis promised.

They demand this clumsy, anonymous participation of me in exchange for my freedom and that of my friends. So what? Today it's the Fleur-de-Lis. Tomorrow, when they're tired of Candini, it will be Shakespeare. If the world can forget, so can I. You used to tell me that memory was every writer's most indispensable tool. But this isn't literature. I will forget. I'll forget about my painful appearance on this stage. I'll forget my humiliation and my shame.

Apart from my life and my name, the Fleur-de-Lis has taken everything from me. Because of compromises made out of fear, my only identity is this flesh in search of air and sun, and the name that keeps it all together. You'll have to try to understand when they tell you that I was there too, an accomplice to crimes and threats, a living part of the shadows whose darkest side are the Security Forces. Will you be able to forgive me, my friend?

God, what escape is there for Renata, whose only courage has been never to ally herself to ideas that her honesty rejected? What faithfulness do they require of one who has only been faithful to an illusion: that of writing to defend not truth but the human right to uncertainty? Why do they force me to kneel before one of these grotesque idols? What is nobler in the mind—to bow down to the Fleur-de-Lis or to die shouting "Long live Shakespeare"? Where is the other door? What blocks it? What pushed us into these one or two corrals of fanaticism and violence? I go along with the others, one more head, mooing submissively but jealously keeping my name to myself for the day when the door to another future opens.

My freedom and that of my friends are at stake, but I'm going to win this game.

They were calling him to board. They were calling the girl, head of the Wardrobe Department, category Z-k, and the girl was slowly mounting the steps, leaning on the other woman.

Bonday saw her jump when they said her name into the microphone. The girl turned to Candini's mistress. The woman smiled and pushed her gently toward the enormous book on the lectern. Father Collins mumbled something that Bonday did not understand. Bonday was only aware of his horror at the change in the nymph from the Jardin des Plantes. The girl was looking at the book, stunned. She was looking at the pen that Candini's mistress placed in her hand.

Father Collins stood up. He heard him say, "Renata." The name was an order, a plea, an exclamation of fear. The girl fixed her eyes, shining with tears, on Father Collins, and imperceptibly shook her head. There was an impatient murmur in the room. The men in the black uniforms took a step forward. Candini's mistress smiled and smiled, and sweat opened up channels down her heavily made-up face, around her red, trembling lips.

"Renata," Father Collins said again, on his feet now.

I knew he would come. And he came. I knew he would say to me everything he did say. I knew Gertrudis was lying. I knew and I didn't want to know, I didn't want to believe it. We always knew. It was more human, less

monstrous, to deny the truth. They, we, all of us knew.
For Ophelia, Claude, Juan, Pedro, and so many others,
it's too late. But not for me. I knew he had a key to the
red office, and that he would open that door. I knew
they gave him the keys so that he could do what they
did not dare to do, and I knew that he would go one
step further in the fulfillment of his masters' orders. I
knew that once he'd been created, no one would be able
to stop him. And no one can.

Neither can I. He holds death in one hand and the
ribbon he has removed from my hair in the other. Obediently, while I repeat my name like a litany so as not
to lose the last thing left to me by this awful world,
these red walls that contain the two of us, enclosed in
the silence and complicity of an entire city, I obediently
allow him to play with the ribbon about my throat, to
play with my life in this rehearsal that will give a different ending to the play if I don't accept my role tomorrow. The ribbon is delicate, but his hands are not.

Without shouting, or struggling, without even any
fear, I let him undress me and rape me. I keep my eyes
wide open. I don't care about his yellow eyes or his evil-
smelling flame-colored hair that rasps against my skin.
I still have my name. And my name is Renata. I want
to see the sun again, Renata. You'll see the sun tomorrow. You'll see the sun after the rally. You'll see the
sun, and you can repeat your name until you wear
yourself out with repeating it, in the sun, amid all the
smells of summer, I want to live, tomorrow, you'll repeat your name, in nights to come, in your dream of
another struggle, alive and writing in the sun, Renata,
tomorrow. . . .

Bonday paid. His wife was waiting for him, clutching
her handbag and avoiding his eyes, her face closed and
sullen.

"What have I done wrong?" wondered Bonday as he staggered through the exit door and they walked toward the plane.

Half-drunk and half-asleep, he waited patiently for the other passengers to rush toward the steps. It wasn't going to rain after all. It was the usual capricious, irritating summer. The sky cleared. The sun dazzled him. "Elsa," he said to his wife, "aren't you glad to be getting away from here?"

Very slowly, with an unfamiliar sharpness in her voice, she replied, "Oh, very glad. You'll really enjoy exile."

At the top of the steps Bonday took one last look.

He couldn't see any houses or squares. From the plane it seemed an invisible city. But through humiliating and unexpected tears he saw the garden at Arroyo Manso, the clump of birches, the gardener bent over the rosebushes, the iron gates of the Jardin des Plantes, the little graveled square, the boy leading him down a tunnel, the nymph in the waterless fountain, the girl refusing to sign and shouting, "No, not my name, not my name," and everyone scurrying to hush up the scandal, to cover up this stain on the Grand Rally, Father Collins being held by one of the men in black, the head of the Security Forces dragging that poor hysterical girl from the stage, and the weariness, the tedium, the tedium of waiting while they patched up the interrupted ceremony, while they sang and applauded, and Bonday, exhausted, smiled once more for the photographers, for the cameras, and patted his pocket to check his passport was there.

Through his tears, he looked down at the drab horizon of the city that lay now beneath a perfect sky and a golden sun. He was safe now, but he still felt upset. A shudder ran through him, and he thought, A man is not much more than this poor thing, his life.

∘ 55 ∘

EMILIO RAUCH LOOKS OUT at the wide, muddy river. The night is clear and starless, open and airless. There are no lights from ships or houses. Down below, a rough, irregular cement wall, half of a wall that was going to be built between the city and the water, ends abruptly, parallel with the window from which Rauch looks out. Like a man leaning over a well with no safety rail, Rauch leans out into the silence and perfect calm of the night. He looks in vain for a face and a name on the smooth, metallic surface of the river, on the flat, bare earth, on the unfinished wall, until a sense of a deeper, wider void than that in the red-painted office makes him withdraw, feeling dizzy and afraid.

"It's late, Rauch."

Bonday is not reproaching him, but pleading. For the first time Rauch notices a chink in the Master's arrogance. It's his vanity that sustains him, like the indestructible masonry of old houses, which, long since empty, still stand with their friezes of cupids and garlands. Even foolish pride has a soul, and Rauch realizes, with sudden compassion, that Bonday has lost his. The tall, elegant man with the gray mustache, and bright, deceptively alert eyes, is like the actor who, in the latter part of his career, knows that he's missed his chance, that he won't be given another role, that he'll die joylessly playing the same character.

"Gentlemen."

Rauch and Bonday both turn toward the door.

"Captain Beh asks if you'll be coming down to the cocktail party. He wants to drink a toast with you to the liberation."

Bonday straightens up. Before leaving, he looks at Rauch for a moment. Undecided, as if he wanted to confess all the bitterness his face reveals. What stops him is Rauch's inquisitive, accusing expression. Indicating the unfinished wall, a fatuous smile on his lips, Bonday says desperately, "Ah yes, for all their faults, one must recognize they've left their mark."

The man in the white uniform sent to find them has red hair and yellow eyes.

A NOTE ABOUT THE AUTHOR

Vlady Kociancich was born in Buenos Aires, Argentina, where she now lives. She has been a journalist and literary critic, and has published one collection of short stories and three novels.